ABOUT THE AUTHOR

Colm Herron's first writing career began at the age of seven when he sold his vampire stories to classmates. Two years later, he was telling cliff-hangers to the wasters in the local gambling hall. Colm's abiding memory is that these ne'er-do-wells seemed to enjoy this weekly break from misspending their lives.

When he was fifteen, he had a play on BBC and later brought his short stories to Brian Friel, an emerging playwright. Friel said "Great. This stuff's better than what I wrote at your age." But Colm was unimpressed and thought "This guy's going nowhere. I don't know why I came to him at all."

So Colm gave up writing, deciding to live instead. Meanwhile Brian Friel's plays became huge hits and over the next thirty years he built up a richly deserved reputation as Ireland's greatest living playwright. And what of Herron? Well, while Brian Friel's plays were showing worldwide to critical and popular acclaim a kaleidoscope of stories was kicking and turning in Colm's head. But they still weren't ready to come out. Till twenty years ago, that is, when he said to himself: "OK, I've lived. Maybe it's time to do the other thing."

And so began his second writing career...

ACCLAIM FOR COLM HERRON'S PREVIOUS NOVELS

For I Have Sinned:

"Perhaps the greatest tribute I can pay to this quirky, funny and deeply affecting novel is to declare that the moment I finished reading it, I immediately turned back to the first page to begin again. And it's even better second time round."
Ferdia MacAnna, *Sunday Independent*

Further Adventures of James Joyce:

"A totally comic novel .... *Further Adventures of James Joyce* could just as easily be entitled *The Further Writings of Flann O'Brien*."
MorrisBeja, *James Joyce Quarterly*, Tulsa, Oklahoma

The Fabricator

"Fascinating, funny, sad and delightful. From its opening lines right through to its final pages *The Fabricator* is not like anything you have read before.
Kellie Chambers, *Ulster Tatler*

The Wake (And What Jeremiah Did Next)

"So funny, so full of charm, so full of great characters and brilliant dialogue. This book is made for the screen."
Paul Webb, screenwriter of *Selma*

COLM HERRON

A MAIDEN SO BEWITCHING

Visit Colm Herron's website:
http://colmherronthewake.wixsite.com/colm-herron

Contact Colm on Twitter: @colmherron
Cover by © Lermagh Graphics
Typesetting: Robin Chambers

ISBN-13: 978-0-9546453-9-7
ISBN-10: 0-9546453-9-1

OTHER NOVELS BY COLM HERRON

For I Have Sinned

Further Adventures of James Joyce

The Fabricator

The Wake (And What Jeremiah Did Next)

For John, Brian and Damien

A MAIDEN SO BEWITCHING

Make no mistake about it. We're all bitched from the start.

That's what Ernest Hemingway used to say anyway. Now Hemingway was one smart cookie – no argument there – but the same boy didn't know the half of it. Take me for instance. I was well and truly bitched nine months before the start. Well, nine months and two days to be exact.

There really is no good way of telling you this so I'll just tell you the best way I can. On the night I was conceived, Momma got out a darning needle and poked a hole in Pappa's johnny before she put it on him. So there you are.

She confessed on my fourteenth birthday and after that I went about for a while thinking the best of me was thrown out with the damn thing. Away in some landfill place with dead cats and crows and squashed hedgehogs and stuff. Guts and giblets and shitty nappies (diapers to all you U.S. folks out there. Hi!) and old tin cans.

The question is though, the real question is, why would a woman do a thing like that? That's the question. Why would she poke a hole in a johnny?

Well she confessed that too. And I wasn't ready for what I heard. How could you be? How could anybody be? So here's what she said:

"See, I wanted a baby and your father didn't. He always had to have his thingamajigger on when he was going to have relations. To tell you the Lord's honest truth Alexis, the man hardly ever had it off. But it was a girl I wanted. That's what I've been meaning to explain to you for ages."

Right, it was a girl she wanted. And she did her level best to turn me into one. You wouldn't believe the things she made me do. God Almighty! I know what I was gagging to say to her and I don't know why I didn't say it. I was gagging to say "It was you, Momma. You was my momma, Momma. Do you not get it, Momma? I could've been normal. I could've had class. I could've been like a normal boy instead of a freaking freak, which is what I am." (I'd just seen *On the Waterfront*).

And she never would have told me any of that stuff either except she was blitzed on near enough half a bottle of Southern Comfort and that's what got her going about how I was a big disappointment to her and all. I'd been her ugly suckling, she said, a cross she'd had to bear, a cross between what she wanted and what I was turning out to be. She had a way of putting things my momma.

But at least I came round then to knowing for absolute sure where I got certain urges from. Nurture, not nature, isn't that what they say? All those dolls and dresses came back to me in a mad rush. And the cute wee panties with no place to pee out of. And the way she got me to walk, like I was modelling clothes or something. And the toys she gave me. I don't even want to think about it. And mother of God, I had more Toodles dolls than you could shake a stick at.

I didn't know what in hell I was half the time, except it was a hell I'd never been taught in school. And believe you me, I got plenty of hell from the Christian

Brothers. Only their hell was narrower and, how can I say it, burnier? It consisted of being constantly reminded of the dangers of the flesh that had to be kept down if we valued our God-given souls. Let me tell you now, there's nothing like a good Catholic education.

And then of course, there were my extra-curricular gender studies which weren't what you would call the best either. I'm blaming John Bartley Stroker for that. He it was who used to keep us informed, if that's the right word, at a workshop down the breakneck steps. We were the Dirtbird gang and he was our leader and the lane jutting off from the breakneck steps was our headquarters.

Some of the other gang members didn't want me in because I was a bit of a pansy, but John Bartley insisted. I always had this feeling that he fancied me, even though he never made a move. He was sixteen I think, two years older than most of the rest of us, but he seemed to me like about twenty at the time. Anyway, most of his talks were about this thing he called corpulation which the rest of us were sorely ignorant of.

"With corpulation," he explained one day, "you've got to get her on her back. If you don't get her on her back your jiz won't go in. Gravity you see."

I think it was Mugs McGuire that asked: "What happens if you pee into her by mistake, Boss?"

"She dies," said John Bartley, and his revelation was greeted with a collective intake of breath.

People like me were sometimes shouted at in the street and called nancy boys, so you probably won't be surprised to know that I'd give nearly anything to have my life over again, right from the very beginning. Only it would be a different life, a very different life, one where I don't have the awful cravings I have now, even at the age of seventy-one.

One night not long ago, after I'd read the first couple of chapters of *The Hitchhiker's Guide to the Galaxy*, I dreamed that I was given written instructions on how to start over. They were really daunting, so daunting that they woke me up, whereupon I got a biro and a pad and wrote down everything I remembered about the dream. Here's what I wrote down.

Go to 666 Eureka Street, walk slowly around the American Pit Bull Terrier that you will find growling on the top step, remembering to pat it playfully on the nose as you pass (that way he'll know you're a friend), break the front door down with an Indo-Persian war hammer and proceed down to the cellar, which you will notice has no steps and no stairs. There, in a locked treasure chest at the bottom of a toilet bowl overflowing with solid human waste, you will find directions on what to do next.

Not very helpful. Dreams aren't up to much of course. But the part about the Pit Bull Terrier puts me in mind now of the dog I groomed back in nineteen sixty, Aubrey Hegarty by name. Two months at it I was. Lovely animal with a backside on it that would have put you to loss. Belonged to the breadman Seamus Hegarty from out the Slaughmill Road and was what you might call a street dog. Allowed to run wild like children you'd see on TV in one of those misfortunate countries.

Hegarty was the kind of boy that's all smiles to his customers and hard as nails underneath. He had a duty of care but didn't bother his big arse. Aubrey was out all day and allowed to wander anywhere it wanted and meet all sorts of disreputables. Irish collie, I think, though I never had much of a clue about breeds.

Notice I'm using the word *it* here. That's because I'm not saying what sex it was. I knew all right. After two months you get to know. After two seconds you get to know, actually. But it doesn't matter anyway. I moved on from dogs after Aubrey took a lump out of my scrotum, tried lambs for a while but found them unresponsive. Not as unresponsive as mattresses though, but as near as makes no difference.

Which reminds me. I was sitting having a cup of coffee in Starbucks last Tuesday and I picked up this free *Irish News* from a rack, and what do you think was down in the bottom corner of one of the inside pages beside the Footsie 100?

MAN ACCUSED OF LEWD ACT WITH MATTRESS.

Beside the Footsie 100. Just think of the speculators that get hit with that when they're playing at the Footsie. Or the other one, the one that's played under tables. Different kind of speculation of course.

Where was I? The *Irish News*. I took just one quick disbelieving look at it, wouldn't lower myself to read the small print. I'd say that particular act must have been in a public place. Otherwise, how would they know? *We're getting reports of a male Caucasian sleeping with a mattress at the junction of Beechwood Avenue and Laburnum Terrace. Members of the public are advised not to approach.*

But anyway, most of that stuff is behind me. I'm seventy-one now, Emeritus Professor of Humanities, respectably and unhappily married, writer of the popular *Steam 4 Teens* site and still looking at girls a quarter my age. What am I saying? Closer to a fifth my age.

But hang on. I should have begun all this by explaining how falling on my head turned me into a genius. I'd intended to tell you about that at the very start but when you get to my age, it doesn't take much to distract you. A knock at the door, a flushing toilet, people out in the street having a row. You bloody forget what was in your head.

So where was I? Being a genius wasn't it? That's it, being a genius. It actually happened after I threw myself out of a second-storey window at the age of fourteen and a half. And now I have this condition known as Acquired Savant Syndrome (labelled ASS by its detractors).

What happened was, Pappa saw me coming out of the bathroom one morning in my bullet bra and *Pretty Polly* panties and he ran downstairs shouting that he was going to put a stop to this nonsense once and for all. If I'd known what was in his stupid mind, I'd have locked my door; but I didn't and the next thing was, he was coming at me across the bedroom with a big claw hammer. There was only one way out and that was the way I went. The window. And the next thing I remember was wakening up in the back yard with Pappa's rottweiler Brando lying stone-dead under me.

Three things resulted from this. One, Pappa went into a state of melancholia which he never came out of. Two, he didn't try to interfere with my wardrobe again. And three, I was transformed into a genius. From the moment I woke up in our back yard, I wouldn't have thanked you for all the back copies of *School Friend* - a weekly comic for snooty adolescent girls that had been my staple diet for years - and to Momma's amazement and mine, I began to visit the adult section of our local library. I quickly developed an interest in a book called *Anna Karenina* by a guy I'd never heard of called Leo Tolstoy, devouring it in two days before moving on to Hermann Hesse who, along with the complete works of Kant, Joyce, Schopenhauer and Descartes, kept me going for the next three months.

How did this happen? you may ask. How does a boy that drools over *School Friend* by day and beats the meat over it by night suddenly drop those kinds of activities and find an interest in the classics? And the answer is that, while a head injury or some other kind of physical disability can kill or cause permanent incapacitation, it can in some cases bring about a rewiring of brain signals triggering the release of dormant potential.

Sorry about waxing technical here but this is more or less what happened to me. According to stuff I've read, it's a bit like people in wheelchairs developing very strong arms. A kind of compensation in other words. In my case, massive over-compensation.

There have been many documented examples of this since history was first recorded, but I'm only going to tell you about three of the most recent ones (and if you don't want to know about them you can always skip the next half page or so. No offence will be taken. To tell you the God's honest, I don't give a toss what you skip, seeing as the only important example is mine).

Number one: a sales trainer called Derek Amato got severe concussion from hitting his head at the bottom of a swimming pool and became a master pianist despite not having had one moment of musical training.

Number two: Ellen Boudreaux is a blind autistic savant. She was born prematurely and had what is known as the blindness of prematurity. Yet she has reproduced hundreds of tunes and styles including *The Supremes* to *Duelling Banjos* (in which she plays both the four-string plectrum banjo and the five-string bluegrass banjo). One of her many amazing feats is with *Whole Lotta Love,* the Led Zeppelin Appassionata in which she replicates every voice, instrument and sound effect.

And number three: Jason Padgett was a furniture salesman. In 2002, two men attacked him in the street, leaving him with a severe concussion and post-traumatic stress disorder. But Padgett was transformed into a mathematical genius who can now see the whole world through the lens of geometry.

I'm just remembering that I meant to tell you earlier about *Steam 4 Teens*. That's the online site I started as a relief valve for my physical frustrations. And I was going to go on to say that I have no shortage of material. All I have to do is keep my eyes open and my antennae out. Write what you know, that's what they say, right?

For example, I was in Foyleside Shopping Centre yesterday and I absentmindedly went up a flight of stairs that's only supposed to be for going down. Anyways, I got near the top and out of the blue all these girls started coming down towards me, what seemed like an endless line of them, these amazing babes, about fifteen they were, that's the age of them I'm talking about now, the age that it's madness for you to lay a finger on them or be seen looking up their miniskirts (or wide-bottomed shorts for that matter) when you're at the foot of an escalator, let's imagine, and they're near the top, or even for you to think about too long, to dream perchance to … with incredible little chests and crotches that jumped out at me – and these mouthwatering zones were alluringly covered with the shortest, tightest tops and shortest tightest shorts I ever clapped eyes on; and then the cutest belly buttons everywhere you looked: the fecking stairs were coming down with them.

Now Derry girls are in the habit of dolling up if they're only going round to the corner shop for a half pound of sausages or a bar of Kit Kat for example, but this was something else entirely. And the most interesting range of colours I've seen since Jayne Mansfield graced the silver screen in *The Girl Can't Help It:* dream pink, Persian rose, cream yellow, baby mustard, burnt sienna, frosted aqua, air force blue, oolala black, Alabama crimson, seal brown, Titian red, tiffany scarlet, papaya whip, blinding saffron, Mountbatten pink, deep carrot orange, dark vanilla, school-bus yellow, Sacramento state green, amaranth pink, tulip red, Mexican fandango, American apricot and shocking salmon, to name only the ones I can remember offhand. (To be honest I couldn't actually swear to Mexican fandango and American apricot because the whole thing got to be a bit of a blur near the end).

And then they were squeezing past, that's right, squeezing past, hips and thighs and all the rest of it squeezing past, chests too, some just starting out and some nearly fully formed or maybe as fully formed as they were ever going to be. I must have said sorry every time one of these nymphets came against me. Sorry Miss. Oops. Sorry sorry sorry. Sorry sorry sorry sorry sorry. I beg your pardon. Sorry about that. Sorry sorry sorry sorry sorry sorry.

I used the word 'nymphets' there. That was actually sort of a generalisation. But make no mistake, over a quarter of these girls were nymphets, which for your information is at least three times the national average here in Ireland. Granted these statistics are entirely non-scientific, based as they are on personal observation, but I am a conscientious and acute observer and my findings are not to be taken lightly. Judging from their exotic complexions, these girls were all foreign and that in itself probably explains the high preponderance of nymphets among them.

It has only just occurred to me that many of you may not know what a nymphet is. OK. First and foremost, a nymphet is a girl who should be not less than fifteen and not more than sixteen. Next, although she doesn't need to have conventional good looks, she does need to have something of the primitive about her.

She should also have dim and distant eyes that go slit when she is either a) annoyed or b) up to no good, a bold and insolent mouth – this is not essential though it is highly desirable - and an almost diabolical charm in her movements that she may not even be aware of, what I would call a *frétillement* (Look at any video of Vanessa Paradis singing *Joe Le Taxi* when she was fourteen and you'll see what I mean). And finally, she must possess the kind of otherworldly face and body that have driven boys and men mad since Adam did a runner on Eve with Lilith.

But wait, I'm just remembering. I got things arseways there. Lilith left Adam, not the other way round. Yes, it's coming back now. According to *Genesis,* Lilith got fed up taking orders from Adam about which of them was top and which was bottom and she hit the road with the archangel Samael instead. That's Samael the sleazebag now, not to be confused in any way, shape or form with Samuel the prophet that's revered by Jews, Christians and Muslims alike.

Samael was the bad seed who spent most of his time preying in Seventh Heaven, the place he took Lil to and proceeded to drive her out of her fucking mind. And just to set the record straight once and for all: sex didn't start between the end of the Lady Chatterley ban and the Beatles' first LP; it started some time before that. And not with Adam and Eve either. What those two did was a biological duty, "go forth and multiply", with the unspoken threat: "because if you don't you're out of Eden on your ear."

No, according to the Apocryphon of John, Cain was born from Eve by intercourse with Samael. So this bad seed fertilised more eggs than would stock a chain of Walmart's, and for all we know he's still at it. But there's me digressing. I should have been telling you how nymphets lose their magic somewhere in their sixteenth year.

Now here's an example from first-hand experience. A bit over ten years ago, an entrancing fifteen-year-old who lived three doors from us used to ride her roller skates up and down the road past our house. She was a morose sort of a girl who was clearly unaware that her greatest admirer in the whole wide world was the middle-aged loser sitting on a chair outside his front door viewing her for all he was worth over the top of a sometimes rain-soaked newspaper, which also served as a fig leaf.

The girl, whose name was Emmanuelle by the way – I kid you not – wore nothing but a dirty grey vest, wide-bottom lime-green nylon running shorts, the cutest yellow ankle socks you ever saw, pale blue trainers and a polka-dot ribbon in her light brown hair. She had long and lovely legs and rode her skates with perfect grace, surging forward on one foot, then the other; and when she did a U-turn (sometimes adding a pirouette, *Mère de Dieu!*) which I timed at roughly every forty seconds, her vest would rise up to reveal her pink abdomen, and some days when the breeze was favourable I would even get a glimpse of her little white bum.

I tom-peeped her many times over a period of about two years until she slowly grew out of my mind, until she and her roller skates finally stirred about as much excitement in me as a Massey Ferguson tractor. And if you think that's bad, you ought to see her now in full bloom nearly twelve years on with her big glossy face, ridiculously large chest, great shaking butt and legs like skittles. Ageing is such a sad thing.

But not as sad as me, I suppose. Until the day I die, there will always be something deeply appealing to my weak and a corrupt mind in the beguiling faces and pale pubescent bodies of these girls in that one-year window from fifteen to sixteen. I am thoroughly ashamed of myself of course and am now throwing myself on your mercy, gentle reader. In my defence I will not even point to the phallocracies that are plaguing the modern world, controlled by dirty old men in positions of power. No, I will only say that all I want to do is dream.

To be truthful, I've started to think the whole thing is too much for me to bear. It doesn't seem right, all that maddening beauty going to waste on pimple-faced boys and hairy-handed seducers. It has got to the stage now that my eyes are drawn as if by a magnet to the feral faces, beautiful little breasts and dainty round bottoms that torture me day and daily.

Sometimes I'm convinced that the only solution is for me to be sectioned, kept out of harm's way - not harm to these enchanting creatures, but to my sanity. And in case you're in any doubt, I must make this clear. I have never, nor would ever, lay a finger or anything else on even the most pouting, brazen, deliberately provocative nymphet. Neither would I view pornographic images of this lot on the internet.

But just in case you didn't know, droolers as old as a hundred or more have been known to think at length about girls of this age. (According to *Biology For Learners:* Scottish Edition, hardback, currently being flogged on eBay for £37.19 sterling, it's the last thing to go in centenarian males except for their hearing).

So, there you have it. All I do is look. Think of the cat and the king and you'll know what I mean. The way I see it, where's the harm in looking? So, I view and that's it. Many of them catch me at it of course and there's a whole variety of reactions when they do. Some roll their eyes in a blasé kind of a way, some are shocked, some pretend shock, some are tickled pink and some screw up their faces in distaste. But they all leave me feeling ashamed, as if I've already violated them.

Yet here's a strange thing about shame. I'm only ashamed of these inclinations because the law here says I should be. You see, the age of consent in the United Kingdom is sixteen. Now if I lived in Angola, I could lawfully sleep with girls of twelve. But if that was too young for me, I could maybe spend a holiday in Japan where it's OK to get off with a thirteen-year-old. My preference would be South America actually. I've heard that a lot of the countries in that progressive continent set the limit at fifteen. This is the stuff of dreams of course, because that's the age certain girls change overnight into nymphets.

And dreams are what I live on. But who can tell what's ahead? I mean, have you heard of William Blake? Prize painter, poet extraordinaire and total weirdo, he's now considered by other weirdoes to be one of the most influential figures of all time. This is the dude that wrote

Tiger, tiger, burning bright
In the forests of the night,
What immortal hand or eye
Could frame thy fearful symmetry?

Why is he weird? I hear you ask. He's weird because he tells us to act out our longings. Just look at this gem from him: "The road of excess leads to the palace of wisdom."

Tiger tiger burning bright indeedie.

So maybe I shouldn't feel too bad about my shameful fantasies. I mean to say, the girl of the great Dante's dreams was only eight. Ever since I stopped reading *School Friend* and took up with Dante, the man has fascinated me. This God-like figure, the father of the Italian language according to some know-all on Wikipedia, would never have written his *Inferno* if he hadn't gone through his private one first – the titillating image of eight-year-old Beatrice whom he first met at a children's party when he was nine. And from then until the day he died he was haunted by that memory of her, a memory that never left him.

He saw just her once more about ten years later, this time in the street, but he didn't have the balls to speak to her. He did dream about her however, day and night, night and day. Poor Beatrice died young and even in death she was his obsessive object of desire. But he never admitted to wanting sex with her – too crude you see – either as an eight-year-old or an eighteen-year-old or anywhere in between.

So he sublimated his shocking need by writing *The Divine Comedy* and having Beatrice guide him through the nine celestial spheres of heaven. Confusing, what? But then Dante was one confused dude. Certifiable, of course.

He's not the only one that had a Beatrice in his head. Hermann Hesse, the Swiss-German writer, had one in a book he wrote called *Demian*. Basically the same doll as Dante's. The central character here is a student called Sinclair who spends most of his time searching for himself (not worth the bother, I could have told him). Then one day he sees this girl in the park. She has the face and figure of a boy and he immediately falls in love with her and he gives her the name Beatrice because Dante is his favourite writer.

He doesn't chat her up or anything like that, oh no, just goes home and thinks about her all the time. Not about having sex with her mind you, but about adoring her as if she was a goddess or a holy altar or something like that. This Sinclair obviously has a taste for boys as well as girls but doesn't like to admit it to himself. The thought of straight sex is disturbing enough without dwelling on any other kind.

And you ain't heard nothing till you've heard about this other screwball in Hesse's book, creep by the name of Pistorious. This boyo is one of Sinclair's mentors that help him on the path to truth. And what is truth? "I'm sure you have dreams and wishes of love," says Pisser to Sinclair. "Don't be afraid. Act them out. One should be fearless and consider nothing forbidden that our soul craves for." Pistorius was actually based on Doctor J. B. Lang, the psycho, analyst and all-round tithead who advised Hesse, the guy that wrote *Demian,* how to deal with his sexual urges. Let me tell you now, this is one mad fucking planet.

You know something? If any of these guys were around in the present day they'd be put away for conspiracy to rape. Just imagine it. You're a healthy sex-driven man and you see a beautiful girl in the street and you immediately want to have her. Or maybe she's a young teenager. But you still want her. So you think, what would William Blake tell you to do in this situation? And he'd probably say "I refer you to these words of mine which are still fawned on by scholars worldwide: "The road of excess leads to the palace of wisdom." In other words, go for it mate.

Did I tell you that it wasn't just Durante Dante and Herman Hesse that had a Beatrice? James Joyce had one too, except she was called Nora. Now James loved Nora Barnacle not as some kind of ethereal creature but as the brazen hussy who gave him a hand job on their first date: 16 June 1904, now known worldwide as Bloomsday.

He'd seen her sauntering down the street, bold as you like, and unlike Dante and Sinclair with their Beatrices, he took decisive action and asked her for a date. She accepted but then stood him up on the time-honoured principle of treating them mean and keeping them keen. And so it happened that he asked her out again and this time she turned up. They walked to Ringsend on the south bank of the Liffey where they sat down and without further ado she put her hand inside his trousers and jerked him off.

By the way, if you think my account of Joyce's experience is graphic you ought to read a copy of the letter he wrote to his Nora that went under the hammer awhile back for £240 000 at Sotheby's. Only don't show it to your mother. And something else. Who ever heard of a man writing one of the greatest masterpieces of all time and setting it in the exact twenty-four-hour period when he got the first hand-job that he didn't have to pay for? Makes you wonder what he might have produced if she'd given him a blow-job.

Looking back at all I've written so far, I suppose the label 'certifiable' could easily be stuck on me. The problem about being a genius is that you live in a different world from most of the rest of the world and of course you see things more clearly than they do. You perceive simple truths that the insane world can't perceive or doesn't want to perceive and this can drive you insane, so insane you could easily end up in the mental. As the brilliant playwright Nathaniel Lee said after they put him in a slammer in Bedlam, England's first hospital for the insane: "They called me mad, and I called them mad, and damn them, they outvoted me."

So make no mistake about it, being a genius can be fecking dangerous. You're better not letting people know you're different. A genius has to try and seem as dull and unimaginative as other people – which isn't easy. Oh no. I had this idea one time of joining *Mensa* thinking I'd find some souls of like mind, but everyone I met there was thicker than a coalhouse door. And arrogant on top of it. You should have seen them. All up their own arses and there wasn't one of them you'd have risked sending out for a loaf of bread or a pint of milk. To hell with *Mensa* is what I say. *Densa* would be a better name.

I stuck it out for two months with these phoneys and then told them I was having a breakdown. Which I suppose was true. When you suffer from too much sanity and too much brain, you're not far off being mad. Like for example, I listened to a five-part programme on BBC radio there awhile back. It was called *Whodunnit* and it was about the fifty per cent drop in teenage pregnancies in Britain over the past twenty years. Big news, but how did this phenomenon come about? That's what the serialised study set out to examine.

It wheeled on these academics by the shitload and they talked about things like government strategy, better sex education, a new sensible generation, cuter use of the condom, more teenagers staying on at college and going to university, less abuse of drugs and alcohol, it being uncool since nineteen ninety-eight for teens to get pregnant and a load of other things I can't remember. Not one of these doctors of drivel had a baldy clue what the real reasons were. If they'd spent less time talking to so-called sexperts and more time jacking off over the problem pages like I do, they'd have discovered a thing or two.

Like what? you ask. Well, like after nearly two hundred years of feminism, it has now reached the pass where a teenage girl will do almost anything to please her boyfriend. And this often means sucking him off or allowing him to bugger them, whichever he happens to be in the mood for at the time and neither of which have yet been known to knock a girl up. These soft-skinned lovely-limbed creatures have become receptacles for boys' semen near enough from head to tail. "It's all about him" sums up what many of them tell the agony aunts.

That's bad enough, but it's the people that go to see plays by the supposedly avant-garde writers that really get up my nose. A few years ago I was asked by the *Irish Times* to review Samuel Beckett's play *Waiting for Godot* that was being performed in the Millennium Forum here in Derry. So I did what was expected of me and wrote an entertaining litter of lies.

Don't be found out is my policy. I had observed this rule of thumb during all those years lecturing in return for a derisory salary, when I'd paid leghumping lip-service to conventional wisdom. Anyway, I sat in my seat for what seemed like all night listening to these two Beckett tramps, Vladimir and Estragon, sitting there spouting their bullshit and to be truthful I spent most of that time fantasising about what I'd really like to do. Which was to make my way to the stage at the end of the first act and say this to the audience:

Ladies and gentlemen, I came up here to explain what's wrong with you. You're sat there thinking you're doing what the upper-middle-class do. Your lives are boring and pointless so you let on to yourselves and others of the same imagined class that you appreciate culture. In pursuit of this, you've now come to a play about nothing happening and sit there not having the first idea about what's not happening.

Now I daresay you have some overdressed frenemies in the auditorium here tonight that you simply can't stand the sight of and vice versa of course, but it's very important for both you and them that you all see each other at this cultural event, if you'll excuse the expression. And so it goes, ladies and gentlemen. Sam

Beckett would laugh his bum off at the whole charade if he was still around, and he might even write a play about it that you and all these others would then go to.

Beckett, ladies and gentlemen, was the smoothest conman ever to tap a typewriter. And he's still getting away with it and him dead years ago. If I'd ever got a chance to talk to him, I know what I'd have done. I'd have got him by the elbow and said "Mr Beckett, here's what it's about. You get born and if you're lucky and work at it, you grow a bit. And then you die. And that's it. That's fucking it. No mystery. Born, live, grow, die. Goodnight."

But I was telling you about Dante. Dante was off his head. A lot of these writers were. James Joyce was mad as a hatter. I mean, when this guy was in his mid-teens he adored the Virgin Mary like she was God, but he had serious problems trying to distinguish between her and some of the whores he was doing business with during those tender years.

He also had a lot of time for Catherine the Great, who he claimed died in the middle of being sired by a horse. Catherine, he said, juggled at least twenty-two lovers and had a special interest in erotic art, owning several tables that had stuffed penises for legs. Can you beat that? Now how did she get her hands on the penises is what I'd like to know. Was she willed them, I wonder, or were they taken by force? Anyway, it's a funny old world, whatever way you look at it.

And by the way, deranged writers who suffered from sex mania weren't confined to just Dante and Blake and Joyce and Hesse. They were legion. And up there with the most revered was the mighty Roman writer

Virgil that was Dutch to me till after I awoke in our back yard on top of Brando.

I wasn't studying Virgil long when I discovered that he was one of the biggest suckers of all time for these little, nymphetic, God-creations, though I also learned that he actually preferred boys. Me now, I got over boys for good when I was thirteen after nearly getting myself castrated while making night-time mayhem on a camping holiday with Saint John Bosco's Boys' Club. That experience drove boys well and truly out of my system and I soon settled for shyly eyeing adolescent demon girls.

And then as the years fell away, I slowly came round to realising that I also had a disturbing penchant for fully furnished males. The thought of these dream men, big in the right places and to my mind as horny as honey bees, affected me greatly, especially if I imagined that they too had a taste for men. It may sound tragic to you but I loved nothing better than the thought of being wielded by a homo erectus, being his bitch, his invert, his permanent plaything.

Reader, don't blame me. It was my mother.

Now I know there will be some out there, some sickeningly solid citizens and possibly virtuous long-nosed country folk, who will still be inclined to blame me and me alone for my wretched impulses. They will say "Don't point the finger at your mother. Get a grip on yourself and behave like a responsible adult." And there will be others who will question the truth of things they will read in these pages and claim that no one person could possibly have gone through as many raw and strange experiences as I will soon be relating to you.

To the first two groups I say this: “Listen, Dipshit, there but for the grace of God go you.” And to the others I say: “Look, Doubter, at the drawings made by almost any five-year old refugee child, and ask yourself if they could really have been through what their drawings show. Well, I’m a refugee too, and here are my drawings.”

I fought and still fight my craving for both nymphets and man-beasts with might and main. I fill my life with stuff to keep me sane, oh yes. For example, I now get my kicks and company by posing as a highly-charged bisexual teenage girl on my *Steam 4 Teens* site, a site that stirs a lot of hearts and maybe more. And going way back to my mid-teens when I first became fully aware of my eclectic inclinations, I made up my mind to channel them in any way that wouldn’t hurt others and possibly land me in prison.

For example, I married Henrietta Bell when she was sweet sixteen and I was less than a year older. She actually looked more like fifteen at the time, and in my state of tumescent fervour I told myself that she would always look the same. But the pity was that within months of being married she stopped being a girl and started being a woman, with the makings of a fine Zapata moustache into the bargain.

Wait, scrub that. ‘Bargain’ isn’t the word I want. This was no bargain. Gone was the fetching limp where she would sometimes do a cute little hop, skip and jump to catch up with me as we walked out – and in its place was a sailor’s bow-legged tread.

But I interrupted myself when I was telling you about that never-ending line of nymphets in Foyleside Shopping Centre. The very thought of them had seriously discombobulated me and I urgently needed something to sort me out. Coffee, I thought. That'll do it. Thinking about this sort of stuff for long could cause a man permanent damage.

Five stairs from the top I smelled the coffee and Starbucks hove into view. I remember reading something about it being wrong to go there because they were cheating on tax. Probably the boy who wrote that would be doing the same himself if he could get away with it. Starbucks it is then. Double espresso please. Strong. What did I order that for? I should be taking a sedative after that kittenwalk. Must try today's newspaper rack here.

DOG FOULING – LATE-NIGHT SITTING OF DERRY CITY COUNCIL

Banner headline would you believe? Christ sake, there's Isis and Assad and Putin and the Turks and the Saudis butchering right left and centre, and Christianist extremists taking out wedding parties and hospitals and there's that jackass in The Oval Office and near enough the rest of the world being run by other nutters and the planet heading towards a war to end all wars, and what is Derry City Council doing? Derry City Council is holding an emergency late-night meeting about dogshit. To hell with that.

Now, where's the death notices? What page does it say? Twenty-seven. Best part of the whole paper. Always get a bit of relief from reading about some bastard I can't stand that's just after shuffling off the old mortal coil. Those girls would destroy your mind.

Hold on, something wrong here. Pages stuck together. Jam is it? And cream. Sticky gooey cream with jam in it. Forget it. Turn over. What's this?

AIR CHIEF MARSHAL FOO FOO CREMATED

Foo Foo, the pet poodle belonging to Thailand's Crown Prince Maha Vajiralongkorn, was recently cremated after four days of Buddhist funeral rites. It will be remembered that in 2007, US ambassador Skip Boyce hosted a gala dinner which Air Chief Marshal Foo Foo attended dressed in formal evening attire complete with paw mitts.

Well, if that doesn't take the biscuit. What is it about these Yanks and their weird names? Skip, Trig, Clint, Track, Chase, Tick. Yeah, Tick. Heard of one guy called Stetson. What can you say? Stetson.

I'll have to go soon. She'll be asking about who I saw, who I met, what they said. I'll have to make up a whole lot of stuff again. I'll tell her I met Mickey McKenna. She'll like that. She still fancies Mickey like mad. He's dead fifteen years but that doesn't matter. She never reads the paper and she's never out the door with her agoraphobia. And she remembers nothing. Well, not much anyway. She hides things on me in case I'll steal them. Hid her eyeglasses in the wardrobe one day and found them two days after in the back pocket of her dungarees. Put her nail scissors under the dog on the mantelpiece and nearly got her little toe amputated when she came across them a week later in one of her house slippers.

STEAM 4 TEENS

NB: Personal photos will not be tolerated. True beauty is on the inside.

A HARD NIGHT'S NIGHT

Denise's letters to her lover, steamed open for your delectation:

Sweet sweetest Huncan
I was working with one of the dildos you told me to use the ribbed kind though nothing's the same as you sweetie and I was trying to bring back that night out in Hawaii last September when you came to me in your beautiful bare pelt and carried me from the shower flat up against you and sat me on the window sill and worked at me softly with your lovely long fingers and then after you did that you lifted me even higher till my legs were round your neck and I felt your tongue reach inside of me and that's when the spasms started sweet heavens but before I knew it you had me on the bed and you bucked me away up off it again and again till I thought I could take no more O Huncan
I wish you were here right now

"Did you get the bread Alexis? And the eggs?"
"I did Henry. They're all out there on the shelf."

"I hope you got the right use-by date on the eggs."

"Course I did. Sure I always do."

"You didn't the last time. I was sick for two days after I ate one of them."

"That's because you let them lie for weeks before you even opened the carton."

"I did not. Anyway, you should have reminded me. But tell us this. You didn't come across anybody I know when you were out did you?"

"I did indeed. I was talking to Mickey McKenna."

"Aw. Mickey McKenna. It's a good while since ... how's he doing anyways? And how's he looking?"

"Great. Doing great and looking great. Actually, I had a coffee with him in Costa. Never saw him looking better. Wearing a new brown corduroy jacket too. And he was asking about you, said it seemed ages since he saw you and he wouldn't mind seeing you again soon."

God but she's an awful sight. Sunken, empty-eyed and a hide like parchment. And those brown blotches all over her hands and arms and face. Liver spots, isn't that what they call them? Funny they're called that when the people that have them are slowly dying. How does the saying go? You're dying near enough from the minute you're born? And the older you get the worse things get? Not for me though, not for me. Ageing doesn't bother me anymore. Just a matter of adapting. Like here I am going down the slippery slope, not sliding mind you, more like edging on my backside and stopping now and then as I dig in the old heels hard and watch all these others whizzing past me and over the edge, some fat, some obese, some slim, some as healthy looking as trout. And obituaries don't depress me either the way they used to. I've actually got to enjoy reading them, seeing ones younger than me going belly up. Did you ever notice? – these newspapers hardly ever give the cause of death when the dead person is over seventy, take it for granted you see that readers won't wonder at that because we're not expected to go on much longer after the big seven-o.

As for Henry, I try not to think about her too much now, those bristles on her chin and that open sore she has on her upper lip from trimming the old moustache. I should never have married her of course. The day she sashayed onto the green wearing those blinding-white hot-pants and twirling her fancy parasol was the day that finished me. And look at her now, just look at her now: not a tooth in her head and chin wagging like a freaking wart. I know I shouldn't bother my backside trying anything in bed but sometimes the old urge gets the better of me and I'm shifting over in a sort of desperation hoping to cradle her big bum in my lap and if she wakens I end up getting a dig in the ribs or worse.

And then other times I put on the frillies and inch over when she's asleep, working on the logic that what she doesn't feel can't annoy her, though the last time I did it she woke up and nearly had a fit. I still have appetite enough but the way it is with her now, she doesn't want to know and always ends up telling me to act my age.

It's quite scandalous of course. As you and I know, seventy-one is far from being finished. Robert Mugabe had three children with his young wife Grace when he was over seventy. Rupert Murdoch was older than me when he and Wendi Deng went at it ding-a-deng-dong and had two daughters in two years.

Not that I'd be looking for offspring at my age. Not like Harry Stevenson from out the Glen that got married again aged seventy-six and had his eleventh when he was eighty-two – all girls, not that that's strictly relevant. And he's still going. Last I heard, his third wife was expecting again. And she's only thirty-seven – well capable of giving him another two or three children. Harry makes mincemeat of what some of these doctors say about men in their seventies and eighties getting heart attacks and strokes from having sex.

Mention of Harry reminds me of a letter I saw from this old woman to a sex adviser in some magazine I picked up at the dentist's. "I'm seventy-nine and in the last ten years alone I have been married twice to younger men and taken a number of lovers," wrote the geriatric. "They're all dead now and, although I had very exciting sex with each and every one of them, what I always enjoyed most was masturbation. Lately, however, I'm not getting the same pleasure from this and I'm wondering if you could advise me on suitable sex toys?"

Well, what about that? I thought. So I stuffed the magazine down the front of my trousers and brought it home and left it lying open at the right page for Henry to see, but the next place I saw it was in the blue bin.

Anyway, I lost my concentration back there when I mentioned old Rupert. Who's this he's married to now? Don't say. It's coming to me. Whatdoyoucallher Hall. Samantha? No. Let me think. Kimberly? Not Kimberly. This bloody memory of mine. Ayesha? Nope. Jerry? That's it. Jerry Hall, big Jerry Hall. Yes. He struck up with her after he divorced Wendi for having a little thing going with Saint Anthony Blair.

But anyway, about the fourth Mrs Murdoch. Jerry, that is. From some of the trash newspapers I read in Starbucks I found out one or two things. This bird has been round the houses. Yep, round the houses is right. Antonio Lopez, Bryan Ferry, Mick Jagger (think of the height of Jerry and wee Mick not the size of two roasted spuds!) and now she's stuck in her thumb and got the biggest plum of them all, the Dirty Digger himself.

I remember reading years ago what Jerry's mother told her was the secret of keeping a man. "Simple," said old Mother Hall. You gotta be a maid in the living room, a cook in the kitchen and a whore in the bedroom." But Jerry reckoned she'd hire the first two and take care of the third bit herself. And, by the way, I heard that she brought Rupert to St Tropez for the honeymoon so as to deliver one in the eye for Jagger Wagger because that's where the Jagger rat pack used to let their hair down in the good ol' days before they got the walking frames.

But there was another reason she picked St Tropez. Oh yes. It seems the place is all hills and there's no transport to speak of. Word was, she had the poor eighty-five-year-old out walking three quarters of the day. So I'd say there wasn't any digging from Rupert come bedtime. Which meant fourteen nights of undisturbed sleep for big Jerry. Most blissful honeymoon she ever had.

Still, I'd rather be Rupert than me. Even though she's a bit on the big side, Jerry would be streets better than my Henry. To tell you the truth, I'd divorce her only it'd be too much hassle. And it would break her heart of course. She thrives on these little tussles with me and I get by with my reading and my *Steam 4 Teens*. Life could be worse.

> And then the other time the time you did it twice in ten minutes after the first time you let me slide slowly down the front of you against your awesome manhood and I nearly wet myself that's the honest truth my kidneys nearly went next you arranged me gently on the bed and tongued me everywhere *everywhere EVERYWHERE* and then you came up on top of me and made love all over again O my God it was like almost too much

Let's be reasonable. Fifty-four years is a bit long to be married to the same woman, especially if she's had a Zorro moustache for all that time. I've already mentioned that particular appendage, I think. My memory is that it became fully fledged about two weeks after the wedding and she's never put any work into it since. The best she ever managed were a few botched efforts with Wilkinson sword edge blades that left her with dark stubble and half-open scabs above those livid yellow lips of hers. And then she's got the nerve to get on to me about my nose hairs. Nose hair I should say. Singular.

You know what happened the other day? I was sitting there in the middle of my dinner and she turned round and said: "You'd really need to see about those nose hairs of yours Alexis. There's one hanging down now and it's nearly in your stew. And there's something sticking to it as well."

"What?" I said back to her and I said it in such a way that I didn't want to hear another word about it.

It was far far better than the time you got me up on the bonnet of that sky blue Ford Pick-up outside the Everglades Hotel remember? when the doorman was away I remember I arched my front to tempt you and you crooked two beautiful fingers till you found where I needed them and when you found it you knew you had me and the things you did next drowned my mind I wiggled and wiggled and wriggled and wriggled and then you drew out your fingers so slow and tempting and then my whole body went all jelly when that beautiful part of you worked its way in growing rising and then OMG exploding I still have a crick in my neck to this day because I remember you kept shifting me to suit the way you wanted and my head was against one of the windscreen wipers and my neck was near broke but I didn't care my whole body was trembling that much with what you were doing to me and then suddenly you were out too short a time it was and I cried out loud when you went because I needed you

there and I was still crying when the
doorman chased us

But once she gets started on that particular subject it's hard to stop her. "I don't know how long I've been telling you and you never see to it. Sure I got you a nose trimmer for your seventieth. Do you never use it?"

"I do use it," I said, "but the hair grows again. That's the thing about hairs. They grow even more after you cut them. Surely you of all people should know that."

She didn't like that one. There wasn't a word out of her for the next minute or so and I knew she was huffing. I gave one quick look and couldn't see her so I knew she was away to try and think of an answer. The woman has clearly never heard of waxing. Sometimes I think the real reason I'm still here is her mince stews.

I heard her shouting from the kitchen. She'd thought of something. "You should ask the barber to do it when you're getting your hair cut. He would do it for you. It's disgusting. How could you stand there talking to somebody when you're out the town and that thing dangling down right in front of them?"

"Didn't I ask him and he wouldn't do it," I shouted. "I offered to pay him extra and he still wouldn't do it. So don't be going on about that again. Do you hear?"

If only I'd known. But sure, what does a seventeen-year-old know about women? Damn all except that they're well capable of driving him out of his fucking skull. This might sound odd when you see what she's like now, but to be completely honest with you and without being the least bit blunt about it, she was the first girl that made me feel like a hundred-percent man.

You know what I'm talking about. I was still putting on lingerie in the privacy of my so-called home at that particular time and trying to get Bilko Hawkins the rugby player from down the street to notice me, and suddenly, just like that, I was all man. Couldn't wait to get her into bed.

I suppose I should tell you here that one of the other people I had my eye on was Father Austin Mathers that I went to Confession to. He had the finest-looking arse I ever saw on a man. It had a powerful furrow in it that always put me in mind of the cleavage a mature woman has in the middle of her bosom. It's hard to know what better way there is of telling you except maybe to say that the two sides of his bum met in the middle like a Donatello and you could tell this even with the coarse, black material his trousers were cut from.

Terrible clothes priests have to wear. I had dreams of him leaving his job to go away with me to someplace where we could sit talking moral philosophy every evening before retiring for another violent night in bed, preferably outside of Ireland, which of course was very backward at that time in all matters pertaining to the flesh and modern morality.

But it wasn't to be. I think I must have given something away when I was confessing my impure thoughts to him because my stumbling compliments about his great empathy may have come across as something more than ordinary admiration. Whatever, he called me a pervert and a predator and told me never to come next or near him again.

Let me tell you now, it's not easy to describe the daily disturbances that tormented my mind and body. Maybe you'll understand if I tell you about something that took place at a dance I went to when I was just sixteen. I was inching around the floor holding a fairly ordinary looking big-hipped girl at a decorous distance to the strains of *Unchained Melody*, a really slow tinker-teaser of a song in case you didn't know, when she casually pressed herself up against me while making conversation about her friend Myrtle who had lost her hairdressing job for being late for work twice in a row because her mother was sick with the shingles, bringing about near-frantic activity in my already jittering genitals.

All fine and normal you might say but, just as I was inconspicuously attempting to pull back from her to prevent an embarrassing spillage, I spied a sight for sore eyes over her left shoulder. A man in mauve shirt and tight cream trousers was practically conjoined with a girl whom I couldn't see properly – but what I did see, and couldn't take my eyes off, was his splendid bottom

Now I have unobtrusively viewed a good number of male bottoms in my day and studied and indeed serviced myself on pictures of the naked David in *Michelangelo: Complete Works* (hardcover £29.24), but here right in front of me was the daddy of them all, perfectly rounded, beautifully grooved and utterly breathtaking. Cue for massive discharge.

But I was telling you about Father Mathers. It actually wasn't my experience with him that turned me off Confession for good. No, it was the thing that happened to Patrick Mitchell. Patrick was an acquaintance of mine in our teenage years, a young man of very nervous disposition given to lascivious thoughts about the half-Chinese woman Fang Clare O'Shaughnessy that lives across the street from him, a woman of boundless bodily beauty who opened her curtains wide every night before taking her clothes off too slow for words.

This caused visible disorder in Patrick's body and it got to such a pass that he was afraid the whole thing might give him some class of seizure and he'd end up dying in a state of mortal sin with purgatory not an option. That was bad enough but when he was describing the whole thing to Father Mathers in the privacy of the confession box, he went into such detail, not only concerning the havoc the experience with the O'Shaughnessy woman had wrought on his organism, but also about closing his eyes tight every time except the first time when the lady in question undressed frontally (because the first time he clapped eyes on the naked front of her, he could see that she was hideously hairy where he never expected her to be) and also about opening them really wide for the second half when she turned to let him see her big backside.

The priest let an unearthly roar out of him (so unearthly that it might have come from heaven itself was what Patrick told me) and then hissed that he wasn't there to listen to disgusting things like that and what was a Catholic doing with his curtains open every night opposite a Godless communist unless it was to steep himself in the cesspit of mortal sin?

Patrick later questioned me on what a priest was doing in the confession box if he wasn't there to listen to disgusting things: because sins were disgusting things and that was what Confession was for; and it was then I made up my mind once and for all that Confession was not for me.

> I want to be awash with you filled from
> you flushed by you that my love is why
> I'm going to insert this here right now
> and close my eyes to try and imagine it
> is that part of you so I can bring back
> some of your wonder and those
> Hawaiian nights that I want to live again
> as long as I live

Right, that'll do it. Just post it for all my lovely young readers and that'll be it for today. You know, it wasn't very long ago that none of these hot little things would take me under their notice. Wait, that's only partly true. Up till I was sixty or so, I looked at them with the hunger of a sixteen-year-old and they just looked through me. But for the last ten years or so, some of them have been smiling at me and sending my body racing, even though I'm under no illusions. They're smiling because I'm not a danger anymore, just a pleasant-looking pensioner, a harmless old git.

And to think I used to sing her that song after we got married. I didn't actually mind the moustache and the sailor's walk then. To be frank, I'd say the reason was that maybe they helped to give me a bit of the man side of her.

> *I love you as I never loved before*
> *Since first I met you on the village green.*

Come to me 'ere my dream of love is o'er -
I love you as I love you, when you were sweet,
When you were sweet sixteen.

And then there was the first poem I ever sent her after we were married. She thought I wrote it myself. Well, I suppose I did in a way. I put purple ink in my pen and wrote the words on a pink sheet of Basildon Bond and sealed it in a pink Basildon Bond envelope. But the words are Alfred Tennyson's. A lot of my writing back then was influenced by Tennyson.

But I still remember what happened the day she got it in the post. She took me by the hand (let's say) and led me from one end of Heaven to the other. How could I ever forget it?

My heart would hear you and beat,
Were it earth in an earthy bed.
My dust would hear you and beat,
Had I lain for a century dead,
Would start and tremble under your feet,
And blossom in purple and red.

For the next six months I serenaded her with the best of Byron, Burns, Baudelaire and Tennyson, not to mention bits from Wordsworth, Goethe, de Larra, Poe, Pope, Whitman, Leopardi and Lawrence, and long before the fire of my venereal appetite was outlawed, my John Thomas had taken on the texture of a chalk-crusted shrimp.

Yes, it was outlawed. And that was basically because Henry wrote to her sister Majella Ann telling her how much she adored love poetry and the interfering bitch responded by buying her a poetry tome as big as a breeze block. It was called The Romantics and had some of my best stuff between its covers. The result was that I was banished from the conjugal bed and had all favours withdrawn to the accompaniment of slurs like *Cheat!* and *Phoney!*

I pleaded with her, pointing out that James Joyce's lover Nora Barnacle had pilfered parts of love stories from women's magazines to use in her letters to him. But it was no good, I was out on my bum. I gave her flowers and posted expensive love cards to her. But nothing doing. I even tried logic. "Listen darling," I'd say. "Would you refuse a love heart from me because it was made by *Swizzels Matlow*? Would you? And listen to me. Please! No, no, listen. Joyce overlooked Nora's little white lies because he knew they came from her adoration of him. Now the question is, Henry, are you as big a man as Joyce?" (I don't think the last bit helped my case).

And then after two years, in the middle of the worst winter since 1947 according to some girl from the Met Office, I was allowed back into the bed, but only as a draught-stopper. So the embargo has now in effect lasted the guts of fifty-four years. Unreasonable of course. Cruelly unjust. Grounds for separation too, except that I do manage to sneak the occasional surreptitious spasm by making contact when she's out cold, and that keeps me going.

Lately, I've been considering spending some time in Edinburgh, actually. It seems they have massage parlours there that could do me the world of good. There's one in particular I wouldn't mind trying out. To quote the blurb I read on the web:

"The closing stages – described variously as a *'finish' or 'happy ending' – focus heavily on the male genitalia. Massotherapists skilled in our treatment are also found in Cebu City, Philippines. Remember, friends, that the true purpose of the massage is to awaken one's kundalini, an enlightened-related energy which when released can lead to eventual salvation."*

Now I'd certainly be in for awakening my kundalini and I wouldn't say no to eventual salvation either, but there are two problems that I'd have to overcome before flying to Edinburgh. Firstly, there's what to do about Henry while I'm away – the woman wouldn't be able to cope – and then there's the embarrassment of asking beforehand if I could have a man as my massotherapist (nymphets are out; no point in looking for the impossible).

But here's something I didn't tell you. And it's bittersweet. Henry and I got married in 1963 around the time The Beatles released their first album. This, as everyone knows, was the beginning of a new age. But not for me, no, not for me. The Swinging Sixties seen but not lived. Still, I stored the image of hot-panted schoolgirls shimmying along the street being chatted up by longhaired, lavishly endowed young men in tight jeans and used that same image as a bedtime aphrodisiac before tucking into my moustachioed wife.

Anyway, must see if anybody's read my latest offerings yet. She's gone upstairs. I hear her feet on the bathroom floor. What's this it was I was going to tell her? Jesus, I really think my memory's starting to go.

YellaRoseofTexas Re: *A Hard Night's Night*

Laguna Vista
Joined: 2 years ago
Wow!

StunGun Re: *A Hard Night's Night*
Booby Dingle, Herefordshire
Joined: 6 months ago
Never try it on a sky-blue Ford Pick-up luv. Coulda told ya :-)

Chubb23157 Re: *A Hard Night's Night*
La Carlota, Negros Occidental
Joined: one week ago
Get right back in there Huncan boy. And stay put this time. Try again, fail again, fail better.

Ding-a-ling-a-ling Re: *A Hard Night's Night*
Limoges
Joined: 3 years ago
Huncan is so toying with u Sweetie. Can't u see? (Btw, is this for real?)

JustineMacAdooey Re: *A Hard Night's Night*
Newcastle, County Down
Joined: one week ago
Slut

Youscratchmine Re: *A Hard Night's Night*
Brisbane
Joined: one year ago

Slut is right. A disgrace to girlhood.

Denise Re: *A Hard Night's Night*
Derry, Ireland
Why don't you two just go eat a grape? You're jealous.

Youscratchmine Re: *A Hard Night's Night*
Brisbane
Joined: one year ago
No, I'll tell you what. ***You*** *eat a grape.*

Denise Re: *A Hard Night's Night*
Derry, Ireland
Listen. Go fack yourself.

Ding-a-ling-a-ling Re: *A Hard Night's Night*
Limoges
Joined: 3 years ago
I give in. This is for real. This is awesome. I think I'm going to die. Puleeese give us more. Puleeese!

Sweetie Re: *A Hard Night's Night*
Boston, Lincolnshire
Joined: 2 months ago
I looooove this. I really looooove it. Oml.

Scoobydoobydo Re: *A Hard Night's Night*
Dublin, Ireland
Joined: one day ago
WwAahhhhhh!!

Doubledeedee Re: *A Hard Night's Night*
Amarillo, Texas
Joined: just now
Jumping jubilees! I'm a girl and I want you Denise. Forever and ever. Is that all right?

Denise Re: *A Hard Night's Night*
Derry, Ireland
You bet it is. Why don't you get back to me?

Littlemermaid Re: *A Hard Night's Night*
Odense, Denmark
Joined: 2 weeks ago
You are a magician Denise. You are part of every girl's fairy tale. I think maybe I love you a little bit.

Denise Re: *A Hard Night's Night*
Derry, Ireland
Thank you so much Littlemermaid. You're so sweet. What age are you? And what do you wear in bed? Isn't Odense where Hans Christian Andersen was born?

Littlemermaid Re: *A Hard Night's Night*
Odense, Denmark
Joined: 2 weeks ago
Yes. And we have the most beautiful bronze statue of The Little Mermaid in

our city. Fifteen. I was fifteen two days ago. And it depends who's with me. Sometimes nothing at all.

My God, she's coming on to me. Is she lesbian? She must be a lesbian. Or maybe she's bi. Or trans. Or what do you call them? There's a whole list. Christ, this is terrible. What am I going to do? This is so wonderful.

Denise Re: *A Hard Night's Night*
Derry, Ireland
I've always wanted to go to Denmark. What kind of a place is Odense?

Littlemermaid Re: *A Hard Night's Night*
Odense, Denmark
Joined: 2 weeks ago
It's a lovely cultural city. Did you ever hear of King Cnut? He was Danish. He's the one that tried to order the tide not to come in on him. We call him Cnutcase. I've actually been living in Somerset, England for a while now but my heart is in Odense. That man of yours is very romantic. Have you ever slept with anyone else? It's funny you say you'd love to go to Denmark because I'd love to go to Derry.

Denise Re: *A Hard Night's Night*
Derry, Ireland
I can recommend some lovely guest houses here if you'd like to come. Or

you could stay with me. I actually live in a house by myself inherited from my parents who died in a suicide pact. I don't own it yet but I will. There are three big double beds in it. Huncan will be away on business all of next month so there would be no problem. You sound so mature for your age.

Good Christ. What have I done!

Littlemermaid Re: *A Hard Night's Night*
Odense, Denmark
Joined: 2 weeks ago
Most people say I look very mature for my age too. I'm left college and am unemployed but I've money saved. Maybe I'll settle in Derry, who knows? What age are you and what colour undies do you most like your partner to wear? I feel I nearly know you already Denise. My real name is Isabella. We have a Princess Isabella in Denmark who is third in line of succession to the throne.

Denise Re: *A Hard Night's Night*
Derry, Ireland
I've seen pictures of her. She's lovely. Anything that's in pink. I could eat Huncan when he comes to bed with his light pink lollipop legband brief panties on. I always start by kissing the

crenulated track left on his lovely brown stomach by his panties. He loves me doing that. Your princess is a dish and so is her husband. Both utterly gorgeous.

Littlemermaid Re: *A Hard Night's Night*
Odense, Denmark
Joined: 2 weeks ago
Is Huncan the first lover you've had?

Denise Re: *A Hard Night's Night*
Derry, Ireland
Well, he's the first man I've had. I'll never forget the night I met him. It was in our local bi bar, Stonewall Stockade you call it. I always think it's a great place to go because it doubles your chances of a good night. Anyway, I was trying to catch the eye of a girl wearing nearly nothing on top and a really short muslin skirt that was starting to make me really damp when suddenly I found this animal smell right behind me and I turned round and there he was. Huncan. We chatted and he bought me a Lucky Devil that when I took my first sip made me want to have him there and then. I'll never forget what we did that night.

Littlemermaid Re: *A Hard Day's Night*
Odense, Denmark

Joined: 2 weeks ago
I'm coming. What's your email?

Denise Re: *A Hard Night's Night*
Derry, Ireland
I don't do email. No security. Just let me know what plane you're flying in on and I'll meet you. Promise.

Hankypanty girl Re: *A Hard Night's Night*
Pozuela, Toledo, Spain
Joined: 6 months ago
Update! I canna wait!! Oh mi dulce Jesús!!!

Minnie1250 Re: *A Hard Night's Night*
Camden Town
Joined: 3 weeks ago
Tears are filling my eyes now. I can't see the words in front of me anymore. This is the most woooonnnderfull book I've ever read. Give me more please!!!

Christ but I love this. It's as if all these little ones want a piece of me. I can see them now. Young Minnie, beautiful gorgeous little Minnie. Ah Minnie, I aim to please. And Doubledeedee from way down in Amarillo. Show me the way Doubledeedee. And Hankypanty girl, my little Spanish chica. Mwah! Forget about JustineMacAdooey and Youscratchmine. You get sour grapes everywhere.

Now I'm remembering that other wonderful night when your heart and your hands caressed me everyhow and I felt as if your fingers were reaching into my very soul I was part of you that night inside the massive beating of your heart inside your beautiful private parts when you opened your thighs to me big and wet and allowed me to bring you along and then do you remember you must remember I took your kingly sceptre in my hands and impaled myself with it right to the core of me once a hundred times a thousand times are not enough I am your subject now I am your slave now I want to live and die in your deep hollows in every nook of you that my precious would be the heaven I crave your fountain courses through me and I feel the rush of you even when you're not here O my darlingest Huncan

Littlemermaid Re: *A Hard Night's Night*
Odense, Denmark
Joined: 2 weeks ago
When can I come? After the first night in your house I'd love to go on a tour of Inishowen. I've seen pictures of the scenery there and I can't wait. We could sleep in a different hotel every night. How does that sound? I just can't wait.

Denise Re: *A Hard Night's Night*
Derry, Ireland
Joined: 3 years ago
We'll do whatever you want Isabella.

Christ.

Scoobydoobydo Re: *A Hard Night's Night*
Dublin, Ireland
Joined: one day ago
OOOHHHHH I love this story. I soooo love this story. What a man!

Kirsty Keeler Re: *A Hard Night's Night*
London, England
Joined: two months ago
Awesome! And then some! Update please. Pleeeeaaassse!

The Ginger Girl Re: *A Hard Night's Night*
Aberdeen, Scotland
Joined: one day ago
Omg so crying right now.
Love your book! Never want it to end.
Don't let it end. Can't wait for an update.

Scoobydoobydo
Dublin, Ireland
Joined: one day ago
Huncan is awesome. I'm reading it all over again. I'm in tears now. This is beauuutiful.

Ding-a-ling-a-ling Re: *A Hard Night's Night*
Limoges
Load of crap. Hunc's just after the one thing babe and don't you forget it.

Littletramp Re: *A Hard Night's Night*
Boston, Lincolnshire
Joined: 2 months ago
Omg! this is like, awesome! amazing stuff rite here!!!!!!!!!! :D:D:D makes my bunny buns go all tingly! upload soon pwease! :D

That's it. I remember now what I was going to tell her. How the hell could I have forgotten?

"And flush that toilet if you're doing your number two," I roared up the stairs. "And you might open the window too."

"Huh?"

She heard me rightly but she always says huh when she needs the time to think.

"You heard me."

"That was you, Alexis. You were the last one in here. The smell in this bathroom would kill a horse."

+++++

I wanted to explain to you properly about my parents. That should have been one of the first things I did. But I tend to ramble. It's got to the stage now where the only time I've got any discipline at all is when I'm making up stuff for the young ones.

Yes, my parents. None of the two of them wanted me. But you know that already I think. Momma was expecting a girl – expecting in the sense of expectation I should add – and Pappa didn't want a child of any description. So I grew up not only wondering what I was doing with male parts but feeling very unwelcome indeed. Therefore, you won't be surprised to be told that their deaths had little impact on me. At the time they passed on, I was concentrating on getting top marks in my A level examinations. Until Henry came along that is. After that, my concentration was divided.

Mais je digresse. Pappa went tits up first Wednesday of the month. Don't ask me what month but I know it was the first Wednesday because that's when I always got my bonus in Mulroney's butcher's where I worked part-time, and I remember being given it just before I heard the news. We got a bonus if the turnover was above a certain amount for the thirty days before that, unless we were absent from work for no good reason. I remember my boss Johnny Pat McGroin gave me the five shillings and I went away and got slaughtered in *Tracy's Nook* that evening to the accompaniment of a drunken hag singing *Love is Teasin'*. Funny how some things stick in your head.

Momma died not long after Henry and I tied the knot. I'm not sure of the date but I know we buried her on a Friday. I remember this because I had bacon, two fried eggs, black pudding, white pudding and three Denny's pork sausages when I got back home from the funeral, and Henry told me that that was a mortal sin because it was a day of abstinence and this meant I shouldn't be eating meat. I wasn't on very good terms with her that particular day because in bed the night before when we'd got finished and we were lying there looking up at the ceiling, I turned to her and said "Was that OK?" and she said back to me "To tell you the truth Alexis, I'd far rather have had a cup of tea and a toasted muffin." So when she started going on about the mortal sin thing I said "Do you really mean to say if I died now I'd go to hell for all eternity just for eating a fry? What's the big deal about a Friday anyway?" and she said "Jesus was crucified on a Friday."

And I said "And?"

And she said "Because Jesus was crucified for our salvation on a Friday."

And I said "And?"

And she said "Because we should do penance for that."

And I said "For what? Sure I didn't crucify him."

And she said "Ah, but you did."

And I said "I wasn't even there. I've got an alibi. I swear. I was in Dirty Nelly's along with Johnny Pat McGroin's brother Grip. But tell me this now Henry. What sort of a religion is it anyway that stitches you up for something that happened two thousand years ago? I doubt even Perry Mason could get a guilty verdict there."

And apart from reminding me that Perry Mason was a defence lawyer, she didn't talk to me for a week after that. I kept saying to her that a God who's bigger and smarter than anybody or anything wouldn't give a damn if we ate pig meat or cow meat or fish meat or bird shit on a Friday when he has to more to think about like the millions dying of unemployment and poverty and suicide and torture and persecution and war and starvation and disease and domestic violence; but she wouldn't listen and wouldn't let me near her in or out of bed. A full week I had to do without. Now that's what I call penance. My entire inside was thrown out of kilter. The heartburn was killing me, I took a rash on my backside, I couldn't sleep, my bowels wouldn't work. God, I wouldn't wish that state of affairs on any man, not even Donald Trump. Well, maybe Donald Trump.

+++++

That stuff about religion puts me in mind of The Collapsed Catholics Society. These three old guys sit round a table down in Sainsbury's cafe every day of the week and that's what they call themselves: The Collapsed Catholics Society. I sit with them sometimes before I do my shopping because to tell you the truth, it's the only social life I have now outside of the computer.

Members of the society, reading from left to right (and you can't go wrong: they're always on the same chairs at the same table) are Harry that wears the nappy and smells of bad plumbing; Len that has it in for the pope and the Clintons; and Mickey that fancies himself as some kind of guru.

"You know what Bill Sharkey used to always say? I'm talking to you, Professor." This was Mickey last Tuesday when I had plenty other things to do and should have known better than to sit down at all.

"No, what was that?" I asked.

Now I've no idea who Bill Sharkey is or was, but I've heard Mickey coming out with the same story about him a good few times and I couldn't be bothered reminding him. So I said "What was that?"

"'We're all in the queue', he used to say. 'We're all in the queue just waiting our turn.'"

The first time he said it to me, I asked him: "How do you mean?" and he said sort of wearily "Do you not see? The older you grow the closer you're getting to the front of the queue."

"Never a truer word," Harry said. "Onced you're over the hill, that's when you start gathering speed." Now I'm ready to swear that's from Schopenhauer. Harry was quoting Schopenhauer. And all he ever reads is *The Daily Star*. I took a sideways look at him. His face had gone all calm and he had this kind of serene air about him like he'd just relieved himself. Harry's favourite line is "I haven't spoken to me wife in years. I don't like to interrupt her." It was sort of funny the first time.

The third guy, Len, is a fat fraud that's full of pet hates. I notice lately he's using a walking stick. Younger than me too. This may sound uncharitable, but it gives me a lift to see him struggling a bit. He used to walk round the store with an empty basket in his hand, never did any shopping that I could see, just walked round and round stopping people he knew and keeping them in conversation for as long as they could stand it. He's got even worse since his wife died. And lately he's taken to using a trolley, empty of course. Looks a bit ridiculous but I suppose it gives him something to lean on.

"I was just thinking this morning," said Len. "D'you see yon one Hillary Clinton? Hillary Clinton went on in those debates about Trump feeling up women and treating them like dirt and sure her Bill's been at it since he got out of nappies. Feeling's the least of what that man did. Sure Yasser Arafat had to sit waiting outside the Oval Office till that girl got finishing sucking him off."

"Jesus," said Mickey. "I didn't think Arafat would've been like that."

"It was Bill got sucked off you eejit," said Len. "And hardly a word about it either. Trump's right about the newspapers and TV. Dead biased."

"He's a dirty animal," said Harry.

"Who? Bill?" said Mickey.

"Trump. Sure you heard him on that tape. What he does to women."

Len was shaking his head. "Touching them? Or more like it blowing his load about touching them? Where's the mistresses is what I'd like to know. You're not going to tell me he paid them off, are you?

"He paid off Stormy Daniels," said Harry.

"Who?"

"Stormy Daniels. She's a porn director. Clever girl, I heard. I think Trump promised he'd get her on *The Apprentice* if she did the business with him and after she did it, she signed a button-your-lip thing for a big pay-off. Over a hundred grand I heard."

"Dear ride," said Len. "But I suppose the man's got the money."

"She's a smart girl all right," said Harry. "Bright as a button. I heard some guy sent her a tweet saying 'Pretty sure dumb whores go to hell' and she tweeted back 'Whew! Glad I'm a smart one.'"

"I wouldn't listen to that stuff," said Len. "I'll tell you this now. Hillary's crowd were wheeling out all these women by the cartload going on about Trump getting a wee feel and there was Bill, not a whisper about him, getting the full whack every time, rutting around like Randy the red-nosed reindeer."

"Aye, it's supposed to be he lay with a whole lot of ones." said Mickey. "That girl, what do you call her, Flora something."

"Flowers," said Len.

"Flora Flowers. Good-looking one too. Did you ever see the back end she has on her? Makes you want to be young again. But sure there was plenty before her. And after too. I mind hearing on the wireless Bill got two state troopers one time to roll him up inside a carpet so's they could carry him up the stairs into a hotel bedroom where he'd this girl waiting for him."

"Any man goes to that bother can't be all bad," said Harry.

"He's a goodun all right. Would you do it? I'm talking to you Harry," said Len.

"Do what?"

"Do what Clinton did. You know, get rolled up inside a carpet and all?"

"I dunno. I'd have to check with the missus first."

"He was some boy," said Harry.

"You're right there," said Mickey. "It was a state trooper out of whatever you call the place Bill was governor in that he got to be his watchman."

"Watchman?

"Aye. You know, lookout. To see the coast was clear when he was going at some woman. Sure he told one of his troopers this girl he knew could suck a tennis ball through a garden hose."

Harry started blinking like mad. "Does that mean what I think it does?"

"Search me," said Mickey.

Harry let a big snort out of him. "Wait till you hear this. Do you know wee Packie Doherty from out by

Prehen?" he said. "Packie thinks oral sex means talking about it. Like over the phone to these sexy women. I swear to God."

"More like them talking to you," said Mickey. "And you pay a packet for it too. So I hear, anyway. Do you know what Packie told me his last phone bill was?"

"I don't understand what the big deal about Wild Bill is anyway," said Harry. "Sure all the presidents were at it. Goes with the job."

"I can't imagine Jimmy Carter all the same," I said. "Very holy man. I remember reading he used to spend half the day on his knees."

"So did Bill, so did Bill," said Len. "And I'm not even going to start about John F. And him supposed to have a bad back. How the fuck did he manage it anyway?"

"And when you think about Kennedy, we used to have him up there on our kitchen wall in between the Sacred Heart of Jesus and the pope," said Harry.

"But wait till you hear what I read about the one came after him," said Mickey. "You know, the next president after Kennedy."

"Johnson?" said Harry.

"Johnson. It seems his wife …"

"Lady Bird." said Mickey.

"What?"

"That's what they called her," said Mickey. "Lady Bird Johnson. She was all into women's lib."

"Right? Never knew that now. I knew she was Lady Bird but I never knew about the other thing. Anyway, she went to the wardrobe one day to get her new Easter bonnet out of it and Lyndon boy was in there humping away at some woman."

"Screw-in wardrobe," said Harry.

"Word was at the time that Lyndon would have fucked the leg of a table and sent it flowers in the morning," said Len.

A store assistant stopped beside us. I hoped she hadn't heard that. Cute young thing she was and bright red hair right down to the back of her knees. "Would you gentlemen like to go and serve yourselves?" she said. "You know there's no table service here."

"Pardon?" said Harry.

"It's self-service."

"No thanks love," said Len. "We're fine the way we are."

The girl hesitated. She seemed nervous but her chin was set kind of firmly. She was just beyond the age bracket I like but I was already overlooking that. "Yousens never buy anything," she said. "Yousens have been coming in here for ages and never onced bought anything."

"Don't annoy yourself about it love. You just see to the diners," said Len kindly. "Leave us whiners to ourselves."

"You can't get wine in the cafe," said the girl. "Just in the store. If you'd like to go to the store. The off-licence is down one of the aisles at the back. The last aisle on your right. Did you not know that?"

She was pale and fresh, new as a peeled egg. Her baggy blue jeans reminded me of the ones Vanessa Paradis had on the time she sang *Joe le Taxi* on the TV. I wanted to take a bite out of the backside behind them. The little cafe assistant's, not Vanessa's. For your information, I wanted to eat all of Vanessa. But Johnny Depp got her. And now they're broken up. Maybe the real thing didn't measure up to the fantasy. What age was I the time of *Joe le Taxi*? Let me think. Late thirties I'd say. Vanessa would have been about fourteen. I know what you're thinking. You're thinking I'm a dirty old man. But I'm not. Not really.

"One of the managers came over to me there a minute ago," said the girl, "and she told me to get you to buy something. She's going to get on to me now."

The girl turned her back on us and suddenly she was away, the seat of her jeans swaying between the tables as she flicked her lovely long hair over one shoulder, then the other. I was in lust again, only this time with one that was just that bit too old for me. A year I'd say. Maybe two. The jeans seemed pretty big for her but when she self-consciously tugged loose a fold of them from her little pale cleft she couldn't have looked any better if she'd been wearing the dress Monroe had on the night she sang that song to Kennedy.

"You know something?" said Len. "There's weird things about every American president ever was,"

"Not them all," said Harry. "There's Carter. And Obama. And what did you call the Gettysburg man?"

"Abraham Lincoln?" said Len.

"Aye, Lincoln. Clean as a whistle."

"You're joking," said Len.

"What d'you mean?"

"Lincoln," explained Len, "used to sleep with his bodyguard when they were away on business. And him with four children too."

"Shocking," said Mickey." I didn't think there was bisexuals in them days,"

"Funny world is all I can say," I said.

"I was wondering when the visiting professor was going to open his mouth," said Mickey. "What d'you mean sir?"

"Well," I said, "twenty years ago you were a pervert if you were gay. And now if you're against people being gay you're a dinosaur."

"You're right there," said Mickey. "You're not as green as you're cabbage-looking Prof. Backsides were never made for that."

"How'd they come up with the word anyway?" said Len.

"What word? Dinosaurs?"

"Gay," said Len. "It always meant a different thing before. Happy and all. Them people haven't much to be happy about. Sure they're getting beaten up and murdered a whole lot of places."

"Aye, and castrated,"

"Gender's only a social construct anyway," I said. It was out before I knew it. That's what comes from thinking aloud. I felt them all staring at me. Silence. All trying to work out what it meant. Bit above their pay grade obviously. So Harry moved things along.

"But do you see that stuff about big Bill getting his end away?" he said. "All that's nothing to your man Tony Blair sucking up to dictators and all."

"Don't talk to me about that man," said Len. "All he's interested in is money."

"Maybe now he's a Catholic he'll turn over a new leaf," I said, just to get them going.

"You fucking joking?" said Len. "He'll be taking tips from the pope about how to add to his pile."

"Is that not going a bit far Len?" I said. "Does Francis not live a very austere life? Doesn't he drive a second-hand Fiat? Or is it a Renault?" Good steam winding these boys up.

Len gave me a pitying look. "Listen Professor," he said. "The man's full of gimmicks. Did yeez hear the latest on the news there? Francis was sitting in his room in the Vatican talking on Skype to these astronauts that are up in the big station away out in space."

"Oh he's very modern all right. Wasn't he talking to them about Galileo?" I asked.

"Is that the astronomer?" said Len. "Naw. Wait till you hear now. He asked them two questions. Where do we come from and where are we going?"

"I coulda told him that and I've never even been on an aeroplane," said Mickey. "We come from tadpoles and we're going to hell in a handcart."

"Tell us something we don't know," said Harry and immediately took a fit of coughing. We all waited respectfully till he'd finished. "Sorry about that, boys. I got a bad wetting going home yesterday so I did."

"You're all right," said Len. "Don't be trying to talk now. Anyway, you see what I was saying there about gimmicks?" said Len. "All these things are to lead you off the track. The Catholic Church has the richest business in the world."

"Save your breath man," said Mickey. "You're preaching to the converted."

"And you know who's the richest man in the world?" said Len.

"Go and sell all you have and give the money to the poor," intoned Mickey.

"What in God's name are you on about?" spluttered Harry.

"Then you can come and follow me," continued Mickey.

"Here, hold on till I get that man a glass of water."

"You're not listening to a fucking word I'm saying," said Mickey. "I'm telling you what Jesus said. The pope wouldn't say a thing like that. Except when he's preaching. The Church stopped believing that stuff after your man Constantine set them up."

"Constantine who?" demanded Len.

"Constantine Constantine. Are you stupid or what? Did you never hear of Constantine? Big Roman emperor. Constantine the whatdoyecallit. After that, it was money money money. Christ was never anywhere near Rome, wouldn't have touched the place with a ten foot crozier. Listen, the Church is rolling around with Goldman Sachs in a big moneybed and so is Tony Blair. Blair's Sachs' top ambassador sure. "

"You're telling me that now?"

"I am. The Church turned over a new leaf after Connie boy took a shine to them. From then on, they followed the money. The Vatican's where cardinal sinners go to prey. With an e."

"Nice one Mickey," said Len.

"They're living a lie so they are."

"Listen," said Len. "That crowd can tell lies better than you and me can tell the truth."

Mickey suddenly turned to me. "Tell us this and tell us no more Professor. Did you ever hear tell of Laura Lee?"

"Of course I have," I said. He wrote Cider with Rosie. And …"

"This isn't a man I'm talking about," said Mickey. "This is a girl that was a prostitute."

"Never heard of her," I said.

"Well, she's into the law in a big way and somebody told me she used to be into Vatican banking before that. She says she turned to being a prostitute to get rid of the bad name of being a Vatican bankster."

"You're joking!" said Harry.

"I am not," said Mickey. "I'd swear on the Bible if I believed in it. Listen, do any of yous know the answer to this one now? What's the difference between a dead cat on the motorway and a dead Vatican bankster on the motorway?"

"You'd better tell us," I said.

"There's skidmarks around the cat."

"That's a goodun," said Harry. "I mind the time I went to get a loan …"

"Wait till you hear," interrupted Len. "You aren't going to believe this. Did you hear about the monastery that's going to close?"

"Naw. So what anyway?" said Harry.

"Well," said Len, "it's been going for donkey's years, so it has, and it's not letting any new monks in. Must have cost millions to build and it's closing. It seems monasteries are closing everywhere. Not enough recruits. And do you know why?"

"Why?"

"Because there's all these gay men's sites now and they don't have to join monasteries anymore to get it."

"Get it?" I asked.

"Aye. You know. Their nuts."

"I don't folly your meaning Len," said Mickey. "Are you trying to tell us monks be doing that instead of praying?"

"Naw, they be praying too. You see, up till things like Grindr and gay clubs started, these people had to go into men's lavatories or join monasteries for it."

"Aye, and cruising," said Harry. "And you see here in Derry, there's a place in Derry, sort of a club I think, something Stockade you call it."

"I heard of that place," nodded Len. "So there you are. They can get it dead easy now. They don't have to join a monastery."

"Hold on. Are you trying to tell me that all monks are gay?" asked Mickey.

"I never said that. There's straight monks and bent monks just like there's straight priests and bent priests."

"And straight farmers and bent farmers," I added.

"We're talking about priests and monks Prof," said Len testily. "Do you know this? Wait till you hear this now. There's supposed to be a monsignor in Rome that's nearly ready to be a cardinal and he picks up these young men that are going on to be priests. Jessica, they call him."

Harry furrowed his brow. "Jessica? But sure that's a girl's name. Aw, I see now what you're saying."

"Anyway, Jessica drops into these Vatican universities and hands out his business card and invites students he likes the look of up to his apartment. And when they come up he asks them if they'd be interested in seeing the bed that Pope John the twenty-third slept in."

"Jesus, that's some pick-up line," said Harry.

I could see Mickey was champing at the bit, raring to get speaking. "Listen," he said. "I bet you never heard anything like this here. D'you know what's kept down in the catacombs under the Vatican?"

"Dead bodies?" I asked.

"Aye, dead bodies. And who do you think one of them is? All wrapped up like a mummy."

"Brigitte Bardot?" I said.

"Brigitte Bardot's still alive Lex. You'd think you'd have known that. Anyway, it's a man I'm talking about."

"General Pinochet?" said Harry.

"Nope"

"I know now who you mean," said Len. "Don't be giving it away now. I think I heard about this. That Mafia boy that made big donations the pope couldn't refuse? Bernadino or something? Right?"

"Hold on. Not Bernadino. Renatino," said Harry.

"Naw, yous are wrong. It's that other mobster. De Pedis. Isn't that him Mickey?" said Len.

"Nope. The pope's got De Pedis in a tomb in some big basilica downtown."

"Who then?"

"Jesus Christ."

Harry's eyes were popping. "Jesus Christ Mickey! What are ye talking about?"

"How could it be Jesus Christ?" said Len. "And how do you know it's him if he's wrapped up like a mummy?"

"Hidden away in this crypt and two blind nuns guarding him," explained Mickey. "See, Rome doesn't want people to know he never rose from the dead."

"Who?" asked Len.

"Jesus Christ! Are you listening to me at all?"

"Where did you hear all that, Mickey?" I asked.

"Me wife read it in a book. She's a great reader. She showed me the part and all."

"God Almighty," wheezed Harry. "That crowd in Rome'd be in deep shit if people found out. Sure that'd be them finished."

"I wonder where all their money would go then?" said Len. "You know, if the whole thing got out."

I heard the telltale cough and half closed my eyes. I knew the sign. Harry was delivering himself of some green mucus, firing it into a big brown handkerchief which he then slipped into his trouser pocket, sticky side first. He sniffed heavily and said "Sure did you not hear about your man Pell investigating the crookery that's going on in the Vatican?"

"Pell?" said Mickey.

"That cardinal from Australia. Did you never hear of him did you not? Big financial expert. He's in Rome investigating a whole crowd of cardinals that's been laundering money since they hit the jackpot with Constantine."

"Aye," added Len. "And the Australian cops are investigating *him.*"

Mickey was all agog. "Pell? You're serious? What'd he do?"

"Messing about with boys," said Len. "Well, that's what he's being arrested for anyway. And they say he covered up for a whole load of other priests doing the same thing. It's supposed to be he's not fit to go back to Australia to be grilled about it. He got some doctor to give him a sick note."

"Did any of yous ever hear the one about Jimmy the Brick?" said Harry. "Jimmy rings up the foreman on the building site one morning and says 'I cannae come to work today boss' and the foreman says 'Why not?' and Jimmy says 'I'm sick' and the foreman says 'We're very short of men here Jimmy. How sick are you?' and Jimmy says 'Well, I'm in bed here at the minute shagging me mother. Is that sick enough for you?'"

"You shouldn't be telling jokes like that," growled Mickey. "That's below the belt. You're a dirty brute, Harry, d'you know that?"

"Me a dirty brute?" said Harry. "What about that Cardinal Law? He should be in jail for all the covering up he did over in Boston and the pope has him back in Rome and made him his second-in-command."

"You're telling me he's number two in the Vatican even after what he did?" said Len. "Well now, I never knew that."

"He is."

"Aye. And number two sounds like a good name too," said Harry.

"Never a truer word. But what about his real name? Law. That's a bit of a funny name for him to have," said Len.

"Aye, well that's true, now I think about it," said Harry.

"And you know why they go for boys?" said Mickey. "Because they used to be boys themselves and they know what boys like done to them. After that, they take a mile out of it. And then they blackmail them you see, like telling them if they spill the beans, people will all say they were to blame too and they'd be put in a reformatory."

"That's it. Crafty buggers," said Len.

"Never a truer word."

"And then as well as that they can do what they want with boys and they still won't get pregnant," said Mickey.

Len was nodding away. "And the priests and bishops won't get pregnant either."

"For God sake. Sure if priests and bishops could get pregnant they'd be turning abortion into a sacrament," said Mickey.

"What is it about them anyway?" said Len. "They think they're a cut above other religions as if they're dead special for not letting priests get married and then they end up having all this sex with children and covering it up. Do they think we're stupid or what?"

"Keep your voices down men," I said. "You don't know who might be listening. Muddlecrass Catholics wouldn't like to hear you saying things like that."

"Middleclass you mean?" said Len. "I'd say you're a wee bit muddled there, Lexie."

"You know how I worked out there's no God?" said Mickey.

"How?"

"It's the awful dirty way children are made. I mean to say, that's where it all is. Down there, know what I'm saying? Think of all the other things that goes on down there all inside of three or four inches. No God with any respect for you would make you to be like that."

There was a thoughtful silence and then a rearward expulsion of gas from Harry's direction. We all sniffed tentatively and then held our collective breaths. When the air cleared Len picked up a newspaper from the table and pointed to something in it. "Hey, did any of yous see this?" he said. "There's a part here where it says they're calling a crater they discovered on some planet after a wee girl."

"That sounds very interesting," I said.

"So it is," said Len. "Just imagine, somebody getting a crater called after them." He blinked then and continued: "Hold on a minute till I read it again." Lengthy pause. "Sorry. She's not a wee girl at all. She's dead. It says here she's dead. But she used to be a wee girl away back in the nineteen thirties and she thought up the name Pluto for the planet. You know the planet that's called Pluto? Well, it wasn't called anything then. Wait till I see what else it says. Aye, these astronomers were trying to think of a name for a planet they discovered and she came up with Pluto."

"So they called it after Pluto in the cartoons," said Mickey.

"I don't think so," I said. "Pluto was the Roman god of the underworld."

Mickey was getting annoyed. "You're talking out of your big smart arse, Professor. Pluto was the dog that was friendly with Mickey Mouse. Sure what would a wee girl know about some Roman god?"

There was no answer to that. The man was right.

+++++

I don't really mind being seventy-one. Well, not a lot anyway. As far as I can see from looking around me, seventy-one is the new fifty. There are drawbacks though. Like when your prostate gland feels like it's the size of a rugby ball. It's supposed to be no bigger than a walnut and it's away down inside of you near the family jewels. That's if you're a man of course. Women don't have prostrates. It's a great article actually because it turns my sperm into liquid so that I can squirt it out. Or in, as the case used to be. Anyway, the rugby ball. When the prostate gets to be enlarged it makes peeing a penance so that's why my doctor referred me to the prostate man in the hospital. Mister Conrad Self, urologist.

Anyway, I'm sitting there in the big waiting area brooding about Isabella coming on Friday and wondering where the hell I'm going to put Henry and suddenly this old guy lands in beside me. He's huge, so huge that the half of his backside that's nearest me takes up his own seat and some of mine as well. He nearly has me off the chair. "Did you hear the one about the Jew?" he says. No hello or how you doing or anything like that. Nothing along those lines. Just "Did you hear the one about the Jew?"

"Pardon me?" I say, moving a bit away from him because I don't like the feel of his big hip against mine, and he says it again, dead loud as if I'm deaf or something. "I'm not sure," I say, frowning. "It's not racist is it?"

"All right," he says, "Did you hear the one about the Scotsman then? Scotsmen don't give a monkey's. Jock's wife died you see and he phoned the newspaper to put her death notice in. Girl said *That's twenty-six words sir. You can have another nine words at no extra cost if you like. Would you like to add anything?* So the Jew, I mean Scotsman, thought for a minute and then said *OK. Could you put this in at the end please? 2003 Ford Fiesta for sale. £3875 or nearest offer?*"

I laugh in a good-natured kind of way and get a better look at him when I'm at it. He's got really tiny eyes and he's very red-faced, with the jaw of a horse and a head of hair on him that would do a lion proud. Somewhere between straw and blond without a trace of grey and falling away down the back of his neck. Dyed of course. He's seventy if he's a day, I can tell by the wrinkles on his neck; they're like the rings on trees, dead giveaway, and everybody knows you don't get to be seventy without your hair showing its age. This puts me further off him than I am already. I always think there's something revolting about men of a certain age dyeing their hair when everybody knows it's faked. And then his scruffy grey eyebrows and the big pouting upper lip like you'd see on a tadpole and the horrible red flakiness around his nose and the way he keeps pushing his false teeth in and out of his mouth. Just my luck to be stuck beside somebody like this.

"I suppose you're here about the old waterworks too," says your man.

"Sorry?" Bloody nerve.

"You in to see Self?"

"Ah. Oh, yes."

"Bit full of himself, isn't he?"

He laughs then, loud and piercing, and says "I see you're number 80."

He's looking down at the sheet of paper I have in my hand with the number 80 on it.

"That's right. 80. Sure we're all numbers now," I say.

"Aye, numbers and bar codes. Did you see that thing they have when you come in the front door?"

"What thing?"

"Thing that looks like a juke box. Big glass front on it. You know, where you check in. You're looking for a slot to put your money in and you're nearly expecting it to start playing *Blue Suede Shoes* or something."

That big laugh again.

"Have you been with Self before?" I ask.

"I have."

"What's he like?"

"Pervert."

"I beg your pardon?"

"He's a pervert. And you know who he looks like? The guy that used to be married to Angelina Jolie, whatdoyoucallhim. Brad Pitt isn't it?"

Scorchio.

I lower my voice. "You said he was a pervert."

A bright mauve rushes to my neighbour's face.

"Oh, he's that all right. I'll give you an example too. The second time I came here to see him he'd the trousers off me before you could say Jack Robinson. Never looked at my face so he didn't. All he wanted to see was my backside. And not just see it either."

He gives me a knowing look and I pretend not to notice. But I'm getting erected.

"I was hardly in the door till he said *I think I'll give you a digital.*"

"A digital?"

The number 77 flashes up on a big screen on the wall in front of us.

"That's not you is it?" he says.

"No. I'm 80."

"Maybe it's me. Let me see. No. Time enough. I'm 79. Anyway, he leaned towards me and whispered all hoarse *I think I'll give you a digital.* That's what he said. And I was thinking to myself, Christ, if that's not a goodun. The health service must be handing out free watches now. And there was me thinking they were being squeezed squeaky by that shower of shitehawks over in Downing Street. So I said to him, Thanks very much, thinking it would probably be a cheap model with a plastic strap and I'd dump it as soon as I got to the first waste bin. But next thing was, he told me to lie sideways on the bed and pull my trousers down. And before I knew it, he had his hand up my bum."

"What!" My heart leaps in joyful expectation. My companion grips my upper arm. "The only other time anybody ever got that familiar with me was back in the Sixties outside Katie's Mountain Dew up in Lower Balix in the townland of Stranagalwilly if you know it. Aw Jesus, I remember it like yesterday. I was feeling a bit desperate that night thinking I was never going to get a woman – you know the feeling yourself I'm sure – and with the talent being very thin on the ground, I went over and sat down beside this big agricultural girl that had shoulders on her like your man Schwarzenegger and chatted her up. And then, after a civil amount of time had passed, like about two minutes, I asked her if she'd fancy going outside for a breath of the night air, if you follow me." Here he smiles, disclosing two decks of yellow dentures. "Got to her feet like something out of Cape Canaveral so she did and we were hardly out the door till she slammed me up against the nearest turf stack. Nearly tumbled the whole thing and overpowered me without the least bother."

He beams broadly at me. "Best night I had in years. O'Hanlon her name was. Catherine O'Hanlon, called after Catherine of Siena she told me, a holy, sacred and devout saint of the holy Roman Church that was well known far and wide for her works of mercy. Did you ever hear tell of her?"

"Who?"

"The Siena woman."

"I think I might have. Was she the one that had visions?"

"You could be right. I was never that well up on saints."

He puts his hand on my knee. "You know, I was working something out," he says very confidentially. "I was working out that this Self boy is probably on an eight-hour day. What do you think?" I don't answer but look down at his hand kind of pointedly and he removes it, though not in the least put out. "Now, allowing an hour for lunch," he goes on, "and half an hour for a snack let's say, that leaves six and a half hours, right?"

"Right." Where the hell is this going?

"OK. So let's say he spends a quarter of an hour giving each patient a digital, I figure he'd be getting through twenty-six arses a day. Do the math as they say in the States. Twenty-six a day." Our chairs shake with his merriment. "What do you reckon?" he says. I force a smile but say nothing. The man is clearly an eccentric.

"Tell us this and tell us no more," he says. "Do you know much about disembowelment?"

I think for a few seconds. "Not really," I say. "It was done in England for treason at one time wasn't it? And the Japanese did it as well I think."

"Aye, and the Vietcong too," he adds. "Whole rake of ones did it. Reason I'm saying is it must be something the same feeling getting disembowelled as it is getting the hand job from himself."

To be honest with you, during this time I can hardly contain myself thinking of the Brad Pitt lookalike that I'll shortly be alone with. Something I can never understand is why the gesture called giving the fingers is looked on as an insult. But there you go. Funny world.

Anyway, my neighbour. He's rambling on now about how if you study history you'll see that they never did the disembowelling or the digital to women and how we don't live in an equal society because on top of everything else they get their state pension five years before us and they live two and a half years longer than us, so where's the justice? Out of the corner of one eye I can see the disgusting way he keeps pushing his teeth out and pulling them in again just in time to stop them slipping down the front of his pullover but that stuff isn't really bothering me anymore because I'm thinking that a fair number of my wildest fantasies are waiting for me just a few feet to my left.

"Did you know about that?"

"Sorry, what were you saying?"

"The Turks. The way they did it was, they made you sit on the sharp end of a big wooden stake that they held up the ways sort of slanted if you follow me. And you know what they did then? They raised the thing upright very slow and the weight of your body made you slide down the pole."

He grimaces then and looks me full in the face. "What about that? Eh?"

"That's going a bit far," I say.

"Them were the boys all right," he says. "The Turks knew how to do it."

"I never heard of that practice before," I mumble for want of something to say.

“Aye, and the Greeks too. Them and the Turks did it to each other.”

“What was their reason, do you think?”

He raises his eyebrows as if surprised to be asked such a question.

“Reason? Them boys didn’t need a reason. Though if you were different from them, you’d likely have been in a bit of bother.”

I nod in agreement. “I know what you mean.”

“We don’t know we’re living,” my companion observes. “Wait till you hear this. I’d a second cousin from Sunderland was in the Desert Rats and he ended up with throat cancer. So count your blessings. That’s what I say. Count your blessings.”

“Terrible disease.”

“Basil Rummage his name was. Dead now. He was based in a British Army camp in a place called Fallingbostel in North Germany.”

“That’s a funny name.”

He looks at me, surprised. “Rummage? I wouldn’t have thought so.”

“No. Fallingborstal. They’ve some funny names out foreign, haven’t they?”

“Not Fallingborstal, Falling*bostel*. I could tell you stranger names than that and you wouldn’t have to go to Germany to find them,” he said. “Did you ever hear tell of a place called Hen Poo over in England?”

“Can’t say I have.”

“Or Once Brewed?”

“No, never heard of it.”

“It’s in Northumberland as far as I mind. What about Anton’s Gout?”

“Nope.”

"Or Compton Pauncefoot?"
"Can't recall that one."
"Slack Bottom?"
"No."
"Happersnapper Hanger?"
"Definitely not."
"Dancing Dicks?"
"I don't think so."
"Kingston Bagpuise?"
"No."
"Throcking? You heard of Throcking?"
"Never."
"What about Barton in the Beans?
"No."
"You sure?"
"Absolutely."
"My sister lives there now. Married to a man called Simon Tamsett."
"Right?"
"From somewhere in Hampshire, Simon is. *Booby Dingle* I think you called it, though I couldn't put my hand on the Bible and swear to that now."
I decide to try and call a halt. "Where do they get these names from anyway?"
His brow is creased with irritation. "You put me off what I was going to tell you. I was going to tell you about Basil."
"Oh, right. Sorry."
"I heard he wasn't too well and I went over to Sunderland to see him. Did I tell you he had throat cancer?"
"You did."

"He was one of a family of thirteen, and I only found out when I got there that his dad was a nutcase called Andy that went round with a loaded shotgun. Andy came over from Donegal when he was in his twenties and never took to England. Never liked the English, so he didn't. Basil told me he had this routine that he always used to come out with. How many dead bodies does it take to make the front page of a British tabloid?"

It takes me a couple of seconds to catch on that he might be putting the question to me.

I shake my head. "I don't know."

"No, I'm not asking you. I'm telling you what old Andy's routine was. How many dead bodies does it take to make the front page of a British tabloid? And you know what his answer was? One English, fifty Irish, a hundred and seventy Afghans and a thousand Iraqis."

"Maybe Andy isn't such a nutcase."

"You could be right there. Anyway, I was sitting all nervous in the living room talking to Basil and wondering if the old boy was going to walk in and open up with the shotgun and Basil suddenly said: 'How's about we go down the pub? What do you say?' So I jumped up and rang a taxi and I'll tell you now, I was never as glad to get out of any house as I was to get out of that one.

"But listen till you hear this. When we got to the pub I asked him what he wanted to drink and he said a pint of Guinness. When it was set up in front of him he took this big syringe out of his overcoat pocket and drew a slug of the drink into it and then injected it into the tube that was tunnelled into his stomach. I couldn't believe what my eyes were seeing and I said to him 'Is there any enjoyment in that?' and Basil said 'Well, when I burp I can taste it.' So what do you think of that, eh?"

Suddenly the top deck comes out from inside his mouth again only this time it slides down his front and would have been on the floor if he hadn't nabbed it just before it could fall off the fork of his trousers.

"Sorry about that," he says, returning the teeth to his mouth and smoothing his hair with the palm of his hand. "These things are giving me a lot of bother. Maybe you didn't notice but they keep slipping out. Adhesive costs a fortune. Anyways, as I was saying, we don't know we're living. Tell us, have you any offspring?"

"Sorry?"

"Children. Have you any children? We've two nearly as old as me and they're a pain in the tool. I'll tell you now about children. All children. They're like farts. You know the way you can't stand other people's farts and can barely tolerate your own?"

I try to laugh.

"They're great when they're young. You're like a god to them, glorified taxi driver and all, running them here, there and everywhere and they look up to you too, it's like you're Solomon or somebody. But you see once they hit sixteen, that's when the rot sets in and they start to treat you as if you're a fucking moron."

"Doesn't seem right."

"Me oldest got his leg broken by a crowd of hoods. They were giving some man a kicking and my boy went over to try and stop them. So they turned on him and got him down on the ground and laid into him and left one of his legs like a whole lot of golf balls in a sock. And what do you think the boy that he saved did?"

"What?"

"Ran off as quick as he could. Never looked back."

"Now there's a lesson for us all," I said.

"That's right. Go to the other side of the road. Did you ever read the parable of the Good Samaritan?"

"I did."

"Well, remember Christ talking about the two boys that walked on by on the other side and never bothered their holes going over to help the Jew? Them two got a very bad press, so they did. The Levite and the priest. Remember them? Two wise men that still aren't appreciated. Tell us this and tell us no more. What is it that makes young men think they have to be heroes?"

"I've no idea."

"I think it's the bloody comics with their heroes beating up the baddies and all these ads telling ones to join the army. You know, a man's life and all that."

"Hollywood too, probably."

"My lot don't know they're living. I'm from Maghera originally and there were nine of us. My four sisters had to go away and work in England when they got to fifteen."

"Did none of the boys go?"

"Didn't have to. There was enough work on the farm. Well, near enough. No, the girls had to go because there wasn't any place for them to lie unless they were going to lie with us. We'd only the two bedrooms and there's no telling what would have happened. You know what I mean?"

There's quiet for a bit while we sit gazing ahead of us. But this man doesn't like silences.

"Would you ever be using the computer now?" he asks.

"I do. Actually, I spend a lot of time on it."

"I use it like an encyclopaedia," he says. "You can pick up some very interesting things on Google and Wikipedia."

"Absolutely."

"Though saying that, you do get a fair amount of shite too. There's this Yank called Thoreau I read about that fancied himself as some kind of philosopher. Wait till you hear what he said. Wait till you hear this. Happiness is like a butterfly. The more you chase it, the more it'll get away from you, but if don't go chasing after it, it'll come and sit on your shoulder."

"That's interesting."

"Do you think so? Do you really think so?"

"Well ..."

"When was the last time a butterfly ever came and sat on your shoulder? Tell me that now."

"I'm not sure. I can't remember."

"Maybe you were too busy chasing it."

"I've never chased a butterfly in my life."

"There you are. This guy Thoreau was talking bullshit. But that's the thing about bullshit. If you've the name of being a big philosopher you can come out with all this stuff from you get out of bed in the morning till you go back in at night and people will say, oh, that's so true." He sets his lips tightly together and shakes his head as if to signify that that particular subject is now closed.

"You know what else I read? The day I got word about this appointment with Self, I looked up some stuff on Google about the prostate gland and all. There was this thing written by a famous specialist saying there were a lot of advances being made in the field of urology. And I thought: 'You can say that again mate. That guy

Self is never done making advances to every man comes in.'"

He flings back his mane then and gives a dirty big laugh that has a whole lot of heads turning. Twiddles his thumbs for a bit and then he's off again.

"Do you think it's possible," he asks me, "that some men at our time of life get off easy?"

"I suppose maybe that could be the case."

"That Robert Mugabe," he says, "president out in Bangladesh. He must be over a hundred. I wonder does he have to go through all this rigmarole. You know, the digital thing."

"Zimbabwe. It's Zimbabwe. And I think he's only about ninety."

"And the pope. This Francis boy. He's no spring chicken. Just because he's the pope doesn't stop him from getting a big prostate. Now that's true, right?"

I nod. "I'd say there'd be very few men would escape it."

"Father Matthew Rodgers is in hospital with it at the minute," he says. "You know him?"

"Sort of a way. He's supposed to be a very saintly sort of man."

"Me and him never got on. Not since the thing that happened with my youngest away back. Tony."

"Right?"

"Yeah. It was around the middle of the Troubles. You remember the way a lot of the young boys from the Bogside and Creggan Estate were giving the cops and the Brits a hard time throwing petrol bombs and all. Well, did you know that there were battles too between the Bogmen and the Creggies?"

"You mean the Bogside and Creggan ones?"

"I do. A lot of them couldn't stand the sight of each other. So these boys were fighting two wars."

"I never knew that now."

"Anyway, me son Tony was a Bogman, you see, and he was going out with this girl Maria Begley from the Creggan. Mad about her he was. They're married now."

"Very good. But how does Father Rodgers come into it?"

"Well, you see, he was the parish priest in the Creggan Estate and he was a Creggie sympathiser. Anything to keep in with the Creggies. And one night, Tony just couldn't wait to see Maria, so he phoned her to try and get her to meet him. Her mother told him she'd gone out to the Creggan Youth Club so he headed up there. Two Creggie bouncers were on the door and they wouldn't let him in so you know what he did?"

"What?"

"He went round the back and climbed up to the wall and along the roof to the skylight and lowered himself down inside. But as soon as he hit the floor, these four Creggies grabbed a hold of him and dragged him to the front door to throw him out. Well, Father Matthew Rodgers happened to be standing right there on a kind of a pastoral visit and he started asking what all this pushing and shoving was about. So the Creggie hoods told him what happened and then they said: 'What'll we do with him Father?' and Father Matthew said 'Take him round the back and beat the fuck out of him.' "

"He didn't say that!"

"He certainly did. Take him round the back and beat the fuck out of him. Now would you say those were the actions of a very saintly man?"

"Doesn't sound like it to me."

"And there he was saying Mass the next morning, Maria was telling me, and preaching about how bad language was getting a bit too common for his liking in the Creggan Estate.

"Nothing surprises me anymore."

"Me neither. But I was saying about the pope there. Did you ever take a good look at him?"

"I've seen him on the television."

"Tell me this. Does he not remind you of one of those music hall boys from away back? Vaudeville wasn't it you called it? Every time you see him he's got this big smile on his face like he's going to introduce the next act. Do you know who he looks like? What did you call the guy in *My Fair Lady* acted the dustman?"

"Oh I know who you're talking about. Sidney James."

"No, not Sidney James."

"Jack Warner?"

"Not him either. Hold on, don't say anything. It's on the tip of me tongue."

"I think I remember. Richard Harris," I say.

"Not Richard Harris. Don't speak for a minute. It's coming to me."

"Jon Pertwee?"

"No. Don't say anything till I think."

"Fred Astaire?"

"For God sake man," he says sort of shrilly. "Give me head peace would you."

Things are threatening to turn nasty at this point so I try not to talk. But I suddenly remember who it is and am finding it hard not to tell him so I blurt it out.

"Richard Burton!"

"Definitely not Richard Burton." he shouts and heads begin to turn. I can see he's getting dangerously edgy now because his right knee keeps bouncing up and down and I can hear the steady thud of his heel on the floor.

"Well if it wasn't him," I say, "it was Sidney James."

"You said him before. For Christ sake, let me think would you! His first name started with an A."

"Alan Rickman."

"Not him."

"Alfred Golden Mayer?"

His eyes light up. "That's it! Alfred!" he says, smiling almost fondly at me. "Alfred Doolittle. Guy acted him was Stanley Holloway. That's who the pope's like. Though now that I think of it he's not really. But you know who he's actually like?"

I say nothing.

"You know that guy that was one of the ... what d'you call it, a double act?"

I ignore the question.

"Aye, a double act. He acted with that big fat man. Oliver something. I've got it! Laurel and Hardy. Stan Laurel. Remember him? That's who he's like. Stan Laurel. Francis is like the spit out of his mouth."

My companion gazes up at the screen. "Must be nearly me now," he said with an air of mild resignation. "Your man never takes more than fifteen minutes for each one. But I'll tell you what I'd like to know. Always puzzled me. How can a man get any work done if he spends half the day with his hand up people's bums? And then there's the other thing."

"Other thing?"

"Aye. Do you think it right and proper that the Northern Ireland health service would employ a man like that?"

He gazes at me with wild surmise. At least that's what it looks like. It's hard to know for sure because I still can't really see his eyes properly. I think I told you that I'd taken in the head and the hair and the teeth and the bulk, but now I find myself actually looking at him full on for the first time and trying to see his eyes. They're the strangest articles you could imagine, so small they hardly seem there at all. Like something you'd see in the distance on a misty day when you're not sure if it's a lake or a cloud.

"A man like what?"

"A man that's a tomato."

"I'm sorry. I don't understand."

"Do you not know what a tomato is? A tomato is something that people think is a vegetable when it's really a fruit. I've no time for that sort."

I don't answer because it's hard to know what to say when I'm half tomato myself. It all depends on the circumstances. Ancient and all as I am, I still get a bit fired up when I see a nice topless young girl in the newspaper with lovely nipples set in a pale brown circle for my watery eye to feed on; and then on the other hand, my knees shudder sometimes when I look at these advertisements showing men wearing the bulging Y fronts, especially if the bulge is deliciously lumpy and you can see particular outlines. I couldn't count the times I've lingered at the men's underwear rail in Marks and Spencer's eyeing the Y front wrappings filled with cotton-covered knobs. Great place to be when you're in need of a lift. And nobody can say a word about a man browsing over men's underwear.

"Give me a straight-talker any day of the week," my neighbour says. "You know about the House of Lords, don't you?"

"Know what about it?"

He leans his mane towards me and his hip makes heavy contact with mine again. "Coming down with tomatoes. Do you see those old boys with their gowns and wigs and all? Fruitcases the lot. Well, not the lot. Did you ever hear of Boofy Gore?"

"No." I want to move away but that would leave me with most of my backside in midair so I hesitate.

"Boofy was straight as a poker. Real name Arthur. He was some sort of a hoity-toity earl, I think, but he was still worth all the fruits in the House of Lords put together. Way back in sixty-seven I think it was he tried to get two bills made into law, one protecting queers and the other protecting badgers."

"That's a funny combination."

"Aye, well. He got it made legal for queers to go at each other but he couldn't save the badgers. And wait till you hear. Some newspaper asked him why he hadn't got the support from all these boys in gowns for the badger bill and he said "There's not many badgers in the House of Lords."

He gives me a big smile and a long slow wink. And then he's back on his hobby horse.

"Listen. I was telling you a while ago about what your man Self put me through." He leans confidentially to my left ear. "But I've come prepared this time."

"How's that?"

"I've been reading up on the web about how to handle pain. You cross your fingers."

"And hope for the best you mean?"

"Not at all. You get rid of the pain by crossing your fingers. Least that's what this blog said."

"Are you serious?"

"I am. These two professor guys that wrote it seemed to know what they were talking about. You know what they said to do if you get a terrible pain? Anywhere? In the backside for example. Just cross your fingers like this."

"I don't understand."

He smiles patiently and holds up his left hand right next to my face. One fat finger is crossed over the one next to it.

"You see," he says, "if you put your middle finger over the index one then it isn't in the middle anymore. So the pain goes away. Or you can put it over your ring finger instead if you want."

Number 78 flashes on the screen, a chair scrapes and a frail-looking old guy shuffles away to the door marked 'Self'.

"That's the one before me. I'm ready for him this time."

He seems pleased with himself, his earlier outrage with tomatoes forgotten.

"Does it have to be the left hand?" Better to humour him, I'm thinking.

"Only if you're strangling him with your right hand at the same time. Now if you're using your left to strangle him, then ..."

He rocks back and forward, pleased with his wit. "I'm only joking. It can be any hand. And if you had no hands it could be your foot. But the foot's a bit tricky. You'd have to train the middle toe to go over the next one and that's not easy, I can tell you, unless you lift it over with your hand and you can't do that if you haven't got a hand."

"Is this not some sort of a con?"

"Nope. These two professors over in England came up with it. They say that when you cross your fingers that kind of way your brain gets all confused and forgets to tell you that you're in pain. So then you don't know you're in pain. See, if the brain thinks your middle finger isn't your middle finger anymore then it's too busy trying to figure things out to remember to tell you you're in pain. It's dead obvious when you think about it."

He seems to have noticed me shaking my head because his tone changes to a kind of sharpness as he tries to elucidate.

"Look. Here's how it works. The brain uses the position of your index finger in space instead of where it is on your hand when it's working out the signals coming to it. Got it now?"

"Ah, I see." Better not to show doubt anymore. "It seems to make a lot of sense. But what are you going to do if it doesn't work?"

"Oh it'll work all right. And if it doesn't, I'll swear."

"Swear?"

"Aye. I'll use swear words."

"You mean obscenities? But Self will throw you out if you do that."

"No he won't. He'll understand. This bird's been around. He'll know that the professors recommend it. That's what these two brainboxes say. Let rip if the finger crossing doesn't work. Scream out of you with all the bad words you can think of. It doesn't make the pain go away completely but it helps a hell of a lot."

He flashes a smart smile at me. "So, when your number's up, you'll know what to do."

He goes quiet then except for the click and suck of his dentures. But it isn't long before he starts again.

"You know what I was meaning to ask you?"

I turn to him and he bends sideways till his mouth is cupped in my ear. "You know with all this prostate trouble you get? What I'm saying is, were you ever taken short were you?"

"Taken short?"

"Aye, taken short. It happened to me one time when I was giving a talk to the Irish Countrywomen's Association down in Carndonagh. I was a landscape gardener for thirty years see, very highly respected, even though I say it myself, and these two women with big hats and tweed suits and fancy accents came to see me one day to ask if I'd give a talk on gardening. So I said I would, thinking they'd be crossing my palm with a good few quid. However, that's another story. Meanest bunch of leeches I ever came across.

"But I'm wandering away from what I was going to tell you. I made sure I went to the toilet before I left the house so that the old prostate wouldn't rear up and put me in bother and I was finishing off my talk by telling them – about twenty of them there were – the six important things to remember when they were watering the garden if they wanted good healthy grass with a strong root system, you know.

"Well, everything went great and I'd got to the end of my talk not a minute too soon, because I was busting you see, when some woman that looked like she just walked out of the big day at Ascot stood up and announced that Mister Rumpole would now be taking questions. Jesus, man, I never knew that was coming. I didn't realise it then but this crowd were so fucking glad to have a man about the place that they weren't going to let me go without a fight.

"And it was in the middle of me answering some question about minor diseases and insect problems that I started the piss. Right behind the podium which was the only thing between me and them. Trousers soaked through, socks and shoes too. You know the way it comes on you sudden with the prostate sometimes and there's damn all you can do about it? Leakage they call it, right? Well, this was no leak. This was the Great Flood. And the questions from the tweediedums and tweediedees kept coming and they went on that long, there was nothing I could do but finish the pee where I was standing. Man, you don't stop in the middle of something like that. Could destroy your system.

"But the worst part of the whole evening was standing drinking tea out of this wee china cup that I couldn't get my finger into the handle of and eating bloody angel cakes and all these dames gathered round me clucking away and me standing in the same place at the podium trying to be sociable."

"That must have been some experience," I say. "How did you get through it?"

"Just brazened it out. None of them seemed to be looking down the ways but that crowd miss nothing. Not that it matters a fuck. I'll never be back there anyway. Bloody leeches."

Number 79 shows on the screen. My companion removes his hip from mine, rises slowly and offers his hand.

"My best to you. And remember what I said about the fingers."

"Thanks. I'll do that."

He trundles to Self's door and I close my eyes and try to relax, relieved to be shot of him. The slob clearly doesn't understand the positives of what is about to happen. Of course there will be pain! Pain is integral to the whole experience, especially as it's going to be performed by a hunk – and how could anybody want better than that? Sadomasochism on the National Health, free at the point of delivery and served up by a highly experienced practitioner.

The word hunk in my head quickly brings me to my own Huncan, my *Steam 4 Teens* creation that will do anything I want. Anything! I'm not sure whether I told you this or not, but I drew him from my four favourite Chinese gods, favourite because they all have this bowel-melting heat in their eyes. There's Tu Er Shen who participates in daily gay wrestling (once pinned to the floor, you cry *I submit!*), Yue-Lan who binds two men permanently together with an invisible blood-red string, Qian Keng, the fun god of numberless health-enhancing ways of sinking the sausage, and the one I crave most of all: King Zhou, notorious god of sodomy *à la Sade*.

The thought of such things makes my mind wander a little as I wait my turn. I smile when I think of how James Joyce was known to salivate over the Marquis de Sade's masterpiece *The 120 Days of Sodom* and how the same Joyce would never have been able to complete his own masterwork *Ulysses* if he hadn't had his daily dose of the old marquis. It is many years since I first committed Joyce's favourite passage from *120 Days* to memory and it has served me well on long nights when I have lain marooned on the far reaches of the conjugal bed.

Blangis stood five foot eleven inches tall, had limbs of great strength and energy, splendid hips, superb buttocks, the strength of a horse, the member of a veritable mule, wondrously hirsute, blessed with the ability to eject its sperm any number of times within a given day and at will, a virtually constant erection in this member whose dimensions were an exact eight inches for circumference and twelve for length overall, and there you have the portrait of the Duc de Blangis.

And when crowned by drunken voluptuousness? 'Twas a man no longer but a raging tiger. Woe onto him who happened then to be serving its passions; frightful cries, atrocious blasphemies sprang from the Duc's swollen breast, flames seemed to dart from his eyes, he foamed at the mouth, he whinnied like a stallion, you'd have taken him for the very god of lust. And his hands necessarily strayed, roamed continually, and he had been more than once seen to strangle a woman to death at the instant of his perfidious discharge.

It is this kind of stardust that I want to feel on me, wonderfully true accounts of life as lived by real men, genital warts and all. Enough of this dust and maybe someday I'll write honestly enough to get myself condemned by my Church. That, in fact, has been my devout ambition since I enrolled in the university of the third age of reason (First age of reason, in case you didn't know, is when you're seven and you're taught that it's a sin to steal. Second age is twelve when you're taught it's a sin to feel. And the third age is seventy when you realise, possibly too late, that you've been conned). And in case you didn't know, getting condemned by the pope of Rome is an invaluable asset in the writer's quest for universal recognition.

Sade and Joyce were, of course, castigated by all right-thinking religious people, by whom I mean thinking people on the religious right, particularly the Catholic pontiff and his acolytes: cardinals, archbishops, bishops, monsignors, priests, deacons and lay lickspittles, the whole church in fact. The reason these prigs gave for their abuse was that written descriptions of sex acts demeaned male and female alike.

Lovemaking, they used to teach, should take place only between married couples in the privacy of the marriage bed and for the express purpose of conceiving a child, and it should on no account be written about for gain, acclaim or pleasure. Such accounts inevitably lead on to unrestrained marital and extra-marital activity as well as sacrilegious sex aids and depraved viewing of sinful pornography.

I feel a tap on my shoulder. "You'll be OK. Finger trick worked a treat. Just keep calm."

"Oh. I've actually been practising it," I lie. "Your appointment went OK then?"

He gives me a big grey smile. "Himself said he'd give me two to three years if I don't have the operation."

"Oh my God. I'm so sorry to hear that. But what about if you do have it?"

"Two to three years."

"But ..."

"Not a great choice, is it? Listen, these boys don't know as much as they think they do. I'm starting a diet today, thing I was reading about on the old web. It'll have me down to eighteen stone in three months."

He bends his mane to my ear. "Just you remember this. Take anything that boy tells you with a pinch of salt. He only wants the one thing and you and I know what that is."

He winks and is gone.

"Mister Cheddy?"

The husky voice came from the large lips of a designer-stubbled raven-haired beast standing at the open door to my left. A thick lump of saliva stopped at the back of my tongue and then went down the wrong way. I began to choke and was still at it when I closed the door behind me, leaving us alone. *Enfin seuls!* (No offence Brad but this guy leaves you light years behind). I attempted to apologise for the choking but this only made it worse and as a result I missed the first part of what he was saying and only caught up with him at the words "... greatly raised prostate-specific antigen doesn't necessarily point to prostate cancer."

"Aaagggh eeeee. Speciwhat? Ump."

"Sorry. Your PSA. It could be that you have an infection in your urinary tract or that ... tell me, Mister Cheddy, do you remember if you ejaculated within forty-eight hours of having your PSA blood test?"

"Ejaculated?"

"Yes. Ejaculated. You know ..." Steady on Lexie.

"Before or after? Ump."

I shouldn't have asked that because it was a stupid question. Of course he meant before. What else could he have meant? The difficulty was that I was so ravished by the sight and the sound and the smell of him that my body was interpreting his words as a kind of early come-on and I didn't really know what I was saying. Ah, the smell. How to describe? Somewhere between fresh human faeces, fox's urine and Jameson's whiskey I think.

"Now now, Mister Cheddy," he chided coquettishly. "I mean before of course. Maybe you can't recall. The test was some time ago. Let me see now. Yes, ah ... more than three weeks."

I had to swallow slowly and loudly before I was able to speak again. "I do recall. I did ejaculate."

"Are you sure?"

"Yes, absolutely sure. I always do."

"I see. Mmm."

My consultant half-closed his eyes. Adorable. He had the most beautiful soot-black eyelashes I'd ever seen on man, girl or dog. My main regret was the demure white coat he had on which hid his figure from me. He ran his long wet red tongue along his lips and my thighs loosened. Easy now. This hasn't even started yet.

"Any blood in it?"

"Sorry?"

"Was there any sign of blood in your sperm?"

"No."

"Or in your urine?"

"No."

"Fine. That's fine. If blood appears in either, make sure and let your doctor know right away. All right? Now, if you wouldn't mind going to the examination table."

He indicated a yoke where the action was to take place, a kind of narrow single bed with no headboard. Above it was the framed picture of a large perpendicular mauve arrow accompanied by the caption POINTING

TO PERFECTION. I did as bidden and somehow he was already there just as I arrived, using big hairy hands to smooth the surface I was to lie on.

"And if you'll just slip off your trousers please."

I heard the slap of latex or rubber as I loosened my belt. "Completely euuugggh?" I whispered.

"Just as far as your knees will be fine thanks. And underpants too please."

Who was I to argue? I slid my trousers and bikini briefs down my legs.

"Ah. Now lie on your left side and draw your knees up to your chest."

"OK."

"Ah. Wait. Just hold on a moment. Stay on your back if you don't mind. Now, let's have a look here. Yes, you have a hernia there. Did you know that?"

I shook my head. Couldn't speak. He gently ran his fingers through my burning bush and pressed on two swellings, one on either side of my trembling member. "How does that feel?"

"Wond – ... OK." Oh my God oh my God oh my God oh my God.

"Not painful?"

"I'm not sure. Would you do it again please doctor? Sorry. I should be calling you Mister."

He did it again and my John Thomas sprang up. Best erection for years, even if I say it myself. Was he impressed? Can't say. Couldn't see his face right. Mist in front of my eyes.

"Oops. I think we'll move on. Now lie on your left side and bring your knees up to your chest. I'm just going to give you a digital. Try and relax."

And so the hand job began. Mister Self slid his sensual fingers into my waiting rectum (two fingers? three fingers? not sure. does it matter?) but suddenly before I knew it he was way way in there, way beyond the call of duty if you ask me. Reader, what can I say? In a twinkling the man had become a glutton. This was pure lust, insatiable, bestial, unadulterated, sadistic, agonising lust. And needless to say, but I'm saying it anyway, my John Thomas collapsed in an ignominious heap – just like that.

I simply cannot describe the pain, except to tell you that by the time the creep had reached the large bowel, the torment was far worse than the night Ditter Doherty grabbed me by the goolies and flung me up against his bedroom wall without letting go of them. And by the time the whore's nails started on my small intestines, I was desperately trying to remember the finger trick my prostate friend had told me about. But no use, my brain wouldn't function.

All this time, my tormentor was muttering things like "Mm" and "Well now" to himself. And then he had the gall to say: "It's a little rough in there, Mister Cheddy."

"You're fucking right it is. Fuck!"

"Sorry? What did you just say?"

"I said you're fucking right it is. Fuck!"

"Really Mr Cheddy, I'd rather not hear that kind of language."

"Fuck fuck fucking faggot!"

"I have to warn you sir that if you don't desist from addressing me like that I won't be able to give you a proper digital examination."

"Dirty bugger!"

"I beg your pardon?"

Is there a place beyond pain where it doesn't matter anymore? No, there isn't. "Pervert!"

It was at this point that he withdrew his hand, quickly, painfully, blessedly. Then with a click and a smack he disposed of his stinking glove.

"You may get dressed now Mister Cheddy." I got myself decent quicker than I believed possible and when I looked up Self was behind his desk as if he'd never been away from it. Prim, proper, coat gleaming whiter than a whited sepulchre. The bastard.

"By the way, Mister Cheddy," he said – and I noticed he was avoiding eye contact – "I'll be in touch with your general practitioner to arrange additional medication for you. Also, I have to tell you that I'll be asking my colleague, Mister Manek, to see you at your next appointment."

+++++

"I can't get used to saying it," Harry said. "President Trump. Sounds bloody ridiculous. The more you say it the stupider it sounds. President Trump President Trump President Trump. Try saying it till you see what I mean. Try it till you see, Mickey.

"President Trump President Trump President Trump," said Mickey. "Naw, doesn't sound right."

"Len?"

"President Trump President Trump President Trump," said Len. He shook his head. "Doesn't make sense."

"Professor?"

“I don’t need to say it,” I said. “I know it’s ridiculous. If Aaron Sorkin had written this and pitched it to Netflix he wouldn’t have got in the door.”

“You’re right there Lexie,” said Harry. “I was just saying the same thing meself the other day. President Trump President Trump President Trump. How the hell did the people over there elect him anyway?”

“That’s democracy,” I said.

“Democracy’s a funny thing, isn’t it?” said Mickey. “D’you see the thing about democracy? It takes a whole lot of stupid people for it to work, right Professor?”

“Yanks wouldn’t like you calling them stupid,” I said. “I’d say there was some funny stuff going on behind the scenes for a showman like that to get elected. Deranged showman at that.”

“I never heard the like of it in all me born days,” said Len. “It’s like some bloody nightmare.”

“Don’t you worry,” I said. “He’s going to self-destruct.”

“You wish,” said Harry. “If that boy doesn’t get pressing up against enough women, he’ll be pressing the war button. I’m telling you he will.”

“He couldn’t be anywhere near as bad as Kennedy,” said Mickey.

“You think so?” I said.

“Sure, Kennedy was hardly elected till he was banging away at some Mafioso’s doll in the first-floor broom cupboard in the White House,” said Mickey.

“Aye, and then he dived into the Bay of Pigs and got his arse whipped,” added Harry. “And sure, the next thing was, he nearly finished us all off with that Cuban missile thing. Jesus, I actually went to Confession that time and I didn't even believe in God."

"Forget about Kennedy," said Len. "That's history. See this new boy? Lexie's right. The only hope is he destroys himself before he gets destroying the world. He's a bloody spacer."

"Yes, and when he destroys himself, do you know who's going to take over?" I asked.

"Who?"

"Mike Pence."

"That's right Prof!" said Harry. "He's the vice-president, isn't he? Very religious sort of a boyo from what I hear. Born again Christian and all. I don't believe in religion as you all know, but he's right about abortion. He calls it – what's this he calls it now? – interfering with the sanctity of human life? I wouldn't use fancy words like that though. I'd just call it murder."

"Hmph! I'll tell you now about Pence," said Len. "He's all for somebody's life being holy when they're inside of their mammies but do you see once they get outside and they're black, once they get outside and they're black, they're fair game and you'd better fucking believe it. Did you ever hear him complaining about cops over in the States shooting black people in the back and getting away with it? Or when his Saudi pals bomb black babies from Yemen or someplace to smithereens?"

"Right on, Len," said Mickey. "But the Yankee cops are improving all the same. The way I see it, they're not lynching blacks anymore. They just shoot them now."

"And d'you see with boys like Pence about," said Len, "with boys like Pence about, you'd be better off staying put inside your mammy. I'm telling you now. That boy'll keep you safe in there."

"Aye, but if you stay in too long it'll only kill the two of yous," said Harry. "That's a medical fact, Len."

"Mike Pence is a fool," I said.

"You're right there Professor," said Mickey. "There's one born again every minute."

+++++

After I left the Collapsed Catholics I wasted half my shopping time in Sainsbury's brooding on Pence and Trump and the whole circus of them, and new clowns appearing every time you looked; and I knew that what I was seeing was the nearest thing to a dystopia since 1984. If Trump went, then Pence would take over the ring and he'd crack the whip like nobody's business.

Who did he remind me of? Who was it? Those eyes, that face. Who? I walked around the aisles not seeing the shelves most of the time and hardly knowing who I was saying hello to, and it wasn't until I saw a promotion poster for some movie on one of the pillars that it came to me. Those pale-faced silvery-haired children in *Village of the Damned* with their staring eyes and flawless skin, and I remembered the blurb on the posters outside cinemas that frightened me back then. *Beware the stare that will paralyse the will of the world.*

And I heard his ringing voice and thought of him leading the ultra-right elites of the corporate media, and our minds would be in their hands. They'd use half-empty vassals like the British Bootlicking Corporation and so-called left-leaning newspapers like The Guardian and The New York Times and The Washington Post to skew our heads.

And by the time I got to the checkout the worldwide web was already coming under the control of spooks, spooks so cunning that they'd developed software which would make it near enough impossible for independent blogs to be read except by the bloggers themselves.

But being disappeared from the web might turn out to be merely an entrée. How soon until *Facebook, Twitter* and *YouTube* are roped in by Pence and Company as associates of the administration, and resourceful bloggers who still manage to work their way back into the web are investigated and maybe even prosecuted by Washington's Ministry of Truth for spreading fake news? And then they'll come for the creators and the dreamers.

Depressing isn't the word for it. Maybe the spooks will get their way and nuke Russia sooner than I think, and then the whole thing will be over and I'll be incinerated along with my publisher and my laptop before this diary gets anywhere near a bookshop. And that would be so maddening.

I shook my head to clear it. Because I had certain things to deal with right now. Like breaking it to Henry about having to park her in Pee Valley Nursing Home while I'm away seeing my publisher. A lie of course. I'd be seeing Isabella. She's coming on Friday.

Friday! The girl has been asking about a threesome for God's sake. What was it she said? 'Maybe you and me and Huncan could get together.' She thinks I'm Denise. But I'm not. I'm Lexie and there's only one of me.

+++++

She held a card saying YOUR LITTLE MERMAID and she was small and slim and just fifteen. Her face was the nearest thing to classic I've ever seen in so young a girl, with high pale cheeks and a certain something which even after all this time I haven't been able to put my finger on. And those eyes, those blue eyes. They knew right away that I was there to meet her and they held me for so long, I thought they weren't going to let go.

She had on a black embroidered strap-front crop-top and neat-fitting jeans with ripped thighs that nearly took the breath out of me. Her silky hair was auburn with curls at the ends and it came right down to below her waist. But my gaze was mostly on her honey-brown midriff with the cute little belly button plumb in the middle and the lips of pink flesh high up on her thighs. Men have had seizures for less.

"Hi! I'm Denise's grandfather," I tried to say but it came out as "Hime Denise's. I'm so pleased to meet you."

"I'm sorry?"

Perfect English, with just the trace of foreign. I shook her hand and felt a faint fragrance of musk. This is wrong. This is so wrong.

"You're Isabella, aren't you? I'm Lexie, Denise's grandfather. I'm afraid she wasn't able to come. Her grandmother, my wife, her grandmother, my wife Henrietta, got an unexpected phone call from her grandmother, Denise's grandmother, Denise's other grandmother I should say, saying she's getting out of hospital after a serious operation and needs round-the-clock care that she can't afford, so Denise went with her because Henrietta didn't want to go alone. We only got the message this morning and it was too late to ask you to turn back."

Words falling over each other, too well rehearsed. She looked confused.

"Oh. I'm so sorry to hear that," she said falteringly, eyes still lingering on my face. "But it's really lovely to meet you. How long will she be away? Denise?"

"Ah, that's what we don't know." A tear glistening at the inside corner of one of her eyes, my lips dry. I brought up some saliva and gave them a good lick. How am I looking? Are any of my nose hairs showing? I should have used the trimmer. Henry says it's a strimmer I need.

"Such a distance. Denise didn't want to go because she knew you were coming but she really had no choice. I wasn't feeling up to it, such a long drive you know. And I get travel sick on buses."

"Oh I'm sorry. Where? Where is it to? Where is the journey to?"

"Kerry. Long way away. Denise wouldn't thank you anyway. She'll be so busy. She'll have to do most of the work you see. Henrietta's not too well herself."

Her eyes brightened. "That's where the Blarney stone is, isn't it? I heard so much about it. I'd love to kiss it. Sorry, I meant to ask. What about Huncan? Is he here or did he go with them? Oh, I forgot. Denise told me he'd be away."

"Duncan?" I whispered. "I'm sorry, who is Duncan?"

"Not Duncan. Huncan. Denise's boyfriend. Oh dear ..." She put her hand to her freckled forehead. "You weren't supposed to know?"

I gave her a series of blinks and my voice came like a gargle. "Denise has lots of friends, boys and girls both. She just likes fun." I cleared my throat and some phlegm sat on my tongue. I gulped it down quickly and noisily. She wasn't wearing a bra. The nipples of her small frank breasts nuzzled her crop top. Look at her face damn you. Dear God she's beautiful, she's so beautiful. And those freckles! "But I honestly don't know the names, there are so many. The Blarney stone is in Cork. Cork, you know. Not Kerry."

Isabella rolled her eyes up and let her mouth fall sideways in a goofy kind of way. No lipstick, none that I could make out anyway. "Sorry. I have lots to learn." So cute, the way she did that thing with her mouth. And the other freckles too, everywhere, on her cheeks and nose and all around it, right down to her red lips.

"Not at all," I said. "I'm sure you know much more about Ireland than I know about Denmark. Maybe ... maybe we should get your luggage. Where is the carousel, I wonder?"

"Here, there," she said, pointing, and quickly led the way that others were taking. I followed closely. Her coltish walk sent a ripple of delight through me and her jeans gripped her little behind so tightly I almost had to look away. Too much, this is too much.

We stood huddled in a chattering crowd watching luggage move slowly around. She was standing very near to me, looking up at me, eyes smiling, trusting, nervous. She still hadn't asked where she would be staying. I should tell her.

"I heard a joke," she said suddenly. "About Donald Trump. Donald Trump is so divorced from the truth, he should be paying it alimony." She had moved closer to me so that I could hear what she was saying. A sweet mild scent of toilet soap was there now with the trace of musk.

"That's good," I cried, a little shrilly. "That's really good." I tried to remember a Trump joke to tell her but I couldn't think of one. So I said: "Sometimes I think he's like a character out of Shakespeare. But I'm not sure whether it's farce or tragedy. Have to wait and see, I suppose."

"Tragedy," she said. "It must be tragedy. I'll bet you things cave in on him. My father says it's only a matter of time."

"He's probably right," I agreed. "Firing rings round him. All that bloodletting."

"It's like a box set, isn't it? There's my suitcase. No it's not. Mine has a blue label. It's like *The Godfather*. What about that man he sacked? What did you call him? Scaramouche was it?"

"Scaramucci. The ten-day wonder."

"And he calls himself 'The Mooch'! Imagine. He looks exactly like ... did he not act in *The Godfather* years before he worked for Trump? Like an enforcer? Didn't he use the garrotte wire on somebody?" she said, wrinkling her nose.

"No, it couldn't have been him. He would only have been a boy when that film came out. Maybe you're thinking of Fat Pete Clemenza. He did a lot of dirty work for Brando. Killed half the cast as far as I remember. Helped Coppola to stay inside the budget, I heard. I actually thought he was there to stay."

"Who?"

"Scaramucci."

"It's like *House of Cards*, isn't it?"

"I don't think you're right. Trump's too way out for fiction."

"But it's so like *House of Cards*."

"I don't agree. Honestly, I think *House of Cards* is like *My Little Pony* compared to what's going on now. This is a horror show we're watching. *Psycho* maybe."

She laughed then, a tinkle of a laugh, a happy-to-be-with-you laugh. The crowd around us had begun to thin out and she had space to move a little away from me but she didn't. She suddenly shouted "There it is!" and darted forward to grab her moving suitcase.

"But did you hear the other one?" she said when she came back.

"Other one?"

"Yes, the other one. What do Trump and atoms have in common?"

"I give in. What?"

"They make up everything."

I tried to laugh. It came out like a woof. "Where do they get these brilliant jokes?" I said. At least I think I said that. I'm not sure exactly what I said.

+++++

We ate at the airport. Chicken sandwiches out of those plastic containers, not exactly appetising, but what can you do? I told her it would be better for her not to stay at my house or Denise's because Denise and her grandmother had left in such a hurry and things were every which way and did she mind if we spent the three days going round Inishowen peninsula? I hadn't booked any hotels or anything but that should be all right. I rabbited on at a mile a minute, trying to focus on a place somewhere behind her right shoulder. When I found the nerve to look her in the eye, she was smiling guilelessly.

"I've read all about Inishowen 100," she said, "and I've seen some of it in magazines. I gave up the phone, you know, after Denise told me she dumped hers. She won't even use email. She calls the whole thing antisocial media. My life got far better after I stopped. I was getting really addicted, you know. It was awful. The only thing I follow on my laptop now is the blog she writes."

"I agree with both of you. I don't use the mobile either. And social media has plenty of pluses, but it's got far too many minuses."

"Denise wanted to take me round the whole hundred miles that I read about. Stunning scenery. Romantic hotels. Isn't that what the brochures say? It's far nicer than Denmark."

"We'll do the best we can," I said. "You'll not see much in three days but that's all you have, isn't it?"

"Yes. My father's in Dublin and he's going to be flying up here for us to go back together." The blue of her eyes seemed for a moment to turn to grey and she began to wind one of her curls around the index finger of her right hand, loosely at first, then tighter.

"Your English is amazing," I told her. "How have you been able to learn it so quickly?"

She smiled. "I just finished nearly three years at a boarding college in Somerset. My father is English and he travels a lot. He's been working there all that time."

Now she was blushing. "We're well off. I'm a spoilt little brat."

+++++

We had nearly reached the top of Glenshane Pass and my prostate was acting up. Time for the toilet. "*The Ponderosa's* two or three miles up the road," I said. "The highest pub in Ireland you know, nearly a thousand feet. And they've opened a new restaurant there. Would you like to stop and eat?"

"I don't think so," she said. "I feel like I've only just eaten. I wish now Denise and I were still using the phone. I can't even talk to her. Or text her."

"She was always funny like that. I've been on to her for ages to get a basic mobile. She says if God had meant us to have mobiles …"

"I know," she said. "I remember that one. She's a funny girl. And mysterious too. But that's what I love about her. And she writes so well."

I smiled appreciatively. "You never know, she may even be back before you leave. All depends."

"Depends? On what?"

"On how her grandmother is."

"I was so looking forward to seeing her." She fell silent then, and when I stole a glance she was gazing wistfully ahead, fingers twining in her lovely lap.

"I'm really sorry she's not here," I said. "It's terrible you have to spend your holiday with an old fogey like me."

She made a sudden movement. "Oh no! You're not an old fogey. You're not even old. I think you're lovely. I'm sorry, what were you saying about that pub? *The Ponderosa.*"

"Yes, *The Ponderosa.* It's the highest pub in Ireland. It was actually called after the watering hole in *Bonanza.*"

"*Bonanza?*"

"The old Western series that used to be on TV. I'm sorry, you wouldn't have heard of it."

"Oh, but I have! I've seen it on Netflix. It's brilliant. And there's a follow-up called *Ponderosa.* I saw some of that too, but it wasn't as good as *Bonanza.* Look at those sheep on the road. Gosh. And the cars going like mad past them."

"Here we are now. Why don't you come in for a minute? I have to use the bathroom anyway."

"It's so quaint. It's really beautiful," she said. "Imagine. A place like this on top of a mountain."

+++++

"I was looking at the plaque behind the bar when you were away. It says we're on the Glenshane Pass. Such a romantic name. And so Irish."

I smiled. "You wouldn't think it was so romantic if you were stuck out there in a snowstorm. A lot of cars were stranded all night on it a few years ago. Some people nearly died."

"Oh dear. That must have been terrible. But I do love the name."

"You were saying about Glenshane Pass sounding Irish. You're actually right. It's from the Irish *Gleann Seáin.* That means Shane's valley."

I began to tell her what history I remembered of this wild place. “Shane was a rapparee,” I said.

“A rapparee? What’s a rapparee?”

“A guerrilla fighter turned highwayman. This was about three hundred years ago. He was one of the Mullans, I think, from a place called Faughanvale outside Derry. His family were evicted from their farm to make way for planters from Scotland and so Shane hit back. He was only sixteen at the time but he formed this gang and they attacked the Brits and the planters every chance they could.”

“What are planters?”

“Settlers. Same idea as what’s going on now in Palestine. You know, the Israeli settlers being given land that’s being confiscated from the Palestinians. The thirty years war that ended here in nineteen ninety-eight goes back in a way to the Brits confiscating Catholic land and shipping in settlers. Would you like something to drink?”

“I’ll have a Britvic, thanks.”

When I came back with her drink she was staring at two girls who had just come in with an older man and woman. The girls were so alike they just had to be twins and to add to that certainty both wore identical casual round neck short-sleeve feather-print blouses. They were wearing very little below the waist, just crotch-tight short shorts that I wouldn’t have minded trying on but which looked ridiculous on these two. They were at least seventeen, with thick hips scorched a patchy red and gross backsides that stuck out like four sore thumbs.

I remembered one day away back dressing up in a cut-out sleeve top not unlike theirs in front of my wardrobe mirror when Pappa walked in, snorted and stamped straight out again, the big ape. He had no idea what was happening, couldn't understand. Wearing that top just felt right.

The woman and the girls passed close to us on their way to the ladies' room and I swear, the pong from them would have felled me if I hadn't been sitting. It smelled to me like denim shorts wedged in crevices for far too long. The girls were the source, no question.

Now if it had only been the rub factor, it wouldn't have been so bad. You don't know what the rub factor is? I'll tell you then. The rub factor is tight clothes chafing your thighs and your armpits. Bad of course, but nowhere as bad as the twin essence these two were giving off.

To be truthful, I spent very little time on the girls. Or their mother, if that's what she was. She was an obese, coarse-looking woman and she was exhibiting far too much of the ugliest bubs that I've ever had the ill-fortune to set eyes on. To be perfectly honest my attention was riveted on the man who was with these females. A gypsy look about him, dark ponytail hanging from one side of his head, short-sleeved pink shirt unbuttoned all the way down and a gloriously golden chest matted with jet wet hair that covered his navel and got noticeably thicker as it stole southwards into close-fitting, glans-mauve trousers, trousers that looked far too tight for his comfort and were definitely too tight for my peace of mind.

I knew in a moment that I would let this guy behave any way he wanted with me. It was a travesty to think of him intimate with the person by his side. For one thing, the physics of it defied me, and for another, it made me wonder at his judgment. He turned suddenly to look up at the wall clock, revealing the clear outline of a remarkable rear-end that must certainly have floored better men than me. And then, almost before I knew it, he was gone, having shouted through the door of the Ladies' that he'd be waiting in the car. Within seconds, the three females reappeared and headed for the exit, fundaments in their wake like slugs' shells.

"Wow!" Isabella whispered. "Did you see those two girls? They're so beautiful, aren't they? Did you see their figures? And their outfits?" She put her hand to her mouth. "I'm sorry," she said. "You must find that kind of talk boring."

"Not at all," I said, my thoughts on the beautiful man and straining to keep a beggar's bliss at bay, "I like looking at girls."

She gave me a tolerant smile. "Of course," she said. "What man doesn't."

"I'm not dead yet," I said.

"Far from it," she said. "I'll bet you're young at heart."

She fingered her little cleavage embarrassedly and then put the palm of her hand absently on her bare stomach. Something was happening around the area of my heart that was taking the air from me and I was suddenly prey to memories jostling for attention. One of these kept bothering me. Years before, twenty years or more maybe, I had thrown caution to the winds and thrust my crotch boldly into the rump of a fine-looking young man just in front of me in a queue and kept it there as the line of us began to inch forward in the teeming rain to board a bus for Belfast. When the queue stalled, I stayed put against him and he turned to look me straight in the eye, smiling sheepishly, either not properly aware of what the beast in me was up to or else wanting it every bit as much as I did.

I quickly found out which was the case because he then proceeded to back in and out of me repeatedly, bringing me all the way to a spasm so sublime that my knees nearly gave way. And when I'd finally paid my fare there he was at the rear of the bus, smiling that silly smile again but now motioning to me by patting an empty seat beside him. Unfortunately, or maybe fortunately, I'll never know which, I ignored his offer after having convinced myself even in the euphoria of release that he was crawling with the clap.

"Are you all right?" she said. "You look pale." Her bright blue eyes gazed up at mine. I blinked and got back to her. This, after all, was the girl who had made it titillatingly clear that she was up for anything with my two soft-core creations. What had she said? 'Huncan is a dream and you, Denise, are part of every girl's fairy tale and I think maybe I love you a little.'

As the thud of my heart slowed, I became aware again of the possibilities in the here and now and I suddenly wanted to reach across the table and touch the soft down of her lower arms. But I knew if I did that she would shrink away from me. The whole thing was ridiculous of course. Pitiable when you think about it, but there you go.

"Sorry?" I said.

"I was just saying you look pale."

"I'm fine." I said.

But then again, maybe not so pitiable. I'm not sure if I've already told you this – and here I probably exaggerate – but I have something of those long-ago matinee-idol looks that a lot of women would still grab with both hands, given the chance. OK, I'm on the wrong side of sixty but I'm quite presentable for my age: tall, slim and dignified, with an endearing head of greyish white hair and a brooding thoughtful look about me.

Unfortunately, it's not women I'm interested in but girls of a certain age and able-bodied men of any age and, apart from the sad incident in the bus queue, I've never had coital experience with either. Unless you count Henry of course and also that five-minute fling with Ditter Doherty when I was fifteen which ended when he fired me up against his bedroom wall.

"But you were telling me about Shane. What happened to him?"

"Shane. Yes. He got caught after about twenty years and he was hanged along with his two sons in The Diamond in Derry."

"Oh heavens."

"Maybe when we're in Derry, I'll show you The Diamond. They were hanged in the very place where the war memorial is now, million-pound monstrosity that's supposed to be for remembering the boys that the potbelly politicians sent out to fight their wars."

"You're so passionate," she said, eyes large and lovely. Look, you fool, look and enjoy her look and bask in her admiration. Because that's all you'll ever do.

I bypassed Derry, promising to show Isabella the hanging place in The Diamond some other time, and drove directly to Inishowen. First stop was a coffee house-cum-cafe in the small village of Bridgend where we ate cod and chips. Then on to historic Grianan Fort.

We had the place to ourselves. The day was clear and warm, but a sharp breeze came in little waves. Isabella shivered as she got out of the car and I asked her if she wanted to put on something heavier. She went to her suitcase and took from it a blue denim jacket which she quickly slipped on and buttoned over her crop top. Perfect match for those ripped jeans. I led the way as we walked up towards the fort by way of zigzag steps. After a minute, I had a feeling she wasn't behind me anymore. I looked back and she was humming a tune and doing a little dance shuffle on one of the lower steps. She stopped, embarrassed, pulled her hair away from her face and shouted that she felt so happy.

"This is like fairyland!" I knew what she meant. Below us was a panorama of the dark greenery of Inch Island and the little windprints on the blue waters of Lough Swilly and a checkerboard of fields and hills that reached into three counties. I named them and pointed out parts of each that we could see and she let out little squeals at the music of their names: Donegal, Derry, Tyrone.

I skipped the history of the fort and instead told her the legend: that inside its walls lie the sleeping giants of Inishowen, and that when the sacred, hidden sword is removed from the innards of the fort, the giants will awake and reclaim their ancient lands. I brought her to the large burial mound close by and her blue eyes blinked in wonderment as I explained about the mound. At some stage in the telling, I remembered with a pang the only girl in my life before Henry, a fifteen-year-old grossly devout Catholic tease called Andraste McEniff, who had stood with me next to this selfsame mound nearly sixty years before wearing wide-bottomed football shorts, dirty white with red trim, and hadn't let me do a thing, even kneed me in the groin when I tried to get her down on the mound. And this was after me going to the trouble of bringing her the whole seven miles from Derry on the carefully cushioned bar of my bike. All she did at

Grianan was go on about her sore bummy, Christ, that's what she called it, her sore bummy, and moan about not knowing how she was going to get through the seven miles back to Derry.

"Who is buried in the mound do you know?" Isabella asked.

"Kings and princes and warriors," I said.

"Gosh. Right here? Imagine."

"And the bodies of the banshees," I added for good measure.

"Banshees? What are they?"

So I told her about the word banshee coming from a Gaelic word meaning fairy woman of the burial mound. "They were spirits that came to a house by night to warn that someone in that house was about to die."

"OhmyGod! Is this true? This didn't really happen, did it?"

I could see she was hooked so I piled it on. Widening my big brown eyes to fullest advantage, I invented a story about hearing a banshee wailing one night just before our next-door neighbour died, and then I smiled mysteriously and said: "Could be there are more things in heaven and earth than are dreamt of in your philosophy Isabella."

"Hamlet!" she breathed and held my arm.

"Your neck of the woods," I said. "Prince of Denmark, right? Hamlet said that in Elsinore Castle, didn't he?"

"That's right. In the play. We did it before I left the convent school. But there's no such place you know. Well there is, but Shakespeare made up the name Elsinore. It's really Kronborg Castle. And it's been destroyed and built up again."

"I remember reading that," I said. "It's like the way Grianan Fort was rebuilt. And aren't there supposed to be spirits in Kronborg Castle too?"

"Hamlet's father's ghost that spoke to him! I remember learning by heart the part where the ghost tells him about Hamlet's uncle killing Hamlet's father and then sleeping with Hamlet's mother. And then he tells Hamlet to kill the uncle. It's so, it's just so awful, isn't it?" She closed her eyes. No false lashes there, or painted-on eyebrows, or mascara or shadow, just an untouched, beautiful, precocious fifteen-year-old. Though maybe not so untouched.

"'Lust,'" she whispered, eyes still shut, "'though to a radiant angel linked, will sate itself in a celestial bed.' I always remember that part." She opened her eyes and looked full at me. Crazy. This is crazy. And then she went on: "But what about Hamlet and his own mother! I think he's sexy."

God in heaven, I thought. So wanting to sleep with your mother is sexy now.

"Maybe," I said and I could feel a falter in my voice. I fancied Olivier when he played Hamlet in the film, especially when he wore the white tights and jock gear in that swordfight. "But he still finds it hard to make up his mind to do what he wants to do. About his uncle I mean."

"That's what I love about him. He's slow to make a move but when he gets started there's no stopping him. But tell me about the banshees. Please."

Her nose and cheeks were a summer haze of faint freckles, so faint in the sunlight I would have needed to look closely to see them properly. Her hand was still on my arm. What was it she had written to Denise? *I'd love to go on a tour of Inishowen. I've seen pictures of the scenery there and I can't wait. We could sleep in a different hotel every night. I just can't wait.*

A recent survey of men between fifty and eighty-three showed that having sex once a week bathed their brains in dopamine, arresting cognitive decline and so improving their memories. For many men, this meant in practice that they would no longer have to write down shopping lists on post-its. So, trying to be a little more specific about all this, what benefits would accrue from having sex three times a day on three successive days, say, at the age of seventy-one? Remembering who won the first ever three soccer World Cups and the exact scores and scorers? Racing blood and generally improved brain power? Serious stroke?

"Please tell me."

"Sorry," I said. "The banshees. Yes. They were hardly ever seen, but when they were seen they were dressed in white, sometimes other colours but nearly always white. Usually they were just heard and their wails would go on for half an hour or more. And then when they were leaving the house there would be a fluttering sound like a bat would make."

"Gosh!"

"I used to hear about all this," I lied, "when I was staying in my grandmother's cottage away in West Donegal, and I remember lying in bed after I got back to Derry and I'd be imagining sometimes at night when I was in bed that I could hear the wailing of a banshee in our back yard and I'd be wondering who was going to die, and when nobody died I realised that what I'd heard was probably only a she-cat in heat."

She sighed. One glance told me she was enchanted. It was in her eyes. And she seemed so relaxed about being there with me, miles from another living person. And in the same glance, I saw she was even lovelier than she had seemed at first sight, her face, her slenderness, the very feline look of her, and the way her hands kept stealing self-consciously to her crotch. This last observation made unspeakably bestial thoughts come and fill my head till for a minute or more I could think of nothing else.

I cringe now when I look back on those brutish fantasies. And yet ... And yet in the state of Sikkim, my reading tells me, in the hills and mountains of Sikkim in the Indian Union, cohabitation between men of eighty and girls in their mid-teens is not uncommon. And is accepted without question. Revolting? Maybe it is. Yet Sikkim is not only the most beautiful place on earth but environmentally the cleanest and safest. It abounds in mists, mountains and colourful butterflies and is a haven of peace and joy in troubled India. So what does that say?

Let me be frank here. I have a sinking feeling that you, gentle upright reader, may very well have recoiled by now from the notion of a man of my age having sex at all, even with his lawful wife of just a year younger. It is quite a shocking image I grant you. The thought of liver-spotted arthritic limbs threshing about grotesquely on a creaking bed is not one for sensitive souls. And if you are of this mind, then how much more distasteful must it be to picture activity of that sort between me and a small, thin and obscenely beautiful fifteen-year-old girl? Something more suited to the dark web, I hear you think; and my mind tends to agree.

"I'm sorry. I have to go to the loo. Is there one here?" Her face had turned crimson and I could see she was all bothered and embarrassed as she clutched herself and moved from foot to foot. .

"There are plenty of loos here but they're all alfresco. Just go round the other side of the fort and if anybody arrives I'll keep them in conversation."

She nodded fast and hurried away. Even in her uncomfortable state she moved with an almost juvenile grace that sent the tremors through me. And I was still watching the back of her when I became aware of the song of a blackbird. I wondered if it had been singing all this time. Had I been so immersed in this girl that I hadn't heard it?

And there it was. Yes, there it was. I could see it now, perched on a tufty hillock close to the burial mound and it was singing its little heart out, two different flute notes that merged for a few seconds, duet for one bird with its golden bill and silver tongue. And then it cocked its tail and gave a sudden change of tone, a pook-pook-pook and a chink-chink and a tut-tut, and before I knew it, he or she had flown.

Isabella was smiling as she came back from the fort.

"I was just thinking there," she said when she got as far as me. "You know at the very start of Hamlet when Barnardo comes to take over from Francisco on guard duty and Francisco says to him 'For this relief much thanks'?" She laughed then, sweet and soft. "That's what we used to say at college when we got back from going to the toilet. For this relief much thanks."

I laughed with her and laughed inwardly too.

"But it's so beautiful over there," she said. "I've never seen so much heather, except pictures of it. Do you see the purple? This is heaven, it really is heaven."

"I'm so glad you like is Isabella. I do my best."

She smiled and then laughed again, giving a mock curtsy, saying, "Thank you kind sir."

"And now will you keep a lookout for me?" I asked. She nodded and looked at me fondly. I hurried away and when I got to the other side of the fort I found I wasn't able to go. I tried and tried but the flow was blocked. I felt ready to burst but between the excitement and the prostate nothing would come.

"Look," I said to her when I got back. "Look what I found wedged between stones in the wall of the fort." I showed her the crumpled pink page of a writing pad.

"What is it?" she said. "Is there something written on it? Oh, that's so mysterious."

"Look at it."

She took the sheet in her hands and smoothed it out, then read, silently at first, then aloud.

My heart would hear you and beat,
Were it earth in an earthy bed.
My dust would hear you and beat,
Had I lain for a century dead,
Would start and tremble under your feet,
And blossom in purple and red.

Her cheeks were aglow and her long white fingers gripped the paper as if she were afraid it might slip away.

"Oh heaven," she whispered. "Some boy must have left this for his girl. It's so perfect."

"It is beautiful, isn't it?" I agreed. "He must love her very much."

"Maybe you should leave it back? Maybe she hasn't read it yet?"

She was gazing at me in a way that I knew she didn't want to let it go.

"I think you should keep it," I said. I could feel my voice wavering. "I'd like you to have it. Just think of it as a little gift. Please."

We stood facing each other and I felt a ridiculous rush of delight rise in me. Dim, misted eyes and bright lips an arm's length away, she just about came up to my chest. And then in a moment her long lashes were matted with wet and her lower lip was trembling.

"Oh that's so, so ... OhmyGod. Please tell me. What happened to Denise's mother and father? Please tell me. Poor Denise. Why did they do it?"

I cleared my throat. I hadn't been expecting this so soon.

"Our son Terence, our only son," I said as evenly as I could, "was married to the most wonderful lady, Adriana, and she was diagnosed with a terminal illness when she was still in her twenties. It was terrible. After about a year Terence felt he couldn't allow her to suffer anymore but he couldn't live without her either so they agreed to end it together."

"Oh."

"Sometimes I find it hard to ...."

"Hard to what?" She was sobbing now and I let her sob. Then she said: "Denise told me a little bit about it but she didn't say that. Did you guess what they were going to do?"

"No. They left letters for Henrietta and me and for Adriana's parents and family. They didn't want to involve any of us in their ... what they did."

"How did Denise ... how did she ....?"

"Sorry?"

"How did she take it? It must have been so, so ... awful for her."

Her cheeks were wet and flushed, suffused with what I can only describe as a beautiful Verrocchian rose. She had folded and refolded the sheet in her hand until she could fold it no more. Then she put it in the breast pocket of her denim top and rubbed at her blurred cheeks with the sides of her fists.

"Yes," I said. "But she is the daughter we never had and we're the parents she has lost. So life goes on."

Isabella collapsed into a veritable cascade of tears then and before I knew it she had her head on my chest and her arms were around the back of my waist. The touch of her hands and the heat of her and the wet from her face on my chest left me more than a little breathless. I didn't dare put my arms round her for fear she might feel my excitement. What had I done? What was I doing?

I held her shoulders in as grandfatherly a way as I could and murmured things like "There now" and "I'm so sorry you had to hear that" and "Oh my dear girl". And that's when something started happening to me. To tell you the God's honest truth I didn't know and still don't know which fluid it was. But whichever it was I quickly put a stop to it. Not a fun thing to do but there you go. Young girls can be a tough gig. Up until now it was just the sight and the sound and the smell and the thought of them. But this one had her arms around me and was holding me tight.

"What does she look like? Please tell me. I've never seen her. I know she has a beautiful soul but I've never even seen her picture. She won't allow it."

"Really? She's still a bit of a tomboy, still hasn't become a young woman. We have pictures of her at home. I'll show them to you before you leave. But you're right about her soul you know."

I abruptly excused myself then and repaired to the back of the fort to assess the damage. Slight as it turned out. And while I was there I thought of running water and managed to empty my bladder of every last drop that was in it.

+++++

"I thought I'd seen the loveliest scenery in the world up at Grianan Fort but this is something else. You didn't tell me."

"No. I wanted to surprise you," I said. "This place is pretty special."

We had just rounded the bend outside Fahan village and there in front of us was Lough Swilly and its beaches and the green hills and great white wind turbines beyond.

"What does that mean?"

"What?"

"That sign."

"*Welcome to Amazing Grace Country* you mean?"

"Yes. Has that anything to do with the song?"

"Everything. It was written by a man called John Newton years after he was saved from drowning out there beyond the lough. It seems …"

But Isabella was singing.

Amazing grace! How sweet the sound
That saved a wretch like me.

I once was lost, but now am found,
Was blind, but now I see.

Her voice was so sweet and the lilt that came with it, something Scandinavian in it I think, stirred what was left of my manhood. And she sang on.

'T'was grace that taught my heart to fear,
And grace my fears relieved.
How precious did that grace appear
The hour I first believed!

She clapped her hand over her mouth then and took it away just as quickly. "Oh, I'm sorry. I interrupted when you were telling me about Isaac Newton"

I laughed delightedly. "You have the most beautiful voice." I glanced over at her. Her head was down and her eyes were fixed on the floor. Demure. Alluring. Utterly beautiful this girl. And she was rubbing her knees together as if not knowing where to put herself.

"Not Isaac Newton," I said shakily, leaning on autopilot. "John Newton. Isaac was the genius. John was anything but. He was a boor and a sexual predator that worked in the slave trade a long time ago. Over two hundred years I think. And one day he was on a ship away out there where we're facing, and it was filling with water and about to sink in a storm. Things were so bad that he actually started to pray and his prayer seemed to be answered. The cargo shifted and stopped up the hole where the water was coming in, and the ship drifted to safety off Lisfannon beach here and the whole crew were able to wade ashore. And then a crowd from around here took care of them and other locals repaired the ship. So there you are. Ireland of the welcomes."

I pulled into a little car park next to Lisfannon beach. "Would you like to take a walk?" I asked. She said she'd love to. As we walked, she kept giving little yelps of happiness, picking up a variety of shells from the sand till they were spilling out of her hands – Venus shells, cockles, mussels, scallops and whelks and others I wasn't able to name. In between times she seemed on the point of hyperventilating over the scene before us: little waves lapping at our feet, the deep blue lough, a man and a boy flying a multicoloured kite, children building sandcastles, the far fairytale shore of Rathmullan, soft mountains up to the sky.

"I'd love to take all these shells home with me," she said, kneeling as she gathered them in her arms. "But how ..."

"Why don't you put them in that little cloth bag you have there if it's empty," I suggested, "and we could wash them later? Unless you need the bag for something else."

"I don't really," she cried, gazing gratefully up at me. She put the shells one by one into the small sack-coloured bag as I hummed a tuneless bit of nothing. The only other girl I'd ever been with on Lisfannon beach was sixteen-year-old Henrietta Bell who was now no doubt giving the staff a bad time at Pee Valley. Out of sight.

We walked as far as the bend of the beach and saw a picturesque marina that had Isabella gasping all over again. "Imagine owning a big yacht and being able to berth it there and go out on it anytime you wanted."

"You could do lots of things if you had the money," I said. "But no amount of money could buy all the other things here."

"You're right. Of course you're right." She linked onto my elbow. "Are there many more places as nice as this?"

"Plenty. Pity you've only got three days."

"It's my father. He insists. He'll be getting a plane from Dublin to Belfast International on Monday and then I have to go back to Somerset with him. I told him I wanted to live here with Denise but he says he won't have that."

"Does he come to Ireland often?" I asked her.

"I'm not sure. He's in the perfume business and he goes all over the place. But he's got other things he's doing in Dublin, nothing to do with business." She was still hanging onto my elbow, for all the world like a little girl. "Could we buy some wine in a convenience store?" she asked.

I looked down at her. "You want wine?"

"Just a bottle between us. Would that be all right?"

"I'd have to buy it. They wouldn't serve you. By the way, I've been meaning to ask. What age are you?"

"Sixteen. I was sixteen last January."

"The age limit for buying drink here in the Irish Republic is seventeen." Like the age of consent. Five miles up the road in Northern Ireland it's sixteen for both. I know this stuff by heart. "They'd be asking you for ID. It's all right, I'll buy it." She told Denise she was only just fifteen. She's aged a year in the space of two weeks.

"Can I ask you something? I don't even know your name," she said nervously. "What's your name? Denise never talked about you."

"Lexie. Lexie Cheddy. Do you not remember? I told you at the airport."

"Oh I'm sorry. I must have missed it. Lllllexie. That's a lovely name. Is it from Alexander?"

"Well, yes, in a way."

"Lllllexie. Can I call you Lllllexie?"

"Of course. It's my name."

"And Cheddy. That's a cute surname."

She had put her other hand on the underside of my arm and I felt the soft swell of her small breast.

"I'll have to tell you about that sometime. There's a story behind that."

"I'd love to hear it."

"What's your surname?" I asked.

She smiled embarrassedly. "You promise not to laugh?"

"Of course I won't laugh."

"Batty. We're Batty." She put her hand over her mouth and her eyes were dancing. "Off our rockers. So now you know."

"That's an English name I think. There used to be a guy called David Batty that played for England. Tell me, is your father English?"

"Yes. He's from Somerset and that's where he put me in boarding school when we left Denmark after my mother died."

"Oh, I'm sorry. How long were you there? In the boarding school I mean."

"Over two years." She screwed up her nose. Lovely the way she does that. "Saint John of God Convent School for Girls."

Imagine being let loose in that place. I read somewhere that boys think about sex once every fourteen seconds and girls once every fifty-three seconds. But what about seventy-one-year-old bisexual crossdressing men with a penchant for nymphets? The thing never leaves my waking mind.

I lost her temporarily then to a little dog, border terrier I think it was. Actually, I wouldn't know a border terrier from a chihuahua, but I seem to recall from the ensuing conversation that that's what it was. Anyway, it arrived from nowhere and offered Isabella a cunning paw. She disengaged herself from me and got down on one knee to pet and hug the thing. The dirty little cur melted under her caresses as you can imagine and then shamelessly rolled on its back, literally rolled over, hoping for the full Monty I'd say, and near enough getting it too.

The dog's owner came puffing along and apologised for George's boldness and then hung on for the customary chat. Tall angular gushing woman, spinster from head to toe, babbling on for what seemed like ages. For the uninitiated among my readers this kind of palaver normally takes the form of two dog owners swapping stories about their stinking mutts, though sometimes the owners are using said mutts as a means of getting into each other's pants. If they hadn't a dog as a proxy they would no doubt find some other pretext for chatting up possible partners.

I've often seen this surrogate stuff going on down by the Foyle embankment, even watched in titillated fascination as two strangers stand chewing the fat while their pets indulge in strenuous daylight congress right next to their averted eyes. This could be described as breaking the ice - and the hymen too, I imagine, if it happens to be the bitch's debut.

Actually, I've been toying with the idea of getting one myself. A dog I mean. I thought I was done with dogs after I got bitten by Aubrey Hegarty who belonged to that bastard of a breadman if you remember, but I've lately been considering buying one. As the means to an end so to speak. I shall explain exactly what's on my mind in due course, but if you don't mind I'd like to get something off my chest first.

I have no love whatsoever for these disgusting fleabags that get away scot-free with shitting anywhere they fancy and of course are allowed by their owners to stop at will and sniff at a lamppost or the root of a tree or some other dog's dirty backside or whatever. If it was a child that they had with them, do you think they'd stand there patiently waiting for their own flesh and blood to finish admiring a weed or smelling a flower or examining a little pebble? No, they'd be pulling the bawling offspring after them.

But back to the ploy that's in my head. There's this damp dream of a guy I see in Brooke Park sometimes that walks an ugly looking little brute of the male persuasion, some class of spaniel I think, though I couldn't swear to that, and I wouldn't mind getting talking to him. Maybe I'll get a girl spaniel that's the same breed as his so we can compare notes. But that's for another day.

It turned out anyway – and you really have to hear this – that the spinster on the beach had called her smelly little cur after George Clooney. In a just world, this kind of disrespect for the second dishiest man on the planet would have serious repercussions. And I don't even want to think about what goes on in that spinster's bathroom when she's bathing little George.

Really, I can't get over the names some of these people have for their dogs. There's one I've seen in my street called Adam that belongs to Harold Gore, a bank official that I'm pretty sure is a Christian fundamentalist. He's been up on every bitch in the street - Adam I'm talking about here - till he's blue in the face. Taking the Master's divine exhortation to go forth etcetera to heart, obviously.

Isabella kept going on about dogs on our way back to the car. "We had a dog called Scout when my mother was alive. A cavalier King Charles spaniel. I loved him." She was tripping along next to me, doing her best to keep up with my long strides, then she began hanging onto my arm and running along beside me. "I thought he was the cutest dog in the world. But then my father sold him."

"Oh dear. That must have upset you."

"It broke my heart. And it was just after Mum died too. Did you ever hear of a film star called Dennis Quaid?"

"Yes. He's very good. I saw him in *Far From Heaven*."

"That was brilliant," she said. "That's the one where he was a gay man married to a woman. But the best film I ever saw him in was *Great Balls of Fire* - you know, the one where he acted Jerry Lee Lewis."

"*Great Balls of Fire*. I didn't see that."

"It was brilliant. I'm sure you remember hearing the song when you were young. I mean younger."

"I did."

"What was I saying there? I know now. I was going to tell you about Dennis Quaid. He's in a new film called *A Dog's Purpose* and it would make you cry, it really would. Dennis Quaid said in an interview one time that he used to have a basset hound and they were everything to each other. She taught him how to live, he said. It was like she had a ... I don't know what you'd call it ... a system. Like, she seemed to live by certain rules, you know, like, live in this very moment, love everybody you can, make people happy and have fun and all."

"Freud and Jung and those lads missed a trick then," I said with a smile. "All you have to do is get a dog. Who needs counsellors and talking therapies?"

"But it's true, Lllllexie. Dennis said in an interview one time that years ago he was in ruins. He just flipped and was into cocaine and he was in a really, really bad way. And even when he got treatment for it he still needed something to take the place of the coke, you know, like the methadone that they give some people that are on heroin?"

"I know about that."

"Well, he tried meditation. He read the Bible and the Qur'an and what do you call the Buddhist book and the other one, the Hindu book?"

"Oh yes. One of them's called the Dhamma something, the Dhammawada or Dhammapada, I'm not sure which. That's the Buddhist one, I think. And the other ..."

"And he went to India nine times and meditated every single day for ten years. And then he got a dog."

"And what?"

"What do you mean what?"

"What happened then?"

"He got another dog. And then another dog. There's an amazing picture of him on his ranch I saw one time. He's got his dogs all around him and one of them is sitting up on a horse. You should see it. He looks like the happiest man in the world."

She let go of my arm when we got to the car and as I searched for my keys she smiled over at me, eyes just about high enough to peep across the roof, beautiful hair shining like silver in the sun, yellow band in it now, heartstopping sight, mine if I wanted maybe, if only I knew how to handle it.

+++++

Buncrana is a couple of miles down the road from Lisfannon beach and the first hotel you come to is Inishowen Gateway, a massive gleaming white place that's as long as a street.

Just inside the entrance was a mural showing a beach scene with muscular men and bite-size nymphets, all in tight swimsuits, as well as herds of large-breasted women sprawled about like basking seals and then scores of toddlers with buckets and spades. Above it was the slogan YOUR IDEAL STARTING POINT ON YOUR WILD ATLANTIC WAY.

My wild Atlantic way. I wish. I booked two bedrooms for one night only. Isabella came over to me when I was signing the book. "I'd like to pay my way," she whispered. "I have the money. And I got plenty of euros at the airport."

"I wouldn't hear of it," I said. "You're my guest, Isabella."

After we left our luggage in our rooms we had a lovely dinner and afterwards went to the lounge. Such a cosy place that lounge. Even to this day I have special memories of it.

"You're better not to be ordering anything alcoholic," I told Isabella. "They might only start asking questions."

She smiled and nodded. She looked relaxed and happy. And damned desirable, sprawled impudently as she was in a deep armchair with her legs carelessly splayed. I've already told you she had on this little denim top and that it was a perfect match for her ripped skintight jeans. Well, now I'm telling you again.

"Whatever you say," she said. "Do you think they'd have ginger beer?"

"Ginger beer? I'll ask."

They had it, the non-alcoholic kind. And I also bought a glass of pinot noir for myself.

We sat sipping side by side, sunk in our armchairs. She said "We used to drink ginger beer at night my first year in Saint John of God."

"Saint John of God?"

She giggled. "Do you not remember me telling you? The convent school. In Somerset. That's where I went to college."

"I remember now. It's no wonder your English is so good. You don't sound Danish at all, you know. Did I tell you that?"

"I think so." She sat looking between her legs at the floor, stayed looking there till I said "Did you like it in the convent?"

"No. The nuns were like ..." She gazed into her glass. "They were like ...."

"Like nuns?"

She looked up at me and smiled. "Yes. Like nuns. Sister Michael was the worst. The time she made us all close our eyes and put our heads sideways on the desk when she was telling us the facts of life. She made it ... you know, the whole thing, seem like a terrible ordeal you had to go through. Unless you were a nun and then you didn't have to go through it. It was mad."

"Good heavens." Steady now Lexie.

"We had to study biology for GCSE and some of the pages in the book had illustrations of people and things about ... ah, a whole lot of things, and when the nuns discovered this years ago, they gummed the pages together in all the biology books. We used to say they'd been gummed together since the time of Methuselah."

"That's shocking."

"And just wait till you hear this. Three doors down the street from the convent there was this place that sold the morning-after pill and STD testing kits. As God is my witness." She placed her right hand solemnly on top of her breast. She's relaxed. She feels safe telling me all this. Good old Grandpa Lexie.

"You know what the nuns were? They were ... I don't know what you'd call it ... sinister. They were sinister like, kind of gliding along in their big grey habits and their arms up their sleeves. They gave me the creeps, honest to God. Half of the girls were drinking before they left."

"You mean in the convent? Drinking in the actual convent?"

"Oh yes."

"How did they manage that?"

"Well, there was a caretaker. Two caretakers actually, but there was one that brought drink in, bottles and bottles of it sometimes, in a waste bin. Some of the girls took turns to pay him."

I stared at her. She was barely more than a child and yet so matter of fact. Was she one of the drinkers? Did she take her turn to settle with the caretaker? And did she bed-hop with other girls in the convent? She fancied Denise, that I knew. What was it she had written when Denise asked her what she wore in bed? *It depends who's in with me. If I'm alone, nothing at all.*

A man and woman arrived carrying drinks and sat next to us. I smiled absently at them. The man didn't respond but the woman smiled back. My eyes flitted over her. She was tall and stately, fading good looks, swathed in pale green veils, hair dyed a bright red, in her fifties I'd say. Her partner was a dour sort of a git entirely lacking in oomph. Stodgy and bald, heavy-jowled and dull-eyed, bulbous nose, flared nostrils, kitted out in tweeds with matching waistcoat, not my cup of tea at all.

Isabella took off her denim top and put it over the arm of her chair. "It's very warm in here, isn't it?" she said, pulling her hair back from her face. The concealed lighting played on her bare neck, her warm apricot shoulders and the soft outline of her breasts and further down on the crooked little lines of perspiration that trickled from her bare midriff to the waistband of her jeans.

"It's warm all right," I said. I was so close to her that I felt sure she could smell the lavender eau de Cologne that I'd hurriedly splashed on in my bathroom to neutralise earlier mishaps.

"You on holiday?"

"Sorry?"

"I said are you on holiday?" Mister Tweedy addressing me.

"Oh. Yes, "I said. "Just for a few days."

"Same with us, Eleanor and me. That's about all I get in the year, a few days." He was talking at me without looking at me, border accent, down by Dundalk, refined somewhat so as not to betray his origins I'd say. His voice went with the rest of him, buttoned-up. This guy was on his summer holiday in a semi-heatwave and he was wearing a three-piece tweed suit.

"You in business?" he asked.

"No, actually. I'm retired."

"What did you do for a living then?" Nosey bugger. But then maybe not. More than likely he's asking about me so that he can wait till I finish and then start talking about himself. Maybe it's time for Isabella and me to go to our rooms.

"I was an academic."

"Yeah, but what did you do for a *living*?"

"I'd call that living. Would you not?"

His jowls twitched. "That's smart. You're smart."

"Magnus!"

The exclamation, mark and all, came from the lady of the veils and it brought about a temporary toning down from her man.

"What I'm getting at is," he said, "did you have a job?"

"I worked in a university."

"A university? Doing what?"

"I taught."

"And what did you teach?"

"Humanities."

He stared blankly at me. Obviously had never heard of it. Didn't deter him though.

"I'd guess there's not a fortune to be made in that."

"You'd be guessing correctly."

"You a professor then?"

"I am."

"El's nephew's a professor. That right El? What kinda professor is he El?"

"Acoustic engineering you call it," she said. "He's unemployed at the moment though."

"There you are," said Tweedy. "Worked himself up from the rocks and what's it all for? May as well be herding sheep."

"Universities are tough places now," I said. "So many redundancies."

"I'm in the car park business myself," he said, running a hand over his big gut.

"Really? In what capacity?" I nearly added "Attendant?"

"I own them. Whole string of them. Came up from nothing and made myself a millionaire."

"That's interesting," I said.

"Yeah, you could call it that. Hard bloody work. I'm at it fifty weeks in the year. Take ten or eleven days off so's I can recharge the old batteries. I've car parks in half the counties of Ireland you know. Started off getting a loan for three quarters of an acre would you believe."

"Do you find it fulfilling?"

"Pardon me?"

"Your work. Do you find it fulfilling?"

"If you mean does it fill the coffers it certainly does. You want to know what's a gold mine?"

I shook my head.

"Hospitals. I've eleven hospital car parks so I have. No shortage of customers there. No sirree. But you have to watch the schemers."

"Schemers?"

"Yeah. There were these consultant guys in three of the parks I own that said they should get free parking. Just because they were top of their tree. I said to them, I said to the whole lot of them: "Look, you're taking in big money so why should you get charges waived? If the visitors and porters and kitchen staff and nurses and all the rest have to fork out, why shouldn't you?"

Nobody spoke for a bit. I asked Isabella if she would like another drink and she shook her head. Time for her and me to go upstairs.

"Reckon I'll sell off the whole caboodle in a few years' time and then travel the world."

"Well, I hope you enjoy your retirement," I said.

"Retirement?" he fired back. "Who said anything about retirement? I want to see around me a bit and then start into something new. Marketing maybe. Or publishing. I've had half a mind to do book publishing for years now."

"Really? You read a lot then?"

"Never read a book in my life. Don't need to read books to do publishing. Did Roman Abramovich play football?"

"Roman Abramovich?"

"The guy who owns Chelsea football club."

"Oh, I see what you mean."

He stood up abruptly. "El, would you like another g 'n t?"

"No Magnus. I'm fine. You take it easy now."

He lurched slightly as he headed for the bar.

Eleanor smiled at us. "Are you enjoying your holiday?" She had a lovely west of Ireland lilt and a warm open smile.

"We are, thanks," I said. "Just trying to get in as much as we can."

"This is such a beautiful place," she went on. "Donegal I mean."

"It certainly is," I said. "Tell me, are you from Galway?"

"I am. The accent always gives me away."

"What part of Galway?"

"Lettermullan," she said. "I'm Eleanor Bastian by the way."

I shook her hand. "I'm Lexie Cheddy and this is ... Isabella."

She smiled warmly at Isabella. "I'm so pleased to meet you both. Our family were Irish speakers so I grew up bilingual. Lettermullan is so rich in culture but such a deprived place." She absently pulled back a veil which partly covered her face. A fine face that was scarred on one side, almost perfect features though. How in under God does someone like her end up with someone like that?

"I know Lettermullan. I've been there," I said. "Actually drank in a shebeen there once."

"Would that have been Mary Rose's by any chance?"

"The very one. Have you been in her place?"

"No, but I used to hear all about it. Do you know what I heard? I heard some of the gardaí would sit waiting in their patrol car till she put the customers out and then go in for their own nightcap."

"I didn't know that now," I said. "Sure it could only happen in Ireland."

I heard a giggle from the side of me. Isabella's face was bright with smiles. "That's so funny," she said. "I love this country."

Eleanor beamed at her. "You're not from here?"

"No, I'm from Denmark though I live in England," said Isabella. "I'm just here on a short holiday."

"I hope the weather keeps up for you," said Eleanor. "I'm sure it will. The forecast says it will last."

"Did you live long in Lettermullan?" I asked.

"Until I was twenty-two. That's when I met Magnus. He was holidaying in Spiddal and staying in a guest house I was skivvying in there. Swept me off my feet so he did. Inside two days he met my parents in Lettermullan. It was a real whirlwind."

"That's lovely," said Isabella. "That's so romantic."

"It was sort of funny too," said Eleanor, laughing at the memory. "I knew I was going to go away with him and I suppose I became a bit careless about my duties and the woman of the house gave me one day's notice to quit. She was a real slave-driver you know. So after I'd got my pay I left a five pence piece on the kitchen table and under it a note saying "This is a tip for Max" – Max was the dog – "for all the washing up he did for me licking the plates clean."

"Nothing like the old Bush." Tweedy was back. "That's what I always say to El. Don't I say that, El? Nothing to beat the old Bush." He winked at her and she quickly lowered her gaze.

To me he said "I was telling you I don't read books. But saying that, El was showing me a thing on *YouTube* that this queer writer was on. What was it called El?"

"*The Importance of being Oscar*. But Magnus. Please."

"Right. *The Importance of being Oscar*. It was done by one poofter about another poofter. What did you call the one that did it El?"

"Micheál MacLiammóir. But –"

"Micheál MacLiammóir. Queer as a clockwork orange. He told on the TV how he gave General Eoin O'Duffy a good buggering away back in the Thirties. That's the lad that was head of the Blueshirts and head of the Garda Síochána into the bargain would you believe. Top bumbardier so he was."

"Magnus!"

"It seems MacLiammóir and this other actor fruit called Hilton Edwards were getting it together for years."

"Magnus! There's a young girl here."

"But here's what I was going to tell you." Nothing if not determined, Magnus ploughed on. "Wait till you hear. Do you know what people used to say about MacLiammóir? They used to say he was up to the hilt on Edwards. You get it?"

I stared at him and said nothing.

"Them were the boys, weren't they?"

Eleanor sat bolt upright, snatched her handbag from the floor, sprang from her armchair and steamed out of the lounge trailing pastel clouds of veils.

"What do you think of that? Eh?" Magnus, apparently not put out in the least by Eleanor's storming exit, sat rocking back and forward, shaking his head and barely controlling his laughter.

"I think it's shocking," I said. "I'm surprised that anybody in this day and age should have such an attitude."

"No no no, you're not listening." said Magnus. "This was, what, eighty years ago? And it was all said behind backs. If the gardaí had wanted to they could have had these two daffodils locked up. But how could they" - and here he was briefly overcome by another fit of laughing - "when their boss was getting his peanut butter stirred by one of them".

"You know what I've always thought?" I said, and I could feel the colour rising in my face.

"What's that?"

"I've always thought extremist homophobes were mostly closet homosexuals. The bigger the attack the bigger the arsehole and the bigger the chance of them being secret gays."

"What! What did you just say?"

"Sorry. Sometimes I speak too softly. What I was saying was I've always thought extremist homophobes were mostly closet homosexuals. The bigger the attack the bigger the arsehole and the bigger the chance of them being secret gays."

"Are you trying to say something, friend?"

"Not trying. I've just said it. I don't know for certain what your inclinations are sir, but I have my suspicions and I'm thinking perhaps a lot of your acquaintances are wondering when you're going to come out."

Magnus shook his jowls and stood bolt upright and then, to let me know that he'd had enough of my company, he threw back what remained of his large whiskey and immediately proceeded to choke on it. The purple of his nostrils spread quickly and brightly to the rest of his face. A case of *à bout de souffle*, I thought. With any luck the bastard's about to drown in a dram of the best Bush.

It certainly looked and sounded serious but I didn't attempt to help. A concerned member of staff approached and I smilingly but firmly waved him away, telling him that we were used to these little episodes. I'm sure the man must have been perplexed because Magnus looked far from all right as, bent almost double and fighting for breath, he proceeded to send out these fearful brays and groans. Finally, he straightened himself, spat some yellow on the carpet and took his leave, but not before croaking out a barely audible attempt at a comeback, something along the lines of "There's one thing for sure. You're one yourself when you're going on like that."

I turned to Isabella. Her head was on her knees, long auburn hair reaching to the floor.

Alarmed, I asked her if she was OK. She didn't reply and it was then I saw that she was laughing.

She sat slowly upright, rose to her feet and hitched up her jeans, doing a teasing little shimmy as she did so. And then, entirely unaware of how all this was affecting me, she proceeded to pull and shake out her hair, some of which had become attached to her wet cheeks.

"That was brilliant," she spluttered. "I've never seen a putdown like that in all my life."

I wanted to touch the golden down on her right arm there and then. I was sure she would be all right with it but simply couldn't bring myself to do it.

"Maybe we should go," I said, "before some gay-basher comes along."

She sighed a smile and wiped the tears from her eyes and cheeks. And then her shoulders suddenly sagged.

"Is there something wrong?" I asked.

"No, it's all right. I suddenly feel so tired. It just came on me."

"Oh dear. I was stupid to keep you up till this time. You've had a long day. Maybe you should go straight to bed."

"I think you're right," she said. "It's all kind of all crowding in on me now. So much has happened since I got up this morning."

"What time were you up at?"

"Half-four."

"Oh heavens. I've been very thoughtless. We'll get you up to your room right now. What's your number?"

"Two three three. Easy to remember."

"Second floor. I remember now. I'm across the corridor from you. Two three four I think. Let me have a look. Yes, two three four."

"Sometimes I don't sleep too well," she said.

"You'll sleep well tonight. You're at the back of the hotel so you won't hear any traffic."

When we got as far as our rooms a young couple were having trouble opening their door which was next to mine. The man asked for our help and I showed him how to use his key card. He seemed in a hurry but still took the time to look me in the eyes and smile and place a grateful hand on my shoulder.

Please don't be shocked when I tell you here that the torrid odour that he gave off stopped the breath in my throat and the heat from his hand went through my thick shoulder pad as if it wasn't there, sending a unsettling sensation rushing all the way to my toes and back up again. And it wouldn't be going too far to say that the old knees nearly went from under me.

Never before had these combined reactions taken place in my brief and virtually blameless encounters with young men – although the bus queue incident came close – but this particular young man was different. Tall and imposing, with a dark curling mop, deep brown eyes, olive skin, simian features, sensual mouth. Clean shaven but with thick black hair on his neck, arms and the backs of his hands. A bloody animal, I thought, and one that's ready for anything by the looks of him.

His shoulders and chest, covered by a tight white T-shirt with an image of Beyoncé on it, damn her, were muscular and downright beautiful. Maddeningly I hadn't time to take in the rest of him because his little blonde partner that looked like a badly botoxed Barbie doll destroyed both my conversation and concentration by gushing out her gratitude to me and then pushing her whole front deep into his, priming him for all she was worth, and I could see in a moment that some unconstrained activity lay ahead. And then their door was shut and he was gone.

"We can have the wine tomorrow night, can't we?" said Isabella.

Still reeling somewhat, I looked more or less blankly at her and nodded mechanically.

"Thanks for a lovely day Lllllexie. You've been so kind." And with that she came very close to me, stood on her tiptoes, put her hands on my arms and kissed me on both cheeks. I felt nothing. I was having trouble getting back to her.

Door closed, light on and standing alone. *Henry and June* had been on my reading list for ages and I'd brought it with me just in case. I had also packed a couple of Runaways comics. Close scrutiny of the pubescent girls that they featured had never failed to put me in the mood. After a minute's thought I decided on *Henry and June*. I took my medication, stripped off, had a shower, quickly dried myself, sprayed on some *Pour Homme Eau De Toilette Vaporisateur* and slipped into my black lace panties and the pink push-up bra with the daffodil motif, leaving my classic vibrator next to Anaïs Nin's book on the bedside locker.

I turned on my *iTunes* nice and low and got Jon Bon Jovi, slid between the cool cotton covers, lingered on the young man next door, then reached for the book and opened it. Ah. *Henry and June* (I read) *takes place over the period of a single year in the life of Anaïs Nin as she encounters love and torment in her no-G-strings-attached relationship with first of all the beautiful and sensual Henry Miller and then with his voluptuous and insatiable wife June. Anaïs becomes the apex of this steamy triangle, playing havoc with the married couple who have already led the most mind-blowing sex lives; but what takes place in the twelve months of the diary will leave the reader staggered. This highly intimate account ...*

The hell with the blurb. I turned the pages fast till I got to the beginning of the diary. Someone tapped lightly on the door, so lightly that I thought for a few moments that it must be someone else's door. Then I heard the voice.

"Llllexie. Please can I come in?"

Good Christ, it's her.

"Yes, just hold on a minute." I scrambled out of bed, slapped my dental plate back in my mouth, turned off the music and dived into the suitcase to get my black silk dressing gown, pulled it on, buttoned it up and rushed to the door. Just as I was about to unlock it I remembered the book and the vibrator, both sitting on top of the locker. *Grand Dieu!* I dashed across, slipped them under the eiderdown and scurried back to the door. What confronted me when I opened it was something I will never forget.

Isabella stood with a bottle of wine in one hand and a book in the other and she was beautiful. Her face was a light crimson, making her freckles seem darker, and the little brown curls at the ends of her long long hair went way below the bottom of the chunky yolk-coloured jumper cardigan that clashed beautifully with the light pink pyjama bottoms she had on. Light pink pyjamas brought to Ireland for Denise to take off. And bare feet. She was ready for bed.

"I'm so sorry," she said, tremor in her voice. "I couldn't sleep and I wondered if I could sit in here awhile and maybe we could talk."

Talk. She wanted to talk.

"Oh no, don't apologise Isabella. There's nothing to apologise about. You're over-tired, that's all. You've brought the wine. And a book. I see you've got a book with you. What is it?"

I hardly knew what I was saying and my words were spilling over each other but she didn't seem to notice.

"I started it on the way over on the plane. It's the first time I've read him and I wanted to ask you something. Can I sit down?"

"Of course. Here, let me take those out of your hands."

Not knowing quite where to put herself she had gone to the bed and sat nervously on the edge of it. She immediately jumped up.

"Oh! I've sat on something. I hope I haven't broken it." She began to feel the surface of the eiderdown.

I left the bottle and book on my dressing table and went quickly to her. "Pardon me a moment," I said. "If you'd just stand for a moment." She half-stood and I leaned behind her, felt under the eiderdown achingly close to her hovering little ass and drew out the book face down. "I tend to leave things in all sorts of odd places," I stammered.

"Oh, you've got a book too," she said. "But that's not what I sat on. It was something else. I'm sorry. I hope I haven't broken anything."

"Not at all," I said. "Don't worry yourself about it. What was it you wanted to ask me about?"

Isabella went to the dressing table and brought the book to the side of my bed. She showed me the cover as she sat where she had sat before. Picture of a shiny black insect, rather like a ladybird, walking across a chessboard, and above it *The Metamorphosis* printed in marble-red font.

"Ah. Kafka," I said. "You're reading Kafka. Good."

"Yes. I read some of it on the plane but I don't understand it. I was hoping maybe, you know, seeing you taught ..."

"What is it you don't understand? Here, why don't you sit in the armchair there?"

"Oh, that's lovely, thank you. Your armchair looks nicer than the one in my room." She got up from the bed and moved slowly and delicately across to the armchair. I blinked a few times in rapid succession to try and clear a mist that seemed to have come between us. "Is it all right if …?" she said. I missed the rest of her question.

"Pardon? Is it all right if what?""

She smiled brightly. "Is it all right if I open the wine? It's a screw-top."

"Progress. I used to nearly always manage to end up with bits of cork in the bottle," I said, now sitting where Isabella had been. "Yes, please do open the wine."

"Can I use these glasses?"

"Absolutely. I'm afraid I'm not able to offer you a proper wine glass."

"All goes down the same way, Teresa Houlihan used to say. Teresa's my second-best friend. It all goes down the wee red brae anyway, she used to say when we were drinking the lager out of cups."

She put a guilty hand to her mouth. "Oops, I gave something away. But I hardly ever took any. "

I smiled indulgently. "We all have our little secrets. So I know one of yours now."

She laughed and I heard the plop and the glug of the wine toppling into the two glasses one after the other.

I wanted, feared, what might be ahead. She walked toward me, trembling hand reaching forward holding the glass of red wine, its beaded bubbles almost brimming over. She was as nervous as I was.

"Thanks Isabella. I'm glad you came in. I'm actually in the mood for talking."

"Oh, that's great. I was scared of annoying you but I just knew I wasn't going to sleep. Are you all right sitting there? You look uncomfortable."

"The bed's just fine thanks."

The bed's just fine. Would it be that shocking, that earth-shattering? The law is a hard-ass. Sixteen or seventeen were arbitrary ages of consent decided on by screwed up judges and lords and the like issuing dishonourable discharges under their robes. And the ages are based on stupid assumptions about every girl's age of emotional reason being the same.

I remember reviewing a play – *Rita, Sue and Bob Too* – set in a run-down housing estate by a young genius called Andrea Dunbar. A man in his late twenties has sex regularly with two fifteen-year-old girls in the back of his car, where he takes them night about. And at the end, Sue's mother recognises that the best that girls like Sue and Rita can hope for in this dead-end place is to get their fun while they can. Is Isabella so different? She's unhappy and unloved, and I suspect her father isn't exactly the anchor he should be. When I look back to the night of the play, what I found most interesting was that the audience weren't in the least put out by what they saw and heard.

"The thing I was going to ask you," she said and then frowned, concentrating. She paused as she eased back into the armchair, legs indolently apart.

"Oh yes. You wanted to know something about your book."

She made a slurping noise as she took her first drink from the glass. "Sorry," she said, giggling. "I'm very rude." She wiped her mouth with the side of her hand. Why is it that every move …? It can't be that she's being deliberately provocative. "It just seems like a horror story, Gregor waking up one morning and he's been turned into a disgusting cockroach."

I smiled. "It's not exactly Mary Poppins."

"And he spends all the time going to the bathroom anywhere and eating disgusting things and hanging upside down like a bat or something. And he's trapped in the house. He can't get out. It's like a movie David Cronenberg would make. It really is."

"You're right. Though it was there well before Cronenberg was born and it'll still be there when he's forgotten."

"But why? Why's that?"

She shook herself, gave a slow wide yawn and laid one limp hand on her lap.

"Sorry," she said. "Please excuse me."

"I think the whole thing is mostly about Kafka feeling different," I said. "You know, alienated. For a long time, nearly everybody he saw and knew seemed pretty normal to him but he himself felt anything but. For a start he was a German speaker living in Prague, and as well as that, he was a Jew living in very dangerous times and he was always afraid of people finding out what he was."

"I didn't know that. You see, I thought ... but I'm interrupting. I've no manners. I'm not even letting you finish."

"You're all right." Her hand still sat dreamily on her pyjama bottoms and her face still held the flush that was there when she came in. It was remarkable how stunning, almost otherworldly she was. So near, so impossible. "And he probably meant too that workers were being dehumanised in a capitalised society. His books mean so much more when you know about his life."

"I'll have to read about him," she said, her little jaw firmly set. "I'll definitely do that before I read any more."

"Tell me, have you got to the part yet where the maid comes in to clean Gregor's room?"

"Yes. That was awful. Poor Gregor."

"Yes. Well, Gregor didn't know it at the time but he could have flown out of the open window and spent the rest of his life rolling dung balls with the other dung beetles down below. That would have been a real happy ending but unfortunately Franz Kafka wasn't into happy endings."

"Gosh. Did he make a mistake then?"

"He did. But sure we're told even God was human for a while. The thing is, you see, from Kafka's description of Gregor the beetle, he had to be a scarab beetle with wing-sheaths so – voilà! – he could fly."

Her eyes were wide and admiring, beautifully blue, innocent like a child's. "Imagine!" she said. "But how do you know all this?"

I smiled. I was glowing inside now and hardening like hell. "I belong to a group called the Coleopterists' Society. We study beetles and compare notes. We're nerds, you see. I've corresponded with all sorts of people from all over the world – you wouldn't believe it –

university professors, doddering old ladies, mental patients, white supremacists, left-wingers, waste collectors, politicians, an ex-dictator that I'm told is on the run right now. You name it."

I felt her fascinated gaze on me and this encouraged me to make something of a fool of myself.

"And do you know how a dung beetle lays its eggs?"

Her expression changed and she shook her head, possibly wondering if I'd suddenly flipped. I got up from the bed and did my best to imitate the egg-laying, inclining my head to my waist and walking slowly across the room in this posture, making dung-rolling movements with my lower arms and hands until my head was buried in them and the eggs were finally laid. "Good Christ," I said, "this egg-laying is bloody exhausting."

She exploded in a delicious burst of laughter that I think could actually have been a release of tension. The truth was, the situation had got to me and I was in a state of what you might call diminished responsibility.

"What's your book?" she asked, looking at me a little oddly. "What's the one you're reading?" Notice the abrupt change of subject.

I had no choice but to take it from under my pillow and show her the cover.

"*Henry and June*!" she breathed. "Isn't that porn?"

"I haven't actually started it yet but I've a feeling it's not porn," I said.

"It's just that the girls used to pass that very book around in college with pages turned in that had ... like ... certain bits in them. I never got reading any of it though."

I laughed. "Just like we used to pass round *Lady Chatterley's Lover*. With bookmarks and bits of newspaper stuck in all over the place. We didn't know it then but *Lady Chatterley's Lover* is a very serious book."

"And is *Henry and June* serious?"

"I don't know yet. But I've read some of Nin's other stuff and she could certainly write. Some of her writing is comparable to James Joyce, actually. What I've read of her is mostly a mixture of seriousness and her search for fame. She didn't seem to have any shame actually, and she'd relations with lots of men, even her own father, and wrote it all down in her diaries."

I made half-closed eye contact, wondering if I'd shocked her. I had.

"Her father," she said. "Oh."

"Pornographic or not, I don't know. Opinion is divided on that. She's a very interesting person actually. She got the fame she wanted a few years before she died and it all happened because the women's movement championed her. And the irony was that she had cheapened herself as a woman, which was the very opposite of what the women's movement stood for."

Her eyes were wide again and that strange, otherworldly look was back and for an off-putting few moments she seemed older than she was.

"Teresa said she slept with women too."

"Yes. June Miller was one I know about. Nin was having relations with a writer called Henry Miller and when Henry's wife June got wind of it, she flew back immediately from wherever she was on the continent. And as soon as she and Anaïs laid eyes on each other, the two of them were hooked."

"OhmyGod."

Isabella's hands moved restlessly on her knees. She began to say something about Nin's father and then stopped, blinking hard.

"Sorry Isabella. What were you saying?"

"Nothing. I wasn't saying anything. Could I see the book?"

"Of course." I brought it over to her. She read aloud from the cover. "*Henry and June – from A Journal of Love. The Unexpurgated Diary of Anaïs Nin, 1931 to 1932.*"

She handed it back without opening it. "I heard that Henry Miller was a real lover boy," she said.

"He certainly was. His books are very explicit about it. There's one terrible scene with his first wife Beatrice. I don't think it should have been ..."

"Should have been what?"

"Sorry?"

"Should have been what? That's a lovely dressing gown. You look really handsome in it."

"Ah ... thank you."

"What were you saying? Should have been what? You were telling me about Henry Miller."

I knew then that I was in danger of losing it. I'd have liked to blame the wine but it wasn't the wine. Preposterously, I had been almost on the point of telling her about when Miller penetrated the frigid Beatrice through her nightdress. Time to get a grip.

"I'm not sure what I was going to say. I think maybe it was about *The Tropic of Cancer*. That was his most notorious book."

"I heard of that one too."

"Male chauvinism at its worst."

"Really?" she whispered, her pink pyjamad knees knocking nervously against each other. She was wide awake now and no mistake.

"Yes. It was really all about male control and the subjugation of women."

"Subjugation? What does that mean? Domination?"

"Yes."

She was agog. Her eyes were sparkling and her slightly swollen lips had a faint uneven rim of purple around them. Suddenly she swung her legs languorously over an arm of her chair, almost spilling some wine in the process.

"We passed round *Lolita* too," she said conspiratorially.

"Yes. Lolita," I said. "It's a remarkable book."

"I never read it all. I got bored when they were travelling all those thousands of miles round America."

"Some people tend to give up at that part," I said, "but I think it's brilliantly written. You should read it again some time. America has such a rich history considering it's still a young country. I'm trying to remember what Nabokov called it. A crazy quilt of forty-eight states, I think."

"Does America not have fifty states?" The top button of her cardigan had opened and some of her little cleavage was sitting there for me to look at.

"It does now. It had only forty-eight at the time Humbert took Lolita on that journey, nineteen forty-seven. Do you know what age Lolita would be now if she were alive?"

She shook her head.

"Eighty-two. She'd be eighty-two."

I could tell that this didn't interest her. "But I was saying about America's rich history," I said. "And the descriptions of landscapes that Humbert gives is like a novel in itself. Actually, the first European writers and landscape artists who visited the States were bowled over by its trees. There's a giant redwood, in Nevada I think, that's three thousand five hundred years old and a pine tree in California that's supposed to have been there for five thousand years. But its exact location is a secret in case some crank gets the idea of burning it down."

Isabella blinked dreamily, picked at some bobbles on her cardigan and said "She was only twelve when she became Herbert's lover, wasn't she?"

"Humbert. Humbert Humbert was his full name. You know, like someone being called Casanova Casanova."

"Oh, right. Humbert Humbert. Dirty old man. I always thought he sounded like a clown with a name like that. But imagine, she was only twelve."

Would it have been all right if she'd been fifteen Isabella?

"Tell me," I said. "Have you ever heard of Groucho Marx?"

"Groucho Marx? Of course I have! I've seen Duck Soup. OhmyGod, the mirror scene!"

"I remember it. Classic. Anyway, Groucho was asked to comment on Lolita after it was published and he said 'I think I'll put off reading it for six more years until she turns eighteen.' "

She spluttered with laughter and left her glass with a clatter on the dressing table. "You're so funny Lllllexie! "The way she said my name, so familiarly she said it, with that lovely little Danish lilt to it, the way she said it. Lllllexie.

And such a very short time we've known each other. Leaving Denise out of it. Denise doesn't belong here. How long has it been? Twelve hours, virtually inseparable for twelve hours, give or take, and she still likes being with me. What does that tell you? She hasn't even mentioned Denise since ... since when? Since Grianan Fort, since the beautiful poem I gave her. My heart would hear you and beat. That poem. It brought such a loving reaction from her that, and try as I do even now sometimes, I still can't feel ashamed.

"It's not me that's funny. It's Groucho. He writes my scripts."

She rocked back and forward on her armchair. "Oh my sweet Lord! Where have you been all my life? I get so depressed when I'm alone. And I was exhausted an hour ago and I'm wide awake now. You're a howl, honestly." Lexie the courting jester.

She took her glass again and almost drained it in one gulp. "Would you like some more?" she asked. "You've only taken one glass to my two."

"How about we share the rest of the bottle?" I said. "There's not that much left anyway."

"OK." What is it about her voice, the lazy way she says OK, the way she stretches out the Kaaaaaay that sends the shivers through me? She got up and brought the bottle over, a mite unsteady on her feet, then slowly and with extreme care poured the wine into my glass. She was so close to me I could smell her, and her smell filled my head, all mixed in with my perfume, but inside the whole blend was *her*, something that must have come from her very pores. I seemed to see through a burnished haze then as the fibres of her cardigan brushed against my left cheek and eyebrow. I knew what was happening of course (I've studied this stuff). Headless corpuscles racing up and down between the knees and the bowels, then settling in the gusset. Partial erection underway.

First time I've noticed how lovely her fingers are. Long, thin, palely clasping the neck of the tilted bottle, then righting it and smiling in the soft look she gave me. There had been girls as young as eighteen in my tutorials that I'm pretty sure I could have had favours from in return for a little personal coaching or indulgent marking, but they were too old, all too old, all too heavy-haunched, too busty, too much like women of the world. There were none like this, none as bewitching, none as beautiful, none as young.

She went back to the dressing table and stood beside it pouring the rest of the wine for herself. Then she sat and slowly settled into a slouch, smiling contentedly. She was very much at home there in my bedroom, as if she had known me for years. Uncle Lexie. Comfortable as a glove. There she sat, athwart the armchair in that ungainly way she had sometimes, pink pyjama bottoms gathered halfway up her shins, folds bunched innocently against her groin. I lowered my eyes and fixed my gaze on her white long-toed feet and their cherry-red toenails.

It was then that we heard the groans from next door. At first it sounded like someone being violently sick but very quickly it became obvious that the groans were those of a male who was at the receiving end of some extremely heavy petting. The East European hunk that I'd helped into his bedroom was obviously now being fingered, fondled and generally pulled apart by the cheap little piece he had with him. I'd always known there wasn't much justice in this world and here was another example at its noisiest.

Isabella was giggling. "Do you hear that?" she said. "*Some*one's having a good time."

"More like some two," I said, putting on a bit of the blasé and hoping my bitterness wasn't showing.

"Shh. Listen." Finger to bright red lips.

I listened.

"Roll me. Do you hear? Roll me over," he barked.

I stole a look at Isabella and knew from her impish face that she was picturing everything that was happening, from his big body being slowly turned over to the beginning of a whole new procedure.

"No! Do my feet!" The words were at the top of his voice. "My feet! Soles first! Putka! Your tongue dammit! Fuck sake!"

His tone was so imperious that there was little the girl could do but comply. And so we entered a period of relative calm evidenced by soft moans, sickening sighs and strangulated gasps from my eastern friend as his partner worked her way north, pausing fearfully here and there along the way. I had a sudden stark memory of his hand reaching out and resting on my shoulder and the savage scent he'd given off. These overlapping images, olfactory, auditory, kinaesthetic, gustatory, visual, vied for primacy and ended in something of a dead heat. Dangerous deep brown eyes bathed in tawny olive complexion, strong hairy hand, face of a primate, lips that had seen it all. No way was this strumpet worthy of him.

I have to tell you now that I will not be giving anything like a full account of what we heard next, not because I don't have the words but simply because it would be far too painful a thing for me to do. So, much as the more voyeuristic of my readers – and it would be a reasonable guess that you bunch are still here – might desire a definitive account, the following will be both light on detail and extremely brief. Suffice it to say that, even with a six-inch wall separating me from the action, I was aware of exactly where Barbie's hands, lips and tongue were at any given time. The noises issuing from my man were giving it all away.

And Isabella knew too. Whether or not she'd been around the block (and how I hoped that she hadn't) she knew. *She knew.* I'm certain of that. Anytime I glanced at her she had an expression of suppressed glee on her lovely face. Naturally I'd much prefer her to have been appalled, but these are modern times and I'm nothing if not a realist.

If you've ever seen a wrestler slamming his opponent to the floor and jumping on him knees first then you've got a glimmer of what we heard happening when it came to my man's turn. The girl clearly wasn't appreciating it. Her unavailing pleas and pitiable cries were muffled, I guessed, by the pillow under her face. He grunted and bellowed like a rutting stag and we could hear the bed rocking mercilessly beneath his brutal thrusts.

Even while trying to keep a lid on my mounting frustration, I couldn't help sensing that Isabella's mood had begun to darken. I didn't want to look at her but found myself stealing a quick glance. Her forehead was furrowed now and her eyes dull and downcast.

"Will we turn on the TV?" I said. She nodded numbly, avoiding my eyes. I found the remote and switched on, turning the volume to high. "Ice-skating?"

She shook her head. "Something loud," she whispered.

"Panel game?"

"No. No, thanks."

"News?"

She kept shaking her head. "Hold on," she said. "There's Kate."

"Kate who?"

"Kate. The Duchess of Cambridge. Would you turn up the volume please?"

I turned it up.

"The Duke and Duchess of Cambridge," someone announced, "have been awarded damages of one hundred thousand euro over paparazzi photos of the duchess topless on holiday. The awards, while high for a French court, are considerably lower than the one and a half million euro the couple's legal team had demanded."

I wondered for a giddy moment if the damages would have been higher if the duchess's knockers had been bigger, but I wasn't going to say that, of course, because for one thing, Isabella might see it as a slight on her own little breasts. However, I did want to lighten the mood. Anything to lighten the mood. So I said "If I was getting a cool million a year or whatever it is that Kate gets, I'd let the whole world take pictures of me topless and put them on the cover of *Vogue* or *Titbits* if they wanted. I'd stop short at *The Sun* though."

"Sorry," said Isabella. "What were you saying?"

I lowered the volume and repeated what I'd said and she smiled at me and then gave a soft peal of laughter. I was surfing the channels automatically now, aware of a sweet musky balm from across the room and the fading whimpers coming through the wall.

"Wait. That's the Trump. Can you turn it up?"

"What is it about the man that makes people want to watch? He's a buck eejit," I said.

"What's an eejit?"

"It's an Irish way of saying idiot."

"You'll have to teach me more Irish words," she said.

"He's actually the embodiment of where America has got to. It's in the open now. His only saving grace is that what you see is what you get. Not like all the ones that came before him."

"Shh," she whispered. "Listen to it. Turn it up."

"Now here," said the presenter, "is a little gem that went viral. Just over a month ago, President Trump signed an executive order to re-establish the National Space Council. Standing right beside him was astronaut Buzz Aldrin, who you'll remember was the second person to walk on the moon."

"Would you look at his hair," I said. "I mean, is that not …"

"Shhh," she said. "Listen. He's talking to Buzz."

"We know what this is," said Trump. "Space. That's all it has to say. Space. There's a lot of room out there, right?"

"Infinity and beyond!" said Aldrin.

"Jesus H Christ," cried Isabella. "He's going on like Buzz Lightyear!"

"This is infinity here," said Trump. "It could be infinity. We don't really know. But it could be. It has to be something – but it could be infinity, right?"

Cut to presenter. "Now let's get serious for a few minutes folks. Just two days ago, North Korea announced plans to fire rockets near the US territory of Guam. And Kim Jong-un claims that he is capable of detonating a hydrogen bomb that is seven times more powerful than the one dropped on Hiroshima in nineteen forty-five. So the question is this. Has Donald Trump got enough wisdom to react in a way that will not bring about a nuclear holocaust? He's warning North Korea not to nuke Japan. Obviously only the US is allowed to do that. Now before I go to my guests for their opinion, I would ask them – and of course you, our viewers – to carefully consider what I'm about to say. Between nineteen fifty and nineteen fifty-three, the US dropped six hundred and thirty-five thousand tonnes of bombs on North Korea. This included nearly forty thousand tonnes of napalm. These attacks killed two million North Koreans – that is to say, twenty per cent of the population. Is it any wonder that this nation hates America so much, and is it any wonder that they see their nuclear weapons as the only way for their leader to avoid the fate of Saddam Hussein and Muammar Gaddafi and for their country to avoid the unspeakable chaos that now pertains in Iraq and Libya?

"And one or two more things. It is entirely possible that this programme will not be going out next week. In fact, and excuse me for being so grave here, it is entirely possible that nothing, and I mean nothing at all – I'm talking about the final void, folks – will be happening in seven days' time. China and Russia are in the mix in a major way and God only knows how this is going to play out.

"I mentioned Russia just now. Even if we can avoid an Armageddon stemming from the North Korean crisis, we may only be putting off the evil day. Russia could well emerge as the agent that ends up bringing out the worst in the US. Remember that Putin has made Trump and company - and Obama before them - look like little boys lost when it comes to Syria. He, with a helping hand from Iran and Hezbollah, has reversed the trend of the war there and turned Bashar al-Assad into a winner. Question is, will the US take this lying down or will blind arrogance make them strike out with a war to end all wars? Remember, even the best of American presidents considered their country to be superior to all others.

"And Trump is not the best of American presidents. No sirree. This guy is crazy and has a praetorian guard of just-as-crazies who think the whole world should bow the knee to the greatest country on earth. This condition, folks, is known in the wise world of art as hubris and it has brought down bigger players than America. Victor Frankenstein, King Oedipus, Macbeth, Narcissus and Achilles, to name but a few. But the big difference between the fate of these fictional puffed-up fools and America is that American hubris will not only bring the US down, it will bring down the entire planet.

"Now, to give you an idea of what nuclear incineration really means, here is a brief account of what happened in Hiroshima on August the sixth, nineteen forty-five. I beg you not to switch off your television set.

"At 8:16 a.m. on the sixth of August nineteen forty-five, an American B-29 bomber, the *Enola Gay,* dropped its first atomic bomb on the city of Hiroshima. People anywhere near ground zero were vaporized instantly, leaving not a trace. Those further away were carbonized into black, smoking heaps. Those further away still had their eyeballs melted and their features burned off their faces or were completely skinned alive.

"So I would ask you all to consider an existential question and it is this: if you knew that tonight was to be the last night of your life, how would you spend it? I will not even give you options. I have too much respect for the sensibilities of both my guests and viewers."

I pressed the off button. "Sorry," I said. "I shouldn't have kept that on."

"It's so terrible," Isabella said. "I wanted to hear it but it's so terrible." She wasn't looking at me. No longer lying asprawl, she had shifted to an upright position and now seemed to have her gaze fixed on something on the wall below the TV. "It could happen, couldn't it?"

"No. Not in your lifetime. Or mine of course. I'm sure of that."

"But why? Why are you sure? Trump could break that North Korean man's temper anytime."

"But he won't. You know what I think? I think this is about two freaks with funny haircuts, and one of them is fighting for survival and the other is breaking as many norms as he can because he's autistic and psychotic at the one time. If Trump got destroying North Korea, then South Korea would then be wiped out too, like the next domino, and that would be the end of one of America's biggest client states. And that's not even talking about California being obliterated. It would be the beginning of the end for the whole of the USA. But it won't happen. Mad Dog Mattis would garrotte him first. Or the CIA would arrange an assassination. They're very good at that sort of thing."

"I wish you were right. But I'm scared."

"There's no need to be, Isabella." (But there is. This fucking showman is a loose cannon. And the ropes around him are in tatters). "Look, believe me, Trump is a dangerous idiot but he's a pussycat compared to what Lyndon Johnson and John F Kennedy were."

"John F Kennedy? I know Johnson did all that stuff in Vietnam but Kennedy was a good man. You only have to look at recordings of him to know."

"I don't agree. Kennedy was hardly sworn in when he nearly managed to start a war over Berlin and then he got badly beaten at the Bay of Pigs trying to take over Cuba, and to get his own back he started this big terrorist war against Castro. And of course, he nearly finished us all off with the Cuban missile crisis. Bad and all as Trump is, he'll never come near that."

She was still sitting upright and her lovely face was deathly pale. She said "But …" and then stopped.

"Somebody wrote something brilliant one time," I said, "and nobody has ever been able to discover who it was. 'War is when your government tells you who the enemy is. Revolution is when you figure it out for yourself.'"

"Was it Karl Marx?" she said. "Maybe it was Karl Marx."

"Could have been."

"But the other thing you were saying. That Trump couldn't be as bad as Kennedy."

"What about it?"

"What if you're wrong? What if he is? You know what I'm thinking now? I'm thinking how I'd spend my last night."

"No Isabella. Don't be thinking like that."

I knew her eyes were on me now but I didn't look at her. She had taken too much wine too fast and was upset and fearful. And for all I knew, the Irish curse was getting to her too. I wondered how I could change the subject. I wondered if I even wanted to change the subject. The girl needed comforting. I was on the bed, she was five feet away, we were that close.

"If tonight was my last night on earth I'd want to spend it with Denise."

"You would?" I said, still not looking. She could be right. What if we really are going to be wiped out? Is that not all the more reason to live now? Or will I end up congratulating myself on my restraint when I'm melting?

"I'd make her happy. I know I would."

"I'm sorry," I said. "Excuse me please. I have to use the bathroom." I grabbed what I needed from my suitcase and went to the bathroom. Once inside I locked the door and tried not to breathe too loudly. I took off my black silk dressing gown which was clinging to my armpits. Looking at me from the mirror was a ridiculous grey-haired geriatric wearing black lace panties and pink push-up bra. Lexie Lexie, O Lexie, is this what you've come to? A rotten old lecher allowing a susceptible young girl to drink herself silly and listen to a rape? If I'd wanted to, I could have drowned out all that foulness and fury with a bit of the Jon Bon Jovi but I hadn't done that. I was the sinister host, the worst of both worlds, loathsome top and yielding bottom.

"I wrenched off my bra and panties and there they were, moobs in folds, belly in wrinkles and penis pointing sou'-sou'-west, *oh dolce mamma.* But hold on, who was the little lesbian I read about that I fell in love with on the spot, the swaggering Argentine badass singer that told the macho men of the South American music scene what for?

"Your dick is not important!"

And she shouted it from the stage too, right in the middle of her gig. I really should remember. The singer that told it all about female pleasure. Ah yes, yes. Romina Bernardo, aka Chocolate Remix, aka the little Chocolato. She sang it and all. What were the words? Real women prefer two well-placed fingers? That was it. Talk about giving the fingers. And giving more than girls reason to hope.

I wet sponged my sweatiest bits, dabbed myself dry and laid on the Denim deodorant as lavishly as I dared. I then put on my love honey push-up Basque set with its flirty lace ruffles, suspender straps and G-string. This took longer than it should have, I think, because of the wine I'd drunk. As I swung my arms back into the dressing gown I swayed and almost fell over. Steady now, steady. This won't take a fizz out of her. She's done it before, don't think she hasn't.

And girls nowadays don't brood on it, they just move on. And she likes me, she likes my company, she thinks I'm funny. Who was it said if you can make a girl laugh, you can make her do anything you want? Yes, Marilyn Monroe. It was Marilyn Monroe. And I'd say the same girl knew what she was talking about.

At the beginning, she'll just want comforted, cuddled to sleep. But that wasn't how it worked and it wasn't what I wanted. I'm a man aren't I? But I'll make sure she enjoys it, to start with anyway. First, I'll give her soft lip kisses and then I'll use the fluttering tongue trick I got the tip about on Dear Shirley. Then I'll touch her softly, so softly she'll want more, and then I'll take her so tight in my arms and hold her all against me and proceed à la Choco.

And then? Maybe she'll want some rough. Maybe she'll want it that way, letting me let myself go, but frightened at the same time. Well, we'll see. It'll be all right. Of course it will. My heart was going like a drum. *If you have dreams and wishes of love, don't be afraid. Act them out. One should be fearless and consider nothing forbidden that your soul craves for.* Then a final check in the mirror.

She was asleep, slumped in the chair, an almost empty glass lying on the floor beside her, leaf-shaped dark red stain on the carpet next to it. She made a little movement and murmured something about water and her legs slowly slithered apart. She's dreaming, I thought. Her long auburn hair had fallen down on her left side and her cardigan was completely open now except for one button at the waist. Her body gave a jerk as if to shake something off, some bad dream maybe, revealing more than before of the whiteness of her little doves and the tarnished silver stretch between them.

I heard her sob and pull back her breath and sob again, and the smell of her filled my head and chest and a feeling of guilt and tenderness and yearning rose in me, and I walked carefully to her and got down unsteadily on my knees and held the arms of the chair for support. This was hardly more than a child. My head swam and I saw her through a grey dimness and then suddenly I was singing, softly so as not to disturb her.

Beautiful dreamer, wake unto me,
Starlight and dewdrops are waiting for thee.
Sounds of the rude world heard in the day,
Lulled by the moonlight have all passed away!

Beautiful dreamer, queen of my song,
List while I woo thee with soft melody.
Gone are the cares of life's busy throng —
Beautiful dreamer, awake unto me!
Beautiful dreamer, awake unto me!

Beautiful dreamer, out on the sea,
Mermaids are chanting the wild lorelie.
Over the streamlet vapours are borne,
Waiting to fade at the bright coming morn.

I ran out of memory. She woke as I was struggling to try and put together what came next. Her eyes half-opened, slowly opened wide.

"I heard singing," she said. "Was that you?"

I couldn't reply at first. I forced up some saliva and said, trying to smile, "Ah. Yes. I apologise Isabella. I think it must have been the wine singing. I'm not used to taking that amount anymore."

"I was dreaming," she said. "At the start, I was building a shell castle but you weren't there. I was on my own, and then suddenly I was on a capsized ship. I couldn't escape and you still weren't there, and I heard the mermaids calling for me to come down to them. They were going to take me away to be their queen. And then it was your voice I was hearing. Isn't that funny?"

"Dreams can be like that. If they're bad sometimes, the only way you can get away from them is to waken up."

"But it was you singing that wakened me. You rescued me."

"I'm really sorry Isabella. I shouldn't have let you drink so much. That's what brought it all on."

"But I'm all right now. You're here."

I could smell all of her, closer now, and it was getting too much for me. I wanted to carry her to the bed. All it would take was one move.

"Did I tell you?" she said. "I don't think I told you. My name on Denise's site is 'The Little Mermaid'. Isn't that funny?" Yes Isabella, it's funny and it's beautiful. Queen of the sea, Aphrodite of the ocean realm.

"That's a strange one all right. You'd make a lovely mermaid, Isabella."

"Ooh, thank you. That's a beautiful thing to say." Her eyes were a deep blue. "This was the loveliest day of my life, Lllllexie. You're the kindest man I ever met. Denise is so lucky to have someone like you. Can I not stay?"

"No. I'll walk you to your room. You'll sleep like a top. I promise."

I rose from my knees and tried to help her out of the chair but lost my balance and sank back down.

"Here," she said laughing. "This is like the blind leading the blind. No more wine for you tonight, mister." She tried to get out past me and just about managed but it was a tight squeeze and I could swear to this day that the hollow of her groin came against my chest and then my cheek. The cleft in the hillock velveted with delicate moss, traced with a scarlet thread.

She helped me to my feet, her soft hands in mine, my body in disarray.

"Could I not stay here?"

"Pardon?"

"Could I not stay here? That armchair's lovely. I could sleep here all night."

"No. Why would you do that? You've got a lovely big bed in your own room. I promise you'll be out cold as soon as your head hits the pillow. Come on now."

She made a little pout and we went carefully to the door, her left hand in my right.

"Look at me. I'm a fright," she said. She had stopped at the wardrobe mirror. "OhmyGod, what you must think of me!"

She took her hand from mine, rearranged her pyjama top and cardigan and took my hand in hers again. "You must think I'm an awful girl, Lllllexie." There it was again, that drawn-out Lllllexie. There was nothing more in this world I wanted than to allow her to stay. But I opened my door and said "Have you your key card?"

She blinked twice, rapidly. "Key card? My key card? I don't know. Where did I put it?" She patted her breast. "Oh, here it is." She took it out from the pocket of her pyjama top.

"OK Isabella. Now let's go." There was still time for everything to be different. It would only have taken a word from me.

"Here, let me open the door," I said.

In a matter of moments, we were in the corridor. I reminded her how to use her key card and as I made to leave she put her hands on my shoulders, stood on her tiptoes and kissed me briefly on the two cheeks and then on the mouth.

"Thank you Lllllexie. You know who you look like? Did I tell you?"

"I shook my head, unable to speak.

"Jeremy Corbyn. The girls in Saint John of God love him you know and they think he's so handsome too. You should grow a little beard and moustache like he has and then you'd look exactly like him. Did you see him on holidays?"

"I wasn't – oh, *his* holiday. I don't think so."

"He was in Dubrovnik on a cycling holiday and he was wearing shorts. We all thought he had great legs."

"It's nice of you to say those things. I admire Jeremy Corbyn and it's very flattering that you think I look like him."

Her hands were still on my shoulders but then she inched nearer and joined them around my neck and I placed my hands lightly on the back of her waist, bare between her pyjama top and bottom. I heard the shifting of her feet on the carpet just before her knees touched my shins. "Did I tell you that today was the happiest day of my life?" she said softly. "And you were so funny." She was on tiptoes again. "And what you did to that awful man Marcus!" She took a fit of the giggles then and shook against me.

"Mag-mag-magnus."

"What?"

"Magnus. That's his name."

"I thought you said magnet and I was thinking, Lllllexie's drunk."

"Do you mind?"

A voice from somewhere near. I looked around. Had to be room 344, my latesummer night's dream. The sound of him on top of her closeness was nearly too much.

"Is that meant for us?" she said, now pressed to me.

"Yes, I'm talking to you. We're trying to get some sleep in here. Do you mind?"

"Sorry," I called back. And to Isabella I whispered "You'd better go on in. Goodnight."

Her lips were tight together and her eyes were laughing. "He's trying to get some sleep," she tittered. "Did you ever hear anything like that in your whole life?" She stepped away from me and then she was gone.

Still aglow I went to my bedroom door. I tried to open it but quickly realised it was locked. I searched the pockets of my dressing gown but even as I did so I knew that the key card was in my room keeping the lights on. I turned round and went to the door of Isabella's room and made a fist to knock, but decided against it. Next thing I was in the elevator and heading down to the lobby.

I was waiting for the receptionist to lift his head when someone behind me spoke.

"Well, look what we have here."

I turned round and there he was, old friend Magnus, drink rattling in his hand.

"The professor himself," he slurred.

"Oh hello," I said and turned back to the receptionist. "I wonder could you help me. I locked my key card in my room. Would you be good enough to give me a spare please?"

"Certainly. Room number sir?"

"Two three four. No, sorry, three four two."

"And your name please?"

"Mister Cheddy. Lexie Cheddy."

"I wanted to tell you," said Magnus. "I owe you an apology Mister."

"Not at all. It's perfectly all right." I said and held out my hand to him. I was a mite disconcerted, what with the sensation of the flimsy underwear beneath my dressing gown and my heart still fluttering from Isabella's closeness, otherwise I don't think I'd have been so magnanimous.

"I'd rather not shake, Mister. Don't know where that hand of yours has been."

I frowned, decided to ignore the remark and turned to the receptionist who had just placed a key card on the desk in front of me. I smiled and thanked him.

"I called you a poofter," continued Magnus, "and you're not. At least I don't think you are. What I do know is that you're a bloody child molester."

I was already on my way towards the elevator but could still hear him speaking to the receptionist. "He's got his little concubine with him, d'you know that? Did you see her? Cute wee dolly bird she is too. Probably he's away up to give her a second dose right now. And did you get that smell off of him? Like he's just raided a Christian Dior factory. 'Cept there's nothing Christian about what he's going up to do now. Tell me this, Mister. Do you really think your hotel …"?

The elevator door shut out the rest.

+++++

I didn't feel like reading. I fingered the dildo, left it aside, and quickly decided it wouldn't be a good idea to put on Jon Bon Jovi given my man's sensitivities. I closed my eyes, bestraddled by pictures in my head of her lovely brown body no more than a few feet away shifting restlessly and her pulling at her panties, tugging at the bedclothes, dreaming awake.

I turned over on my stomach and started. I brought up the day picture of her too, frail and beautiful, face hazed with freckles, soft auburn hair ending in curls just above her bottom, black crop top embossed with two little buds and then down to her honey-hued midriff, low slung jeans with their ripped thighs and sweating seat that clung to her every time she moved.

I underwent my customary contortions and came more quickly than I think I've ever come before, and then the tears came too. I rocked on my hands as the shame and the longing and the release convulsed me. When it was over, I began slowly to breathe easier and then turned on one side, hunched myself forward and drew my knees up to my chest. I felt alone.

How absurd it was to have let myself in for this. An unhappy young soul, kind and trusting, gentle and admiring, my guest, my dupe. Sex tourists of seventy walk the streets of the Philippines hand in hand with children as young as ten, as old as fifteen. I was in this for one thing only and that thing was a disgrace. Bastian wasn't far wrong. Out of the mouths of braggarts and drunkards.

There are two and a half days left. Time enough to show her some proper care. But will she let me? She would give herself to me in a moment and my very diffidence might even make her want this strange, unlikely fruit all the more. She's not afraid, not afraid at all, so why should I be? What harm can come? I straightened myself and turned to my hands again.

+++++

After my shower I dried myself, wrapped the towel around my waist and went to the window. A perfect morning. Rays of blue air streaming from behind white clouds and the whole day ahead. Then, a single tap on the door.

"Yes?"

"It's me. Isabella. Can I come in?"

"Not yet. I'm not decent."

"When will you be ready?"

"I'll tell you what. Why don't you go on down to breakfast and I'll join you in a few minutes?"

"I don't like going down on my own. I'll wait for you in my room, is that all right?"

"Yes. Give me about ten minutes would you?"

Two long grey hairs were tickling my upper lip. Must have been last night's blubbering or maybe the shower that dislodged them. I used my two little fingers to push them back up my nostrils. Then I got dressed and viewed myself in the bedroom mirror. Could be worse. When I stepped into the corridor my heart was pounding. She swung her door open before I got a chance to knock.

"Morning!" she said. Her eyes were shining. She was wearing very short frayed white jeans and the tops of her little breasts were just about visible above her light blue blouse. And oh, there was a red rose in her hair. Where did she get it? "What do you think of me?" she said and did a mock curtsy. She had told me her knees were knobbly. They weren't. They were perfect. And her legs. *Mère de Dieu!*

"Ah, you look lovely Isabella. You really are a most attractive girl."

She blushed crimson and hooked her arm in mine, pulling me along. “I’m ravenous,” she said. “I think I could eat a horse.”

“I don’t think they serve them here,” I said, high as heaven itself. “But I do know this place down the road.”

She laughed loudly and leaned her head on my arm. “I’m really sorry about last night, Llllexie. I had far too much wine. You must have thought I was terrible, falling asleep on you like that.”

“Not at all. You’d had a long tiring day. I thought you held out brilliantly.”

“What are we doing today? Do you know yet? I’ll bet there’s so much to see.”

I don’t remember what I replied or anything else until we were in the lobby and she was pulling me by the arm to a poster near reception. “A Sixties night tonight,” she was saying. “Look!”

INISHOWEN GATEWAY
SWING WITH THE SIXTIES
TONITE - EIGHT TILL LATE
BRINGING IT ALL BACK - THE BEATLES, THE STONES. DYLAN, ORBISON, TINA TURNER, DUSTY SPRINGFIELD .... AND THE REST!
DEEJAY: DANNY WANG DOHERTY

“Can we go?”

“Of course we can go, Isabella. You’re my guest after all.”

We went to reception and she chattered happily while I stood there waiting to book us in for a second night.

"It's going to be great, Lllllexie, I just know it is. But would it not be too noisy for you?"

"Noisy? Sure the Sixties was my time. The decibel decade. I was the original Sixties swinger, you know." Like hell I was. Under Henry's thumb and not even allowed near the sidelines.

She was holding back a smile. "Do you know what you just said? A swinger? But maybe it didn't mean then what it means now."

"Why, what does it mean now?"

"I don't want to say. Have you booked? That's brilliant. Can we go in for our breakfast?"

She let go of my arm as we entered the dining room. Right away I saw Magnus and Eleanor and steered Isabella well away from them. No sign of the eastern hunk or his Barbie doll. Having a nice lie in, no doubt.

We both had an Irish breakfast – bacon, egg, sausage, toast and three pots of tea – and the sight of her tucking into it did my heart good.

"This stuff is bad for the system but good for the mood," I said as we munched away.

"It's delicious. Maybe you're just taking it because I am. Probably you're on a diet."

"Not exactly," I said.

"You're staring at me, Lllllexie. Is there something on my face?"

"Sorry, I didn't realise I was staring. You were asking if I was dieting. I'm not really. It's just that I'm supposed to take it easy on salty things. But it'll do me no harm this once. Are you looking forward to tonight?"

"Tonight?"

"The Sixties and all. Great time for pop music. And then there was Woodstock of course. I don't think anything could beat sixty-nine."

She exploded with laughter, spluttering bits of bacon over the tablecloth.

"Oh I'm sorry, Llllllexie. I'm so bad-mannered. I'm so sorry. It was just ..."

"Just ...?"

"It's nothing. Something rude came into my head and I just couldn't help laughing. I'm terrible." Her face was scarlet.

"Not at all. What was it?"

"Nothing at all."

"Could you not let me into the secret?" I asked playfully.

"I'd rather not say."

She didn't have to. I'd just remembered. 69 the sex positions. Two lovers giving and getting oral sex at the same time. My God, she's only fifteen. Innocence gone. Something is wrong.

"What about you?" she said. "Are you looking forward to the hop?"

"I can't wait."

Someone placed a hand on my shoulder. "Good night?" a voice said. I turned my head and looked up. The bold Magnus.

"Would you mind"" I replied. "We're trying to have our breakfast here."

He removed his hand but wasn't for leaving just yet.

"El tells me you're from Denmark," he said hoarsely, glaring at Isabella who was looking down into her plate. "That's a funny coincidence because I heard someone saying on the TV this morning that ... let me think now what it was ... ah yes, Danes enjoy closeness with pigs that goes beyond the bacon sandwich. That's what the man said. What do you reckon? Do you reckon that's fair comment?"

A strident voice from somewhere behind him. "Magnus!" It had to be Eleanor. And in a moment she was there by his side smiling determinedly at Isabella and me. "Good morning. It was so nice talking to both of you last night. You brought back such lovely memories of Lettermullan."

"I'm delighted to hear that," I said. "We really enjoyed your company."

"And now we'll leave you to finish your breakfast," she said, taking Magnus firmly by the arm. "It's very bad-mannered of us to interrupt you." And then they were gone.

Isabella wrinkled her nose. "I think that awful man's still drunk," she said. "Did you hear him saying goodnight?"

+++++

I parked my car at the far end of Buncrana and we walked along the back shore. The back shore is the name given to a long pathway overlooking Lough Swilly. Neither of us spoke for the first few minutes, and all we could hear were children's calls from somewhere behind us and the soft sounds of the lough to our left. The lough was as calm as I'd ever seen it, though now and then disturbed by little ripples that came with the faint breezes. When we got to the plaque marking Friar Hegarty's Rock I told Isabella that this was the place where Friar Hegarty had been martyred three hundred years before by British troops.

"Please tell me about him. What did they kill him for?" she asked.

"He was saying Catholic masses and that wasn't allowed because the British were trying to wipe out the Catholic religion. He would sometimes celebrate Mass in the open air at this remote spot and one day the Mass was raided by the redcoats. The worshippers escaped along the shore path that we're on now and Friar Hegarty got away by jumping on his horse and riding it straight into the lough right there below us. He let the horse find its own way back to the shore and swam for his life. But some of the soldiers shouted to him that they had come to change their religion and begged him to baptise them."

"And did he do it?"

"His conscience made him swim back to the shore but there was no baptising done. The soldiers pinned him down and then beheaded him right where we're standing. It's never been forgotten and there are still masses said here often to remember that day."

"What a thing to happen. He must have been a really good man for coming back."

"Yes. Foolish maybe, but he chose to believe that those redcoats wanted to start a new life."

"And people still come here to remember," she said. "Isn't that great?"

"They come from all over the world," I told her.

"Will we say a prayer?" she asked. "Right now?"

"Just a silent one, OK?" I felt like a hypocrite as we stood, heads bowed, with people passing behind us and me athrob at her nearness. She had one foot childishly sideways half on top of the other and my downcast eyes were on the slender brown of her thighs and her lovely tomboy knees.

We walked on then and she linked her arm softly in mine. The day had turned into a scorcher. It will be cold tonight, I thought. It always seems to turn cold on August nights after days like this. Only two left and then she'll be gone.

"There's a story still told about the ghost of Friar Hegarty," I said.

"Really?"

"Yes. I've heard it often."

"Please tell me about it," she said, jerking at my arm, breast warm against me.

"Well, it's supposed to have happened twenty or thirty years ago. Four teenage boys were out quad biking on this very path one moonless night. It was complete madness of course because they had no lights on their quads and they could hardly see their hands in front of them. Parts of this path are very near the edge as you can see and there's a drop of about fifty feet to those rocks, just down there, if you look now. Well, it was around here, I think, that the boys saw the friar."

"You mean his ghost?"

"His ghost. And the ghost of the white horse he was on and it gleaming away in the dark. It reared up on its hind legs right in front of them and they screeched to a stop. And then they saw the friar turning the horse to face towards the edge and he suddenly spurred it to leap off the path onto the rocks or the lough or maybe both. The boys were scared nearly out of their wits and turned and went straight home."

"That's amazing," she said. "But how do you know about this?"

"It's common knowledge here in Buncrana."

"And what about the boys? Are they still alive?"

"They are, and the last I heard was that it's very hard to get any of them to talk about it. They'd all be around their forties now probably and very glad to be alive I'd say. I've never met any of them myself but I've spoken to people who have."

"Gosh. So this isn't just a beautiful walk."

"Right. It's loaded with history. One of the most famous Irish freedom fighters that ever lived anywhere was taken prisoner by the Brits when he was on a ship out there in the lough. A man called Wolfe Tone."

"I've never heard of him."

"Sorry. He was one of the founders of the Society of United Irishmen. They were looking for peaceful reforms in Ireland, mostly for Catholics, but the British wouldn't budge."

"Was it a Catholic Protestant thing?"

"No, it wasn't. The United Irishmen was made up of a lot of Protestants and Presbyterians and Methodists as well as Catholics. Tone was a Protestant himself actually. These people saw how the American War of Independence and the French Revolution had worked out and they were ready to use violence if the Brits didn't improve things."

"And did they?"

"Use violence? They did. The Brits wouldn't give an inch so the United Irishmen fought them. After Wolfe Tone was captured he was tried and condemned to death."

"Oh. They didn't kill him right here did they, like Friar Hegarty?"

"No. How he died is sort of a controversial story, but all Irish Republicans still look on him as their dead leader."

"Gosh. I never knew about any of this."

"How could you? I didn't know either till I was older than you. We were very ignorant about things. I was actually brought up believing that Brian Boru freed Ireland from the Danes."

"Us? Our people? I never knew we were in Ireland. And who was Brian Boru?"

"He was the high king of Ireland about a thousand years ago. A real tough nut. And your people really were in Ireland you know. But you were never actually driven out. And you didn't conquer us either, like I was taught. You came, you saw and you surrendered."

That silver tinkle of laughter again, holding my arm tighter, pushing her hip playfully against mine.

"Surrendered?"

"Yes. You were part of the Vikings and you were great seafarers. And real cool pirates. Did you know that your men founded the biggest cities in Ireland and the same men were taken over by our Christianity and our women? You ended up sticking around, speaking our language, getting married to us and stealing our clothes."

"We stole your clothes!"

"In a manner of speaking. You became more Irish than the Irish themselves and you really did start to dress like us too. All blacks and greys and browns. Dull as be damned. Do you know that nobody wore pink or blue or red in this country till Elvis sang Heartbreak Hotel?"

"You're so funny, Lllllexie. You really are a scream."

"I'm serious. We were the dullest place on earth. Except maybe for the Soviet Union."

"I saw pictures of James Joyce," she said, "and every picture he's in, he's wearing black or grey."

"That's not strictly true. He had a white shirt. One."

"We always heard he was a dirty writer," she said, laughing. "The parts where –"

"He definitely did go too far at times. He let Molly Bloom get ... did you ever hear of Molly Bloom?"

"Molly Bloom. Yes, I heard of her."

"Well then you probably know that she was married to Leopold Bloom, the main character in Ulysses."

"Oh yes. I know some parts where it gives her thoughts."

"Really?" I glanced sideways at her. She was looking away from me out at the lough.

if that's all he harm ever we did in this vale of tears and God knows its not much doesn't everybody only they hide it I suppose that's what a woman is supposed to be there for or He wouldn't have made us the way He did so attractive to men then if he wants to kiss my bottom I'll drag open my drawers and bulge it right out in his face as large as life he can stick his tongue 7 miles up my hole as hes there my brown part and then Ill tell him I want £1 or perhaps thirty shillings – Ill tell him I want to buy underclothes then if he gives me that well he won't be too bad I don't want to soak it all out of him like other women do I could often have written out a fine cheque for myself and write his name on it for a couple of pounds a few times he forgot to lock it up besides he wont spend it Ill let him do it off on me provided he doesn't smear all my good drawers O I suppose that can't be helped

"Well, in the most famous passage of the book," I said, "things get pretty obnoxious at times when she's thinking about men and women. Some of the stuff Joyce had her thinking was far too crude. It actually took away from the novel. But you can't say that to Joyce scholars. They won't hear a word against this sacred cow of a thing. It's as if these people are indoctrinated."

"Remember I was saying in the hotel about girls passing around Lolita and all at the convent school?"

"I do remember that."

"Well, they passed around Ulysses too. But it was just the Molly thing you were talking about there. Or the parts of it that the girls underlined."

"I know what you mean. Although a lot of what she thinks in that same monologue is really about love and how she wants to be loved and how she doesn't want to be loved."

"You mean the ways?"

"Yes, the ways."

"Is it, like, girls underlining parts then that don't show the whole thing?"

"Yes. That's a good way of putting it Isabella."

yes when I put a rose in my hair like the Andalusian girls used or shall I wear a red yes and how he kissed me under the Moorish wall and I thought well as well him as another and then I asked him with my eyes to ask again yes and then he asked me would I yes to say yes my mountain flower and first I put my arms around him yes and drew him down to me so he could feel my breasts all perfume yes and his heart was going like mad and yes I said yes I will Yes.

"Did you teach James Joyce?"

"Pardon?"

"I said did you teach James Joyce?"

"How could I have? I wasn't even born when he was a student."

"No, I mean, did you teach about him?"

"I did. Sorry for the corny joke Isabella but I couldn't resist it."

She had got so close now it was as if we were joined at the hip really and my John Thomas was working its way up to a jig that I don't think Saint Vitus himself would have been at all happy with and by the way did you know that his feast day is on the very eve of James and Nora's walk to Ringsend on their first date that ended with her frigging him till he could be frigged no more and then in the middle of it all I stumbled and nearly fell when her foot went in front of mine?

"Oh dear, I'm sorry. Did you teach about him in Derry or did you go away to other places to teach?"

"That's OK. My fault. Just in Derry. Though hold on, I did give a talk one time in Dublin to Joyce scholars in what they called a colloquium."

"A what?"

"A colloquium. It's just a fancy name for a conference."

"Gosh. That sounds really swank. Don't you be falling now."

She reached her right hand over and put it on the back of my left hand that was holding her arm. Don't wish for this to last, wish for it to end. Go back now. Be your age.

"Some of the Joyce scholars were intelligent enough," I told her, "but mostly they were what you would call chancers."

"What's a chancer? Somebody that takes risks?"

"No. A chancer is someone who bluffs their way. A kind of a phoney."

"Really? Were there phoneys there?"

"So many I was tripping over them. And all men. There were only two women speakers and they were head and shoulders above the men. It was nearly like back before the suffragettes started, honestly. There were three big Joyce scholars with alphabets after their names and you could have heard a pin drop when they were giving their talks. But they wandered off their topics and talked mostly bullshit. Very impressive bullshit if you didn't know better. One of them was French I remember. I'm convinced his accent seduced most of the scholars there, young and old alike. You know, left bank of the Seine and all that. I think very few people there really took in what he was saying."

"And he got away with it?"

"The three of them did. One of them spent an hour talking about the furniture in all the houses or apartments that Joyce lived in. It was pretty excruciating stuff. And there was another doling out advice to younger Joyce scholars, encouraging them to do what he called creative research. Creative research in my book means waffle. These guys actually drove a coach and horses through the whole sham without realising it and the three of them naked as the day was long. And believe you me that was one long day.

"It's a racket Isabella. People using Joyce to try and get ahead. I like to think the man himself was having a good laugh about it wherever he is. The same three celebrities or others like them descend on cities in Europe and the States as well giving more or less the same talks to more or less the same people about the same book and they're ripping the soul out of the blooming thing. P. T. Barnum was an amateur compared to these guys."

"P. T. Barnum? Who was he?"

"He was a huckster that lived in America away back. Spent his life looking for money and fame. He had this big con he called a travelling museum of freaks and animal menageries and zoological curiosities. And he fooled a lot of the people a lot of the time."

"But is *Ulysses* really a great book?" she asked. "Or is it a con too?"

"It's not a con. It's probably one of the half dozen best novels ever written. It all takes place during the twenty-four hours of the sixteenth of June 1904 and it's about love and loyalty and truth and friendship and goodness. It's a book that celebrates the ordinary man and woman and it's ended up being dissected in mostly the wrong places by a bunch of charlatans that wouldn't know how to conduct themselves if they were trapped in an elevator with an ordinary man or woman. But you were asking about Molly Bloom there. Molly is earthy and sexy and she cheats on her husband but she has a reason for it."

"What reason?"

"Well, her husband Leopold loves her deeply but he hasn't really made love to her during the ten years since their young son Rudy died, and Molly is a woman who needs to be physically loved so she tries to find it with a guy called Blazes Boylan that comes and sleeps with her after Leopold has gone out."

"Oh, that's terrible. That's so sad."

"It is sad. The hero of the book is Leopold himself. He's the Ulysses. Before he leaves home for a funeral on the sixteenth of June, he goes to Molly who is still in bed and tends to her and takes note of the errands she wants him to do. And then he goes out to face the day, even though he knows that Blazes Boylan is at that moment on his way to Molly's bed. He also knows that some acquaintances in Dublin are laughing at him behind his back because of what's going on between Molly and Blazes. But all this time he never loses his goodness or his great love for her. The poor man is tormented by dreams of earthly beauty and the kind of bliss that can only be found in, you know, complete love. And he doesn't even realise that he himself is the embodiment of it."

"Oh dear."

"So it's no wonder that day is called Bloomsday and is commemorated every year all over the world."

She was sighing now and her hand tightened on mine but then the sigh stopped abruptly and she said: "Oh look. Look at that lovely beach. And I don't think there's anyone on it. Can we stop here awhile?"

"Maybe we should turn back. Time's getting on." Yes, turn back now.

"Oh please. I'd love to sunbathe. Can we not sunbathe?"

Bloody hell, I need a leak. The beach it is then.

"Just for a little while, OK? I'm feeling pretty hungry and I'm sure you are too. We'll be fainting by the time we get back to Buncrana."

"Oh Lllllexie, thank you. It's such a beautiful day. What way do you get to it?"

We shuffled our way down a little banking. There was only a handful of people there and three of them were getting ready to leave, a woman and two young children with sweet papers and empty crisp bags littering behind them. And two figures lying sunbathing near the far end of the beach.

I was looking around me for somewhere to pee and saw that the only place I could find privacy was a line of rocks near the two figures about fifty yards away. Fifty yards. Seemed like touch and go.

I was already on my way as I called to Isabella "I'll be back in a minute." Question was, would I get there in time? Funny, once I've made up your mind to go, my body just won't wait. It's always the same. I quickened my step trying not to think of my screaming bladder. Hum a song. Anything. If you're going to San Francisco, be sure to wear some flowers in your hair. All across the nation, such a strange vibration. People in motion people in motion …

Wrong song. I realised I wasn't going to make it to the rocks so I stopped and knelt down, crouched forward, unzipped and let fly, nearly did it on myself.

Ahh. For this relief ... I shook myself as dry as I could and tucked it away, looking around, trying to appear nonchalant. What's happening over there? Funny sight. The guy looks like he's wrestling with a conger eel and it's got him pinned to the sand. Can't be. Ridiculous. I closed my eyes and opened them again. That's no eel, that's a girl and she's on top of him and there's her big white bum. Good Christ.

Now they've switched and he's on top of her and it's his bare brown bum up in the air, up and down like a fucking piledriver, and very fine it looks too, wouldn't mind, going like fucking mad it is. What's the world coming to anyway? In broad daylight. No, not really like mad now that I see it right, more like rhythmic, controlled, up and down and in and out. Bloody tease.

Twenty or thirty seconds was all I looked but I saw plenty. I saw her hands flailing above his big back and then coming to rest on his bum. And that seemed to make him go even harder. Is she liking it? Who knows? Stop the tom-peeping for Christ's sake. They'll see you. Stop and go now. Now.

"You're here Lllllexie. I saw you coming out of the side of my eye. I missed you."

She was lying on her front looking up at me awkwardly and the red flower that was in her hair had fallen on the sand.

"It's the most beautiful day," I said, my shameless eyes on her lovely shanks and little round bottom and frayed tight white denim shorts. I don't remember the exact statistics at the moment but I'm sure I mentioned to you before about how often boys and girls think about sex. Once every minute is it? Can't think just now but in my case it's at least twice every nanosecond.

The blasted thing never leaves my waking mind, nor it won't till the moment I die.

Look at President George Bush for heaven's sake. Not the Dubya. The da. He's ninety-three and he's in a wheelchair and the bastard has to keep apologising for feeling girls' bums. What in heaven was God thinking of when he made men?

"Are you not going to sunbathe?" she asked.

"I will in a minute."

She turned on her back and looked up at me, shading her eyes. A single dark hair had stolen out from the frayed bottom of her shorts and lay curled against her right thigh. The late afternoon sun pulsated above me in a cloudless sky. "You've got a great complexion," she said. "You'd never turn red like I do. Why don't you lie down?"

"I will in a minute. Did you not bring sunscreen?"

"Didn't even think of it. It's sitting in the hotel. I'm a silly girl."

I sat beside her and wrapped my arms around my knees. I think I started rocking back and forward then but to be honest I hardly knew what I was doing.

"Why don't you lie down? This is so lovely."

I knew the couple were heading in our direction and hesitated to look. But then I did. I really couldn't tell you much about the girl because all my curiosity was focused on her partner. He had a fine build, tall and athletic, plain spotty face, stunning body though, adorned with only flip flops and tight black bathing trunks. His great big bully bag swayed wetly as he walked, apparently replenished after the evacuation. I looked from it to his face again and he smiled lightly.

"Perfect day, isn't it? he said. I nodded and smiled back, emitting an agreeable grunt. Perfect for some people. Well, one person anyway. And she said nothing. One glance told me that she was small, redhaired and fully dressed. Also, that she was well over the hill, nineteen or more.

"Those seem like nice people," said Isabella.

"Lovely. Will we go?"

"Oh Lllllexie. Can we not stay awhile? Why don't you lie down?" She patted the sand close to her and tugged at her shorts. The hair rose like a question mark.

"I'm sorry Isabella but I'm hungry and tired. And it's going to take us ages to get to Buncrana. I should have brought a lunch for us. I feel stupid."

"But it took us an hour to get here and we've only been here ten minutes. And now we're going straight back?"

She didn't speak again on our way up to the path or on our long return journey to Buncrana, didn't respond to anything I said, even when I asked her to forgive me. Very soon I missed her hand on my arm and her innocent softness against me and her eyes on me and the sound of her voice. Trust me to turn what could have been an idyll into the opposite. I thought of a cartoon I'd seen in a newspaper that showed a dog pursuing a cat out of the front door of an ugly rundown house and beneath the drawing was the caption 'This is life – one damn thing after another'.

I felt weary from the walk as I drove us to the Drift Inn for dinner. All this time she said nothing. While we waited to be served she looked down at the tablecloth and out the window and over my shoulder and still didn't say anything. During dinner I apologised again and when her silence persisted I became irritated and quietly asked if she didn't think she was overreacting but still she said nothing, all the while avoiding my eyes.

Time to try another tack. I told her that the Drift Inn was originally the Buncrana railway station but that trains didn't run here now and then I tried to entertain her with the story of how my Uncle Tommy had once bought a new sports coat and trousers in Buncrana and tried to smuggle them in the train when he was going back over the border to Derry.

"If the customs men at the border had caught him with them they'd have confiscated them so Tommy had this brilliant idea of locking himself in the train toilet a few minutes before it was due to get to the customs post, and dumping his old jacket and trousers out of the toilet window and putting on the new outfit. That way he couldn't be accused of smuggling. But after he'd thrown the old coat and trousers out of the window he opened the wrapping paper and discovered that the shop assistant had forgotten to put in the new trousers. So when the customs men boarded the train and checked him he hadn't any trousers on."

During the story her eyes had started to dance and she was keeping her lips tight together to try and keep from laughing. But I'd got through and she knew it.

"Is there a customs post now?" she asked. "We weren't stopped on the way down."

"No, there haven't been customs posts between the north and the south for about twenty years."

I was so relieved to hear her voice again. But then it hardened.

"It was a perfect day and you ruined it. We were only there for ten minutes and you ruined it. You're just like him."

"What do you mean? Like who?"

"You suit yourself, just like him. You're no different really."

"Who are you talking about?"

"My father. He used to get round me with his funny stories. You're all the same deep down."

And that was how it stayed. She didn't speak or come near me even when we parted outside our rooms, even when I said "I'll see you about nine for the Sixties night. OK?"

+++++

I knocked on her door at nine o'clock and there was no answer. I called her name four times and still there was no answer. So I went downstairs and followed the sign to the ballroom.

It was already more than half full, mostly with middle-aged and older. *Summertime Blues* was on and the glittering ball in the ceiling gave me enough light to have a good look around. I very quickly saw her jiving with someone. She was wearing a candystriped unitard playsuit that had me palpitating down there and everywhere. Where did she get it? I wonder if they have my size.

She was amazingly well-formed for her age, better even than I'd realised, and the tight candy stripes made my breath come short. They showed off those beautiful contours - soft shoulders, enticing breasts, cheeky bottom, audacious little mound. And the way she moved, graceful as a ballerina. What did the song say? A wave out on the ocean could never move that way? I shifted in my seat, hardened, got mad when other dancers obscured my view of her.

After we get back to our rooms tonight, I'll ask her to let me in and I'll go on my knees again, only this time it will be to tell her how stupid I was and I'll promise to take her to that beach tomorrow and we'll bring a big lunch and stay as long as she wants. She spun like a spinning top and seemed to connect telepathically with her partner each time he turned to catch her waist or arm or hand. *Summertime Blues* came to a thudding finish and they stood side by side, arms around each other's waist. This guy was good but she was better. She was standing quite near and with her back to me and my heart was going in my head. Lovely hips, not even flared yet, and between them the soft roundness of her little bum.

The music changed to slow. *A Whiter Shade of Pale. Oh mio dolce Signore*, sexiest song of sixty-seven's long Summer of Love, known to have loosened the loins of even the most vestal of virgins, and her hands joined loosely round her partner's neck and his around her waist. He drew her roughly closer and she went willingly as if it was part of the dance routine. She didn't resist either when he thrust himself forward into her playsuit and took all of her little bottom in his big hands as if he owned it and instead of objecting she leaned away back from the waist to look at his face and say something to him and I felt their pleasure as she pushed right up into him and then I saw him properly. My man from room 236. How could she? How *could* she? And where was Barbie? Where the fuck was Barbie?

Turmoil doesn't come near to describing it. If grief is the price of love, what price does lust exact? And what did it matter? I had to have her. Now I knew it. No more turning back. I had waited long enough. I had stood apart from her when all she wanted was love. Her love and mine might not exactly coincide, the gap in years might be unclosable, but how many lovers were compatible, I mean really compatible? People of all sexes everywhere were connecting every moment of the day and night and here was I beating myself up over the most natural thing there was.

I turned my eyes from them and didn't look again till the music ended. They had left the floor and she was sitting alone just three tables from me. I watched without turning my head. Chin resting in her palms she was gazing ahead at the embracing couples shuffling to the music of their youth. Very soon my Apollo appeared with drinks and I saw her look up and say something. She was going to have her pound of flesh, no question about that.

The lights from the rotating crystal ball played on their faces, his impassive, hers partly hidden. After a minute he suddenly stood bolt upright and loped towards the exit, half crouched like some kind of predatory thing. A few more paces and he turned sharp left and headed through a doorway. *Gentlemen*. I got up and followed him in, heart thumping. He was standing at a urinal and no one else was there. I was too keyed up to take in the back of him properly although I could tell in a millisecond that his arse was nothing ordinary. I stood next to him and unzipped. My lowered eyes fell sideways on his dong which he held casually at the hilt between two brown fingers and the piss spitting out of it. The girth, the length, oh my God, look at it, it's like one of those wild mushrooms. Or a serpent you'd see on Attenborough. A hornsman. No, not a hornsman. What the fuck do you call it? An anaconda. That's it. A bloody anaconda.

"The girl you're with," I said without looking up.

"I beg your pardon?" There was some kind of elemental smell off him that more than neutralised the chemistry floating up from the urinal cakes. Urinal cakes. What a name.

"The girl you're with. She's under my care."

"What are you talking about?" Bulgarian. I hadn't been able to pinpoint it last night but now I knew. He was Bulgarian. His voice, deep and velvety, sent the shivers up me. One of my students from that country once told me she couldn't understand James Joyce and his accounts of moral transgressions because people in her country didn't have any concept of sin. I remember thinking it would be a wonderful place to live, a place where you could really live and finally put the mark of Catholic guilt behind you.

"We heard the goings-on in your room last night. I'm the one who helped you get in."

"Oh."

"How's your girlfriend?"

"Sorry?"

"The blonde. The one you slept with."

"What are you talking about? You're being a pest."

"We heard you. Your goings-on, your ..."

"You're out of your little mind," he growled. My brain was becoming fogged with his nearness and something was happening to my tongue.

"I was ..."

"Yes? Yes? You were what?"

"I wanted to ... ah ... I'm here to talk to you about the girl who's sitting waiting for you out in the dance hall right now. Isabella. She's here from England on a short holiday and she's my granddaughter's best friend and she's under my care. You ..."

"Yes?"

My mouth had gone completely dry.

"What are you saying?"

I dredged up what saliva I could, moistened my tongue and reluctantly raised my gaze, taking in properly what I'd been peripherally aware of, the tight Taylor Swift T-shirt that hugged his stomach, pecs and shoulders, and then his olive skin, clear blue eyes and voluptuous lips, and to crown it all a head of curling coal-black hair. The man was a fucking Adonis.

"She's fifteen years of age," I croaked. "Below the age of consent. I just wanted to warn you –"

"She told me she's sixteen."

"Trying to make herself older than she is. You must understand, girls of her age tend ... tend ... girls of that age ...."

"Say it! Can you not speak man?"

"In any case," I whispered, "the age of consent in the Republic of Ireland is seventeen. And ignorance of the law is no defence. Statutory rape is what you'll be looking at."

My voice was coming a bit better but my bladder had downed tools. I was standing there trying to pass water and I couldn't, it just wouldn't come. He lowered his head in my direction and I thought he was going to head-butt me. I recoiled and that's when the dam broke. Right away I felt a wet heat on my left thigh and knee. I finished the pee, no choice, it kept on coming. And when I got to the dregs I reached down and felt the left side of my trousers. Soaking. Good Christ, hair caught behind my foreskin probably. Age will be the death of me.

"I'll drive her over the border then," he whispered in my ear and then leered. Beautiful large lips, absolutely beautiful. And his personal essence up close was making my head spin. Take me, I'm Spartacus. "I imagine their laws are more advanced," he continued.

"One year more. The age of consent there is sixteen. Isabella is fifteen."

"She knows her own mind. Who do you think you are anyway? The pope? The Archbishop of Canterbury? Some kind of fucking patriarch?" His ape-like features were working like something let loose.

"I'm her guardian and I'll be watching your every move. Reception will give me your name and address and I have your car registration."

"My name and address are confidential. Reception won't give you that information. And by the way old man, you've just pissed yourself."

I ignored his nasty and unnecessary remark. Did he not think I knew?

"They'll give it to the gardaí," I said.

"And who is the gardaí when he's at home?"

"Not he. They. And they are the Irish police. Wet or not I'm now going to go back into the dance hall and if I see you with Isabella for one moment longer I'll be reporting you as a potential paedophile. You'll be ruined my friend, you'll be in all the Irish newspapers. And I'll be making sure Bulgarian newspapers copy the story. Just think about it."

His eyes flashed. "What makes you say I'm Bulgarian?" As he said this he shook his knob gently dry, shaking it between his first and second fingers the way you might a smouldering cigar, holding it mouthwateringly for far longer than he probably needed to, then tantalisingly tucking it away.

“What do you think you’re looking at?” The words came like a whip. “And that’s not the first time either. Pedal!”

I’m a bit of a linguist and though I have only a smattering of Bulgarian I was under no illusions about what he was saying. He was not telling me to get on my bike. He was calling me a faggot.

“I didn’t come here to be insulted,” I said haughtily.

“Of course you didn’t!” he rasped. “We both know why you came.”

The toilet door opened and two men walked in arguing.

“Look, I’m telling you,” said one. “It was Martha and the Vandellas sung *Dancing in the Street*. Sure wasn’t I there for God sake? You’re too young to remember.”

“And you’re too senile to remember. It was Marvin Gaye. Martha and the Vandellas only covered it.”

I zipped up and left the toilet.

+++++

I don’t think I’ve ever taken a quicker shower in my life. In ten minutes flat, I was washed and dried and in less than twenty seconds more had administered four or five well-directed sprays of *One Million* eau de toilette. Only then did I pause to decide what I should wear. I decided on the pressed cream chinos and striped button-down shirt and light violet panties. Yes. Couldn’t do better than that. I arrived back at the dance hall a little out of breath and looked around. Isabella was sitting exactly where she had been and she was alone. My seat hadn't been taken so I went back to it. *Twist and Shout* was playing and the place was thumping mad.

How did she look? Hard to tell. Psychedelic colours got in the way of seeing and the floor was moving with the dancers. The bastard was here, I knew it. I couldn't see him but he was here. And there he was too, among bumping swaying couples, writhing like some kind of dervish and the girl with him half gone as well. This wasn't Barbie, definitely not Barbie. Unless she'd dyed her hair dark. I wanted him. Christ how I wanted him. Even if I were to die after, I wanted him.

What am I anyway? What I am, that's what I am. A freak fucked up by a fucked-up momma. I'll wear a petticoat for him or whatever he decides, my short one if he wants so he can see me right, so he can pull it roughly over my head and do me big and hot.

Purple Haze came on. A man went to her and spoke and left without her. Hendrix had my heart going. She rose from her seat and was swallowed up when people crossed between us. It was all too quick. What age would Hendrix be if he was alive? Let me think. *Purple Haze* cut short. What the hell's this Deejay playing at anyway? Now he's started *Runaway*. Ah, Del Shannon. Simpler times, lovely singer. Good looker too. Fine body but somehow didn't turn me on. I remember him well though.

She was back at her table with a drink in her hand. A tall skinny figure leaned down to speak to her. She shook her head. Eight till late the poster said. How long will she stay? Don't be stupid, she'll stay till he comes for her. Etta James singing. Poor unfortunate girl, poor brilliant incomparable unfortunate woman, telling us what she never had. I found a dream that I could speak to, a dream that I can call my own. She went to the bar three more times and almost fell the third time. I watched him leave alone and this time he didn't come back.

I waited to bring her to her room. I listened to the Sixties and saw black and white body bags in Vietnam and Laos and Cambodia and Indonesia and half empty dance halls echoing to bands we paid to play to our needs, and boys and girls pairing off but not with me. I heard a dead man sing *Three Steps to Heaven*, a man that lived more in his twenty-one years than I have in seventy-one.

Step one - you find a girl to love,
Step two - she falls in love with you,
Step three - you kiss and hold her tightly –
That sure seems like heaven to me.

I brought her to her room. She fell into the armchair, humped up her knees to her chest and cried. I sat frozen on the edge of the bed. Not four feet from me tightly wrapped in red and white candystripes was the outline of the underside of her thighs and the triangular gusset between them. I wrenched my gaze away and there on the dressing table were seashells and pebbles all formed in the shape of a heart and in the middle of it a pretty coloured drawing of a mermaid. Cockleshells, scallops, mussel shells, Venus shells.

"They're all the same," she slurred, sniffling, rubbing under her nose with her knuckles. "They're all just, just ... they're all out for ... they're all the same."

"Who do you mean?"

She stared glassily at me and her eyes were a luminous grey. "I hate them, boys and men. They're brutes."

"Oh Isabella. You don't hate them all, do you?"

She blinked. "I didn't say I hated *you*. I don't hate you. You're not one of them." More tears came and that was when I took a soft cotton handkerchief from the breast pocket of my shirt and put it in her hand. She gave me a grateful *vin triste* half-smile and her fingers touched mine. The crying had brought that patchy rose to her cheeks and her nose was inflamed and her lips were swollen and I wanted to hold her and comfort her right there.

"Thanks. Thanks, Lllllexie." She dabbed her eyes with the handkerchief and then gave a thunderous blow into it from her nose. "I'm sorry I did that on you today. I didn't mean to. It was just the wrong time for me."

"Wrong time?"

"Of the month. You know. It wasn't your fault. You must have things wrong with you too, the age you are and all and you still brought me on that brilliant walk and showed me all those places and told me ... I hate what he did."

"Who?"

"This man I was dancing with. He hurt me."

"He offended you?"

"Hurt."

"Hurt?"

"When we were out dancing. He hurt me. He hurt me with his hands. But I still wanted him. I'm disgusting. I still wanted him and I thought he was going to stay with me but he never came back and I was dying for him to. Is there something wrong with me?"

"What do you mean?"

"Like, am I ugly for instance? Do you think I'm ugly? *I* do. No, not think. I know."

"You're beautiful," I said. "I think you're the most beautiful girl I've ever met. And I've taught some beauties in my time." Christ of Almighty. All those young men desperate for good marks. And you couldn't afford to put a step wrong with them. You just knew. Her lovely blue eyes brightened for a moment and she said "You're just saying that. You're so good and kind. But do you see me? Do you see me? I hate myself, I hate the way I look."

"But why? Why do you hate yourself? You're perfect. I love the way you look."

"Do you not understand? I hate my body. I don't even want to be a girl. Teresa told me one time that her mother said the dances in Ireland used to be like cattle markets. Girls standing in a big line along one side of the hall and the men standing opposite like people going to bid. And they'd walk up and down sometimes and pick whoever they wanted to pick. Like cows."

"I remember that myself. But a girl could refuse if she wanted."

"Teresa thought it was terrible, but it's worse now. You're like an ornament, what do you call it, a thing in an exhibition? They expect you to go around with the front of you and the back of you stuck away out like, like, like toys and ... did you ever see the jeans some of the girls have on? I don't know how they get into them. And it's all for men to look at them and want them."

"But don't girls like to look attractive anyway? You know, to feel good? And men don't come into it a lot of the time? I've heard that."

"If you go off with a boy now," she went on, "he thinks that means he's going to get to do what he wants, and if you don't let him, you know he's going to get doing it with someone else that very night. All I ever wanted was for someone to want me for more than ... you know. But they're all the same. They just take everything they can get and then try and do the same on the next one. It's like animals do."

"Isabella, listen to me. You're very young. You're only fifteen. You've plenty of time to meet the right person."

"Sixteen. I'm sixteen."

"Sorry. Sixteen."

"And maybe the right person isn't a boy." she said.

"What?"

"Did I tell you about my father?"

"Yes. You did. You were saying –"

"He told me it was love. And do you know what he's doing now?"

"He's in Dublin. Isn't that what you said?"

"Yes, but do you know what he's doing?" She covered her eyes and mouth with her hands for a few seconds and then looked up at me again, face blurred with tears. And a lovely little pink rash had quickly formed between her nose and lips. "He'll be coming up from Dublin the day after tomorrow and he'll be meeting me at the airport and I'll be going back with him."

My head wasn't properly processing what she was saying. What was distracting me was the question and answer in my head. If I had transitioned, what way would I be now? And my mind answered that I'd probably be just the way I am except for the different parts. I'd be a screwed-up septuagenarian with a craving for beefcakes and a criminal obsession with nymphets.

Who was it said that the most important thing for a child in their first three years is to have two adults that the child can totally trust? Yes, the chimpanzee expert, Jane something. Jane ... Jane ... it doesn't matter. So, with parents like I had, what kind of a wizened chimp does that make me? And what kind of a world is this anyway? Gender-fluid, gender-neutral, gays, lesbians, intersex, cisgendered, pangendered, genderqueer, trans men and women, transvestites. And straights of course. Don't forget the straights. And how happy are they?

"They showed porn at my school in Denmark," she said "and it just seemed stupid."

"Right?"

"Yeah. Like, you know, ridiculous. That's how it seemed to me anyway at the start. Would you like some more wine?"

"No thanks. I'm fine here."

She got up from the armchair and filled her glass to the brim.

"Oh dear, I've spilled some on myself." She rubbed at her pyjamas with the palm of her hand.

I brought her a towel which she left absently on her lap as she sank slowly back into the deep armchair. Her eyes had taken on a somewhere else look. She took the glass in her hand again and sipped from it, looking at me nervously through slit eyes.

"I think," she said, and paused for a long moment before she spoke again. "I think ... I think ... I remember the stuff they showed us." She took a deep breath. "My father got me to watch some other stuff with him. Except the ones he showed were terrible. He said the DVDs they had in school were laughable and couldn't really happen the way it showed. He said he was educating me but he didn't say that was why they showed them, to make us see how ridiculous porn was. But his stuff was the very opposite. It was real violent. It was just so awful what the men in them were doing. Old old men and young girls all in together."

Say something. Say something to her. "Could he have been trying to help you?"

"Trying to help himself more like. And he's so religious too. That's what I used to always think anyway. He was, is ... you know that name ... born again. I think sex should be beautiful. It should make you ... It should be ... but it doesn't, it isn't. Why do we have to try and look beautiful and boys don't? They don't care about what you're really like."

She seemed about to cry again. "Will we turn on the TV?" I said.

"He got me to watch things with him that made me want to run away. Just run away. Anywhere. He showed videos too about these men, you know, that were in court, with all the wives and some of them were only young girls. Fundamentalist something of Jesus Christ. It was awful."

She tilted her glass and in two or three gulps drank all that was in it.

"I've been thinking now for ages," she said, feeling her nostrils with her fingers and then giving her nose a quick rub with the back of her hand, "that I wanted to be a boy. But sometimes I get scared. You can have it done when you're sixteen you know. And you can't be diagnosed. That's the amazing thing. You can't be diagnosed. The only test is not being happy with what you are now. I found out that all trans people have a brain that's right for what they want to be and it doesn't have to be the gender they're born with."

"I didn't know that. But you're right to be scared Isabella. What if you changed your mind when it was too late?"

"You get hormone treatment to start," she said as if I hadn't spoken. "And then you go back and get a double ... what is it you call it, you know, when you get ..." She lowered her eyes. "And then -"

"But you're a girl Isabella. I've never seen anyone so feminine. Why would you have yourself mutilated like that?"

She hit the arm of the chair with her fist. "I know all about that," she said. "It's not what you say. And you can change back if it doesn't work out for you."

"But that means more interference with your body. You couldn't do it, it's far too serious a thing to get done."

"Well at least it would be doctors and surgeons interfering and not sleazebags doing what they want. You know Bono got it done? And look at him now."

"What! Bono out of U2? I never knew he was a woman."

She blinked hard and suddenly squealed with laughter, rocking back and forward in the armchair. "Not *that* Bono. That Bono was always a big hairy man with swimming goggles! *Chaz* Bono. His mother is Cher. You know Cher, don't you?"

"Of course. *I Got You Babe*."

She stared at me, mouth wide open, laughter gone. "What did you say? Did you say I got you babe?"

"Yes. The song she and Sonny Bono sang away back in ... oh, away back before you were born."

She squealed again. "Of course. I know now what you mean." And she laughed again. "Oh Lllllexie," she said, "You're so good for me. I really am going to miss you."

She was gazing fondly at me now, eyes asparkle. Funny old Grandpa Lexie. But her mood seemed to suddenly darken again. "Do you want to know what's the worst thing about being a girl?" she said. "The very worst? You're third class every way, that's what. Men rule every way. And girls have even stopped thinking. That creep Trump, what he said about women and bragging about what he did to them and what was it, fifty-three percent of white women voted for him even after they heard him saying it? Did you hear about that, fifty-three percent? Stupid hen turkeys. Men control everything. Everything."

"No, Isabella. Things are changing. It's happening right now."

She wasn't listening. "Do you know trans people in Ireland are allowed to put their new sex on passports and all? That's why I want to live here with Denise."

"I didn't know that."

"Didn't know what?"

"I didn't know you were really planning on living here permanently."

"I told you that. I told you already."

"Sorry. I'm sorry Isabella, but you've got my head spinning."

"Oh Lllllexie, I'm the one that's sorry. I shouldn't have annoyed you but I thought I could tell you because you're so clever and experienced and all. Now I've upset you."

With that she got out of the armchair and came and sat close to me on the edge of the bed. She put an arm around my shoulder and held my wrist tightly with her other hand. "And I should have said before now. I adore what you're wearing. You really know how to dress, Lllllexie. You're such a handsome man. And you really are the kindest person I've ever known. And you smell lovely too."

"Thank you." Sweet Lord.

"What is it you're wearing? Is it Brut?"

"Brut? No. I think maybe it's the hotel soap."

"You never talk about your wife, Lllllexie," she said softly. "Tell me about her. Please. What's she like? Is she pretty?"

"Pretty? She used to be. She's getting old Isabella, a lot older than her age."

"Oh dear. But is she good to you? Does she make you happy?"

I hesitated. After what seemed to me too long a time I said "I suppose it's like what my Aunt Maggie used to say. Before you marry the girl of your dreams, it's all sunshine and roses. And then with time it rains and then it pours and love goes out the window."

"No!" she cried and I felt her soft hip against mine. "I never told you Lllllexie, but I've hardly even thought of Denise since I came yesterday. And you know why that is?"

I shook my head.

"You. It's because of you. I've never met anybody like you. These have been the two best days of my life. Honest they have. And I'm so sorry I made you unhappy."

I couldn't look at her. I stared straight ahead.

She stood up then and came round to face me. She wedged her soft knees between mine, placed her hands on my shoulders, leaned forward and kissed my forehead. "Oh," she whispered. "I love the smell of your hair. And you're so Jeremy Corbyn."

"Pervert!"

The shout from the corridor was immediately followed by loud banging on a door and then more shouting, less distinct than the first exclamation.

"Come out here you slimeball! I'm reporting you to the desk, sicko! The guards will soon have *your* number!"

Isabella pulled back from me and stared at the door. "It's that man Marcus," she whispered. "He's drunk again. OmyGod." She put a finger to her lips and moved again to sit beside me, head on my shoulder, both arms around my waist.

I knew who it was. And it wasn't Magnus.

"That must be your door he's banging at," she whispered.

"Govno!"

She breathed into my ear "He's talking rubbish. Do you hear him?"

He wasn't talking rubbish. He was talking Bulgarian. And he was talking Bulgarian because he was Bulgarian.

"Kuchka!" Bulgarian for bitch I think.

And then in half-falsetto: "Kon da te ebe!" I could be wrong about this but to the best of my recollection that means something along the lines of get fucked by a horse.

"I'd better go out there," I said.

"Don't! Please don't, Lllllexie! He's mad and he's drunk! You wouldn't know what he might do!"

"Keep the door locked Isabella. I'm going out there. Don't even peek now. You hear?"

She tugged frantically at my shirt as I headed for the door. "Please, Lllllexie. Don't be brave because of me. If we just sit here and keep quiet he'll go away."

"I'm not going to take any more of this," I whispered. "He has to be confronted. And after I get rid of him I'll be reporting him to reception. This nonsense has gone on long enough."

I pushed her firmly away, opened the door, stepped out and let it close behind me just in time to hear him make a comment about my mother that I couldn't quite make out.

"Hello," I said, attempting a smile.

He turned around, goggled and then erupted.

"Hah! Kuchka!"

"I know you're angry," I said as calmly as I could, for my heart was beating very fast, "but please don't be disturbing the other guests. If we can just go into your room for a minute I'll explain everything. Or my room if you prefer."

"Umri! Lainar!"

What an incredible specimen! And the fact that he had just called me a shithead and told me to die only drew me to him all the more. It is a well-established fact that by far the biggest impediment to true sexual fulfilment is indifference in one or other of the partners, but this bodacious beast exuded passion like none I'd ever come across. And that wasn't all he exuded, for even at a distance of four of five feet the smell of him was already firing up my loins to near combustion. And those loins told me that even if tonight were to be my last one on earth, this was how I should spend it.

I attempted a wider smile. "I'm really sorry about the way I looked at you in the toilet earlier but it was just that I couldn't help admiring your physique."

"Physique! Is that what you call it? Hah! Would you like to hear another word for it?"

"Surely that was a compliment sir. I think you are the most handsome man I have ever had the excitement to meet and that's the truth of it. Do you really wonder that I couldn't take my eyes off you? Please tell me, what's your name?"

"Mainata ti!" That was not his name.

"I understand your annoyance with me," I continued, "but when I warned you off the girl, it was only to protect you from prosecution. If you'd gone on and had relations with her and she'd told the guards you could have ended up in prison and your life ruined. I apologise with all my heart for handling the whole affair so clumsily. Please forgive me. But I have something even more important to tell you which should really be said in the privacy of your bedroom."

He was still glaring at me but for the first time I detected what I took to be a trace of uncertainty in that divine face. I figured that maybe he hadn't clicked at the Sixties hop for some reason and was sorely in need of an outlet. Every cloud, as they say. Or as someone without my style might put it, strike while the iron is hot.

He was beginning to breathe harder now and I was aware of Taylor Swift seductively throwing her top half back and forward, her body undulating with every breath he took. Ah Taylor, you don't even come close. And anyway, you're too old.

“You spoke about the girl,” said my man evenly. “I take it that’s her room you just came out of?”

I nodded. I was trying to decide if there was really a softening in his tone when suddenly his eyes flashed and he said “And you accuse me of seducing young girls! You, you are the seducer!”

“No, no, you don’t understand. She had too much to drink and I have simply helped her back to her room, that’s all. I would never dream of doing anything to her. I’m her host for just one more day and then she flies back home. Do you think we could go into your room? Or mine if you wish?”

Silence. I waited and held my breath. Then he spoke.

“For a start,” he said quietly, “we’re going to have to use a douche. Are you into that?” Well, you could have beaten me down with a feather.

“A douche?” I said.

“I have some in my room. The last thing we want is a mess.”

I followed him into his bedroom. As the door closed and the lights came on he turned and pulled me towards him and then I felt him hard against me and he held me really tight. I cried out of me with what he was doing. “Hey, you smell good,” he said. “I think maybe I’m going to like this.” His beautiful lips brushed against mine and his tongue worked my mouth open and circled the inside of it over and over and over again as I shared the brandy and sweet garlic of his saliva and my legs shuddered as he thrust repeatedly into me and my dental plate came loose and a rush ran through me like I never remember having before and the buckle of my belt hit the carpet and I knew without looking that my panties were at my ankles. Slave to a Slav, gagging for whatever he wanted.

"How's your heart? Medical wise?" he inquired, thrusting even harder while he held my backside in his hands.

"Heart? Heart heart heart OK." *Mon Dieu, mon doux Dieu!*

"Oops," he said. "Bit of privacy wouldn't go amiss here." He took his hands from me, went to the window and closed the curtains, shutting out the stunned night. He came back and held me as before, only tighter this time.

"Blood pressure?"

"OK. No, up and down. Ooooh my God. Up and down." His thick black hair was tousled now, curls hanging over his eyes. I tried to breathe deeply but couldn't because I was engulfed by his fragrance and what he was doing to me.

"Up and down? How much up? I don't want a stiff on my hands," he growled and then he laughed. "Not that kind of stiff anyway. Have you done this before?"

I didn't answer. He had me so tight, and then he began to thrust again, really violently now, lifting me off the carpet each time he did it.

"You haven't, have you?"

I couldn't answer. He slowly lowered me to the floor and shifted his hands to my front and fingered me roughly. Beads of sweat ran down and around his comely cheeks. He kissed my lips full on, long and slow this time, then tongued some places I'd never known were there between my lower lip and lower gum.

After I'm not sure how long he withdrew his tongue. "And you're coming already, aren't you? Little early bird. I think I can feel it. Yes, I can feel it."

I couldn't speak.

"You're coming already, right?"

"I don't think so," I gasped. "I think that's the ... the ..."

"Ah. The cowper."

"Sorry?"

"Precum. OK sir, take everything off, everything. We're going to the shower."

He stepped back from me.

"I already had a shower tonight," I said as I fumbled with my striped button-down shirt.

"Shoes. Socks too," he called from the far end of the room. "Everything. You know you're not going in there to have a shower don't you?"

I undressed to the skin and turned around. "What do you mean?" I asked and what I saw then had my heart doing the maddest dance it has ever done. For he too was naked and man-oh-man, what a sight! This was the god of them all - except this one had thick black hair nearly everywhere I could see, nearly everywhere. What a way to die! He walked towards me holding an odd-looking red pear-shaped ball in the hollow of one hand and – *quelle magnificence!* – his great big glossy knob was up in the air and the whole thing swinging like a metronome.

"Right. Into the shower sir," he said quietly, taking me by the hand. "What's your name by the way?"

"Alexis. What's your –"

"Alexis. Interesting name. I've never had an Alexis before."

Once in the bathroom he pushed me firmly into the shower enclosure. "Let me explain," he said. "This here in my hand is the douche I was telling you about. It's just a simple device for cleaning out your little ass. Stand still whatever you do now. I've done this before and I know what I'm doing. It's what I call the aperitif and you'll love it. And don't be impatient, the starter and main course will follow straight after. By the way, Alexis – good name that, I like it – you'll be glad to hear I won't be using a condom. Better for us both. And just so you know, I'm good at this."

As he finished speaking a jet of something came shooting into my behind and the dental plate flew out of my mouth, hit the wall tiles and landed on the shower floor, shattered. Obsessively intact for fifteen years, now lying in pieces at my bare feet.

I bent to pick them up. As I did so a pikestaff crashed up my bum. Ohhhhhhhhhhh

Rumplesplitskin bledbuttentity purgatorious calafragilistical puncturous sphinctorous. Now I thought not in words but in shadows, wordless, speechless, languageless, languageless landfish, Mister Doctor Conrad, my dear Self, fuck me, my language, so sorry, take me pikestaffed, do to me, take me away, take me back, stop this, stop this now, now, let me back, get me back, take me back, get me away, get him away, this vulgar bulgar peacock jutting strutting in and out of me, elevator hushing shut, sounds of shadows in the corridor, Isabella sits waiting, soft slender girl, dreaming of me where all has failed, waiting to be fixed

I heard him hiss "What the fuck?" and then "Look now what you've done! You've broken my fucking nozzle! Putka! Get the fuck out! Out of here, now, now!"

+++++

Out I was, out in the shivering corridor, naked as the night was touching zero and feeling like a bag of cold sick, three fragments of dental plate tight in my hand and clothes and shoes at my feet chucked petulantly after me by that brute. *Mon Dieu et Sa Mère!* Where do I go from here?

Out of shock my first dread is that she might open her door before I can get dressed. Key card in breast pocket of shirt. Holy Mother of God where is it? It's not there, it's not in the pocket. Think. *Think!* THINK! I know. Get dressed anyway, right here, go down to reception for spare, meet Magnus of the clinking glass, nothing more certain, nothing. Hell with Magnus, forget about him. Is that a movement in her room? Is that her door opening? Holy cow! It's her door!

Wait, no, it's the elevator. Whew. But that's only ten yards away. My breath, my breath won't come. Man and woman step out *and walk in the opposite direction without looking near me.* Thank you, Mother of God. For that I will join a monastery. But hang on. Aren't modern monasteries dens of same-sex debauchery? According to the Collapsed Catholics? One of them said that anyway. Ken was it? I could nearly swear it was Ken. And he may have been right for once.

This vocation thing deserves some thought. For a start, what would I do about Henry? Put her in a home? Now there's an idea. These three days will get her into the way of it. But they charge the world now, don't they? Thousands of pounds a month? Accordingly, I will go and sell all my possessions, give the money to a nursing home and get me to a monastery.

But my key card. Where is it? Could it be in the Bulgar's room? Indeed it could. *Aiutami, Madre di Dio.* I rummage praying through my things and what do you think I see? Yes. There it is, nestling in the gusset of my light violet Calvin Kleins, sticky, damp, discoloured, but still usable. I think.

+++++

I checked my backside with the compact mirror and amazingly the damage appeared to be minor. And there was no pain, no pain anymore. God was in His heaven and Mary too. All in all, not a bad night. Because tonight I'd had a hefty slab of fresh cream strawberry cake and then got nearly the whole slab to eat. What about that!

Now for the dental plate. I laid out the three jigsaw pieces and they came together neatly – no missing splinters. My dentist does same-day repairs but Isabella would be gone by then. So what to do? She mustn't see me like this. I searched in my suitcase for my old plate. Had I packed it? Of course I had. Glory be to God on high. And on Earth peace to all. So I washed it and whitened it, stuck it in and consulted the wall mirror. Cripes, a two-tooth gap! Still, I'll get by, I'll get by.

I've never in my life dreamed better than I did that night. The bad wine came first and was blessedly just a tiny tot of a tipple – crude comments about my pale pink polka-dot panties from precocious little pricks in the school toilets, but after I got that out of the way it was all idyll, streamlets glinting over mossy crevices and so on, a reception roomful of unaccompanied nymphets waiting to be seen singly by charming Doctor Cheddy, green brooks beckoning me as they murmured and gleamed and glittered and danced with the daffodils and the whole thing climaxed with Isabella stealing into my bed at first light.

+++++

She was wearing very tight black vinyl high-waisted trousers and matching high-heeled boots exactly like Vanessa Paradis wore that time she sang *Tandem* on the TV. And a little white blouse low at the neck. She kissed me on my two cheeks when I opened the door. *Comme le font les Français.* "I know you told me ten minutes but I couldn't wait," she said and her eyes were morning-blue.

"And I'm delighted to see you. You know what you are Isabella?"

"What?" she said, and I was suddenly aware of the cute little white handbag in her hand.

"You're a breath of pure air. That's what you are. Did you ever see *Gigi*?"

"Gigi? What's that?"

"Oh it goes way back. It's a musical about a teenage tomboy called Gigi who turns into a beautiful girl overnight. You're the beautiful girl. Except you were beautiful long before this morning."

"Oh Lllllexie." She was all flustered and I could see she didn't know quite how to react. So she talked. "My father buys my clothes. He lets me choose them but he pays for them. He likes to see me wearing nice clothes. But I'm so sorry. I fell asleep again last night and you out in the corridor alone with that awful Bastar.

"I listened and listened but I couldn't hear anything and the next thing was, I woke up on top of the eiderdown with all my clothes on and it was the morning and they were sticking to me. I nearly slept in. It was the birds and a collie dog that wakened me. I saw it out the window. Lovely black and white thing."

She was hanging onto my arm a little bit out of breath as we stepped into the elevator. "I'm disgraceful, I really am. I'm not ever going to drink anymore. Never. Don't let me have any tonight, won't you not? Please. You be my teacher and I'll do whatever you say. But I forgot to ask you. How did you manage? Did you get rid of him all right? You look different. Oh my gosh, what happened to your mouth? Oh Lllllexie, did he hit you? Open your poor mouth and let me see. Please!"

I gave her a slow self-conscious closed mouth smile. "I'm all right. Just a minor mishap." I opened my mouth a little then and she reached up and pulled down my chin with the soft fingers of one hand.

"You've teeth missing! He broke your teeth! I'm going to report him! Oh Lllllexie."

"No, don't do that Isabella. It was an accident, honestly. He was just being a bit abusive and I pushed him and he pushed me and his elbow hit my mouth. It's only two teeth but they were loose anyway. He didn't attack me or anything. He was drunk. Here, this is us now. I'm ravenous."

She trotted to our breakfast table beside me holding my arm in hers. "You call that not attacking? That was an assault! Poor Lllllexie. And it was all my fault."

"What? It had nothing to do with you. Honestly, it was handbags at ten paces."

"Handbags at ten paces? What's that? What does that mean?"

"It's two men who don't really want to fight with each other but go on as if they're ready for a brawl."

"Oh. I thought you meant real handbags. But then there's man-bags, aren't there?"

She piled her plate with enough Ulster fry to keep her going till the evening. I decided on a continental breakfast because I wasn't happy about the thought of the chewing that goes into bacon and sausages.

"This is your last full day Isabella."

"I know. I'm trying not to think about that. Have you thought of what we're going to do? Oh your poor mouth."

"I was thinking we might take a drive over Mamore Gap."

"What do you call it again? More Gap?"

"Mamore Gap. It's one of the most spectacular places you'll ever see."

"That's terrific. I'm so looking forward …"

"Well now, what have we here? Did you two have another good night?"

Magnus was standing there kitted out in the same tweeds as before, his face a dark red. My God, will he ever go away? I heard a choking sound from Isabella and looked quickly at her. She was in the process of drawing out a long stringy bit of bacon from her mouth. "You! You pig!" She spat the words at him and then choked again as she held the bacon between thumb and forefinger and looked around for some place to leave it. I put my hand on her arm. "Please Isabella."

"You!" she shouted. "Do you see what you did? Look what you did!"

Magnus stood gaping at her, jowls twitching, eyes blinking rapidly.

"Open your mouth and let him see what he did Lllllexie. You brute!"

I sat tight-lipped, restraining hand still on her arm. Soft flesh, frail little arm.

"Show him Lllllexie, show him!" She deposited the bacon onto the tablecloth.

"Please Isabella," I said. "I'd rather forget about it. Really."

Her bacon hand was suddenly on my lower jaw, slippery, trying to prise it open. "Do you know you could sue him for assault and ... what do you call it? ... battery? Why won't you let me open it? Am I hurting you? Oh I'm so sorry Lllllexie." She removed her hand, coughed and started on Magnus again but not before removing the skin of a sausage from between her teeth and laying it on top of the predigested bacon.

"And now you're adding insult to injury! What do you call you anyway? Ah, now I remember. Mister Bastar." (This misnomer flung disdainfully at him). "We have your name and everything so you can't get away."

"Bastian," I corrected. "Magnus Bastian."

"What?"

"His name's Magnus Bastian."

"Lllllexie, you should report him to the police. Or guards, is it they call them here? Report him to the guards and they'll make him pay you compensation. And then they'll put him in jail. I'll report him if you don't! Who does he think he is anyway?"

"Magnus, come and eat." The dulcet tones of the lovely Eleanor, somewhat later on the scene than I would have wished, veils flicking nervously between lower face and shoulders. She smiled in a strained way at Isabella and me. "I do hope you enjoy the rest of your breakfast. Sometimes Magnus forgets himself. He's such a social animal. Come on Magnus."

But Magnus was not for moving. "Hold on. Hold your horses one wee minute El," he hissed. "This little concubine you see in front of you just accused me of doing something to this queer's mouth. And she's got the nerve to call me a pig too when everybody knows that the only pig in this here hotel is that poofter beside her."

He then addressed himself to Isabella. "I'll tell you what you'll do now, little Lady Chatterley or whatever your name is. Here's what you'll do. If you've any sense in your head you'll save up whatever money it is he pays you and book him in at Lourdes. That's the only place a dirty pig like him has any chance of getting cured."

Isabella stood bolt upright and looked around the breakfast room. "I'm calling the manager!" she shouted and then sank to her seat again as if she had suddenly taken ill. I stared at her. Her eyes seemed to be fixed on the dining room entrance. I looked where she was looking and then I understood. The Bulgarian beast was standing there talking to a waitress. He had Lady Gaga on his chest and was wearing light beige short shorts that were so short they were straining to contain him. This is outrageous, I thought, simply outrageous, flaunting himself like that in front of all these hotel guests. I felt like I could have eaten him.

Isabella spoke. "That's ..."

"What?" I said, heart going like the hammers of Jericho. Eleanor and Magnus were nowhere to be seen. Absent. Taken from our sight.

"That's ... that's the one I was ... I have to go. I can't stay here," she whispered, but didn't move. She seemed frozen to her chair.

"Excuse me Isabella. I need to go to the men's." I scraped my chair back from the table.

But now he was walking unmistakably towards us. And smiling. *Smiling. SMILING!* I stayed seated. I couldn't leave them alone together. But then she wasn't there anymore. Gone. And I hadn't even seen her get up.

"So how are we today? All shipshape I hope?"

I think I nodded.

"I'm sorry you had to leave so suddenly last night. Did you manage all right after you left?" Voice sympathetic, silky, smooth as brass.

I said something back, I'm not sure what. A large empty space had opened up between my neck and my knees.

"I hope you weren't thinking of checking out today," he continued sweetly. "I was actually wondering if maybe you and I could meet up again tonight? You know, to iron out any misunderstandings?"

I nodded. Vigorously. Repeatedly. I was all for ironing out misunderstandings. But while nodding hard I suddenly became aware that my bladder and bowels were close to crisis. His milky mellifluous voice on top of the sight of him was becoming too much.

"I'd love that," I stammered.

He extended his hand then and I took it in mine. Live wires touching, burning ice up my back, genitals colliding.

He left me with a half wave and I sat on empty air. What did he see in me? He had the pick of the hotel and he was taking me. I blinked, tried to breathe deeply and couldn't, got up from the table. Mine not to reason why.

I don't remember getting to the elevator but I knew I was there when I heard a hunchbacked old lady say "Would you press number three please?" which I did while sniffing the hand he had held. "Looks like another nice day," she said. I agreed. Smells like ... What does it smell like? "Isn't this a beautiful hotel!" she said. I agreed. She then asked me if I knew of any opticians in Buncrana and I agreed. I thought she looked strangely at me as we stepped out of the elevator.

Once in my room, I was able to breathe in the balm properly. I lay on my side and cupped the anointed hand over my mouth and nose. Stacks of musk there, that was for certain, and the heavy pungency of his perspiration, but topping all that was the delirious suggestion of some of his personal poop, like a bouquet that might once have been offered to the gods, and all of the aforementioned threatened to turn my insides out, *dolce Gesù.*

I rushed to the bathroom and emptied myself, nearly not making it in time. In the middle of everything an urgent knocking started on the door of my room. It continued for what seemed like ages. Maybe he can't wait till tonight. I cleaned myself well, rose from the toilet bowl and flushed it. I washed my hands, grabbed my Versace Eros spray, applied it strategically and pulled up my trousers.

It was Isabella, flushed and distraught.

"Can I come in?" So saying she came in anyway, walked right past me and then did a quick about turn.

"I saw him talking to you," she said breathlessly. "Does he know you?"

"Who?"

"That man I told you about. The man that went on all lovey-dovey with me at the dance and then walked out on me."

"You mean the man in the dining room that came over to talk to us?"

"Yes, him. I kept the door of the ladies' open a bit and I saw him talking to you. What was he saying? Was he talking about me? I saw him shaking hands with you. He seemed as if he knew you."

"Oh yes, he's the one I helped with his key card. Do you remember? He was thanking me again for what I did."

"Was he talking about me?"

I shook my head. "No, he never mentioned you."

"I hate him. He's a brute. He's worse than all the rest put together." Her tears were welling and her nose was running. I hurried to the dressing table and pulled a tissue from the box.

"Thanks." She blew her nose in a most unladylike way and then rubbed at it furiously with the tissue. "Oh Lllllexie, I don't want to stay in this hotel. I want to leave."

I blinked. "You mean today?"

"As quick as we can get packed. What time do we have to get out of our rooms?"

"I'm not sure. There's something on the back of the door about that. Twelve I think."

"What time is it now?"

I looked at my watch. "Nearly a quarter to eleven. But listen Isabella, we don't have to leave today. He's leaving. He'll be gone within the hour."

She stared at me disbelievingly. "What? How do you know?"

"He told me. That was why he was shaking hands with me. He was wishing us all the best."

"I thought you said ... I thought ... Do you believe him? *I* don't believe him. If he sees I'm staying, he'll check in again. He'll want to rub my nose in it. What time do you say it is now?"

"Nearly a quarter to eleven."

"We've got time then. More than an hour and a quarter. That's plenty of time." She came over and weeping quietly she put her head on my chest and her arms crept around my waist. What's this? She's different, she's higher up my body than before. She must be wearing heels. Whole new experience. *Ah, mon Dieu!*

"How is it you always smell so good? You're so masculine, you really are, Lllllexie. Oh, I wish I'd known you before you were married." Was she going to reward me? She looked up at me with eyes big and blue, and there it was, there it was again, that Verrochian rose around her nose and mouth and her eyes still wet and now her red lips parted and waiting. I felt the pressure of her lovely young limbs on me and my hands gripped her high-waisted trousers as I drew her closer.

Someone was tapping on the door. Open-mouthed she kissed me on the cheek.

"I'm bristly," I whispered. "I haven't shaved yet."

The tapping stopped but then there was a thudding, loud and persistent.

“I don’t mind if you don’t mind,” she whispered back. Dear God, what am I doing? I thought of tweedy old Bastian. The fool was right of course. I need a cure. And better the Bulgarian beast than this. At least he would be natural.

I pulled away from her and called out “Who is it?”

There was no reply but the thudding stopped.

“Who is it?” I called again.

“Sorry,” said a woman’s voice, faintly Caribbean, “but may we clean your room please?”

“Could you come back in half an hour? I’m checking out today and I just have to pack.”

“Yes sir, that’s OK. Thank you.”

She came against me again, her face bright with smiles. “Thank you Lllllexie. You’re the best person I ever knew.”

“I don’t think you got finishing your breakfast,” I said, “and I didn’t take all of mine either. What would you say to a snack here in the hotel before we hit the Gap of Mamore?”

Her eyes were shining. “I’d say yes, I could devour you.”

I blinked and my heart stopped for longer than it should have. And then, as it steadied up again, I thought: God but she’s quick. “So we’d better start packing right away.”

“Whatever you say sir,” she said. Wide-eyed and mischievous she made no effort to disengage. I knew for certain she wasn’t wearing a bra because I could feel her nipples moving on my upper stomach with only my light summer shirt and her flimsy blouse separating us from madness.

"And I still have to shave," I said, standing back from her. "I suppose you'd better get going Isabella. I'll see you in a while."

That was abrupt but she didn't seem to mind. She kissed my cheeks, smiled happily at me and turned away. And then she went out the door and across the corridor with the almost juvenile swing that she has sometimes, the little butt of her trousers protruding bizarrely.

+++++

The weather forecast on the car radio said that rain was coming in the mid-afternoon.

"We've maybe three hours," I said. "Let me see. Dunree beach and then Mamore Gap. We should have time if the forecast's right."

"Oh Lllllexie, this is my last full day. I don't want to go back. Could I not stay?"

"Where's the sign? I see it now. Dunree. We'll be there in about fifteen minutes. How can you stay? You father's coming for you."

"That's why I want to stay. And you. And Denise. I want to stay and wait for her to come back. And meet her boyfriend. Could I not stay with you till she comes? Your wife doesn't have to know. And you still didn't tell me what she looks like. I've never even seen her picture."

"Denise you mean? Right, what does she look like? Let me see. She looks like me, only she hasn't as many bristles."

"Stop, Lllllexie. What's she really like?"

"No but it's true. She does look like me. People always say that. And they say she takes after me too. It's a pity you won't be able to see her this time. Maybe she'll go over to see you. She's talked about that."

"I've made up my mind. He can take a running jump. I'm not going back."

This wasn't good. Time to put a stop to it. I decided to look for somewhere to park. After a few minutes we came to a lay-by and I pulled in and turned to face her. "Now listen Isabella. You can't defy your own father."

"I can do whatever I want! You don't know what it's like with him!" She was breathing hard and I was aware of a heady fragrance that hadn't been there all morning. How could that be? Her little breasts rose and fell fast and what cleavage I could see was a soft silvery brown. Is that glitter in there? I raised my eyes to try and keep them fixed on her face and even there the freckles got to me.

"But where would you stay? What would you live on?"

"She told me I could live with her and Huncan." She gave a little gasp. "Oh gosh. Me and my big mouth. You didn't know they were together, didn't you not? I shook my head and gazed through the windscreen. A sparrowhawk darted silently from a hedge in front of us, long tail steering it just above the tarmac and over a low churchyard wall opposite, moving so fast it was hardly more than a blur. "I've lots of money saved and I could get a job too. And do my A levels and go to university. And you could coach me. Would you? I would pay you."

"I wouldn't dream of you paying me." Though no doubt I would.

"I really could. I'll be earning money."

"You think you have it all worked out, Isabella. But you haven't even done your GCSEs yet. Speak to your father when you see him at the airport. And even if he agrees you'd have serious trouble getting residency in Derry. You know, with Brexit and all."

"I've thought of all that!" she said excitedly. "I can stay with Denise for a while and then I'll live in a flat here in the Republic of Ireland that's still going to be in the European Union. See? And I'll get a part-time job here and travel up to the university in Derry. And maybe I can go to your house some days to get coached? I want to do English literature. I've got ten GCSEs you know. I was allowed to do them early."

She was animated, flushed, her eyes a stunning bright. On top of being the most beautiful girl I'd ever seen she turns out to be a freaking brainbox. Christ, just think what she and I could produce.

"Are you all right Lllllexie? You seem restless. I've upset you."

"No, I'm fine. Took a while to get to sleep last night, that's all."

"Poor Lllllexie. Let's just sit here and relax. There's no hurry is there?"

I didn't answer, just sat letting my shoulders sag and wondering how all this might end.

"That's a lovely church," she said after a minute. I looked to my right at Desertegney chapel, almost blinding white in its grassy surroundings.

"It's a funny shape, isn't it?" she said, leaning sideways for a better view, her right arm across my legs. "It's nearly like a boat."

"It is like a boat. It was designed that way. Star of the Sea you call it. A lot of men earn their living fishing in the lough here and further out to sea too and the architect had the great idea of giving the church a nautical look."

"And the windows are like portholes! That's brilliant! Were you ever inside it?"

"Once or twice. It's very tasteful. But I have mixed feelings about it."

"How do you mean?"

"Well, not so much it as what it stands for. I have a cousin buried in the old graveyard over there but he very nearly wasn't. He had to be buried secretly."

"Secretly?"

"Yes. Eunan was stillborn and the Catholic belief then was that he couldn't be buried in consecrated ground because he hadn't been baptised so his soul went to a place called Limbo. Well my uncle Jim, whose wife's people are from near here, made a little coffin for him and drove him down from Derry in the dead of night and buried him in the family plot that's over to the left of the church. Do you see the graveyard there?"

"Yes, I see it now. Oh, he was so brave, wasn't he!"

"He was. If he'd been caught and reported to the priests, he'd have been condemned from the pulpits. And heaven knows what else would have happened to him."

Her arm was still on me but then she shifted her position and it was back resting on her lap.

"Where were they buried then? Babies that weren't baptised?"

"Anywhere that wasn't consecrated, I suppose."

"You mean it was like burying a dead cat?"

"Actually, I never thought of it like that. I really don't know. I gave up taking their teachings seriously a long time ago."

"But that teaching was ridiculous. How could people have swallowed it?"

"Good question Isabella. My uncle was a very intelligent man but he was indoctrinated like billions of others were down the years. Sure, even Dante believed the same stuff."

"Dante. I read something about Dante. Didn't he write *The Divine Comedy*? The same name as that brilliant Irish band."

"He did. Hey, you certainly know a thing or two. Dante was one of the cleverest people that ever lived and he had Limbo in that very manuscript you're talking about. He was really daring because he made sure atheists like Socrates got a place in Limbo. But I don't know how he would have handled the situation in Belfast City Cemetery where there's a wall separating Catholics and Protestants."

"I heard of that. It's called the peace wall isn't it?"

"No. This is a different kind of wall. There are about a hundred peace walls in Belfast still separating Catholics and Protestants that are alive. But the wall I'm talking about is the one that keeps the dead apart. It's the underground one in Belfast City Cemetery and it separates the Catholic and Protestant dead. It goes down about nine feet and it runs for a good distance. I'd challenge any corpse to get through that."

"Dead people separated by a wall? But that's crazy."

"I suppose you could call it a gift from the Brits. They controlled us by setting Protestants and Catholics against each other and these walls are part of what we're left with. But listen. We'd better get moving on. I know this country and the rain's never far away."

+++++

Dunree beach still takes my breath away. I was brought there a few times by my Uncle Jim when I was a boy and I've never forgotten it. The rock pools with strange little creatures in them that I always tried to identify but never could, the pirate caves that seemed inaccessible behind jagged rocks and sea spray near the end of the bay, the sand that was pure white in some places and silvery in others. It's the most beautiful beach I've ever been on and the miracle is that so few people know about it.

And today there was no one on it except for us two, just us two. And the memories from childhood came racing back and I told her about them and I told her that nothing had changed and she took my hand as we walked back and forward from one end to the other and back and forward again and again. Nothing had changed. She was silent for what seemed a long time and then she said, pointing to a massive fort that stood on rocks high above us: "Isn't that exactly like the fort out of *Where Eagles Dare*? You know, where Robert Beatty was kept prisoner?"

"I suppose it is," I said absently. "I haven't been here since I was about nine. There was word a good few years ago that Paul Newman was set to buy it."

"Paul Newman the film star?"

"Yes. He's dead now of course but what happened was that the Irish Ministry of Defence put it on the market and Newman wanted to turn it into a holiday camp for children suffering from cancer. But it didn't happen and I read somewhere that it has a military museum now and a museum of natural history as well."

"Why was it built?" she asked. "It seems a funny place to build a fort."

"I don't agree," I said. "I think it's a perfect place to build a fort. If you were up there you'd see why. You'd have a perfect view of approaching ships. It was actually built by the Brits during the Napoleonic wars."

I needed the toilet in a hurry but I didn't want to let go of her hand. It felt good in mine and I had a feeling that she didn't want to let go either. I think my closeness felt natural for her. But the prostate doesn't wait and the sight and sound of the crashing waves weren't doing anything to help it. In fact every time they hit the sand they threatened to open the weir.

"Excuse me, I have to go to the toilet," I said. "I'll only be a couple of minutes. Mind those waves Isabella. That tide's coming in fast."

"OK," she said. "And don't you be long now. I won't be able to hold them back on my own."

"Not like King Cnutcase," I called as I walked away. Immediately I felt as if something inside me had caved in. Idiot! I wasn't supposed to know the joke that Isabella and Denise had shared on *Steam 4 Teens* about King Cnut of Denmark trying to order the tide not to come in. Had she noticed? I looked back quickly and saw her bent double picking something up.

When I came back she was sitting on the sand crying. I knelt beside her. "What's the matter Isabella? What's the matter?"

"You won't let me go, won't you not?" Tears streaming, nose and cheeks inflamed, words hiccupping out of her. "He'll win you over, I know he will."

"Oh my dear girl. I'll talk to him. I promise. I hate to see you like this."

She was shaking her head and her nose was running full steam now, onto her lips and chin, into her mouth. I wanted to kiss it all away. I'd have swallowed it if she'd let me, tears, mucus and all, I'm telling you, but seeing as I belonged to the old-world fraternity of losers that always carry hankies, I decided it would be more seemly to offer a handkerchief.

+++++

She moped all the way to Mamore Gap, but once we got there her mood brightened. It did me good to hear her cries of delight and admiration and I had to stop the car at least half a dozen times because she demanded it. "Could you reverse a bit so I can see that again? Pulllease! Oh my God, this is, like, spiritual!"

When we crested the top of the gap, the slope of the road began to get really hairy but the view was spectacular. It was almost as if we were looking down from the sky. We saw Leenan fort and the towering waves of Leenan Bay, we saw Lough Swilly and the Fanad peninsula and the strip-farm fields of Urris. We saw Dunaff Head and the long winding road leading into Clonmany where I hoped we might sleep on our last night together.

I showed her the part of the Gap that's known as the magic road, knowing it would intrigue her. I stopped at the bottom of a slope and left the car in neutral and it seemed to roll uphill for a few yards. She was amazed of course, even when I explained that the whole thing was an optical illusion to do with the surrounding land and the horizon. We stopped at the wayside shrine to the Virgin Mary and I explained that many pilgrims climb the gap barefoot to pray at the shrine every fifteenth of August, one of Mary's feast days. And I told her that about two hundred years ago, the Gap and the hills around it became the second republic in Europe after France.

"Republic?" she said. "What do you mean? How could hills be a republic?"

"Because the Brit writ didn't run here. You see, some people from this area distilled an illegal drink called poitín, and drank it and sold it and exported it to Scotland and other places. The British government didn't like this one bit because they weren't able to collect any tax from the proceeds, so they ordered the Redcoats to raid the stills. But the locals put barricades across the roads leading to the stills that were up in the mountains here. And they used to place iron rods across a lot of the roads too so they'd hear when the Redcoats were on the prowl."

"Gosh. It's like a movie."

"I suppose it is. But it didn't have a happy ending. After about three years the Brits staged a massive attack on this area and that was the end of the republic."

"Imagine. What was the name of the drink again?"

"Poitín. It was very strong stuff, a lot stronger than whiskey. It can still be got too."

"Poitín. Is that an Irish word?"

"It is. I got its name from pota, the Gaelic for the copper pot that was used by the poitín makers."

+++++

We had pub grub in a place called The Rusty Nail and the place was jammed. We had to wait half an hour for a table and another while to be served, but it was worth the wait. And a young lady harpist was performing. She did six or seven pieces while we were there, but it was only when she played a haunting one called *Róisín Dubh* that the pub went very still, almost as if the air inside had become enchanted. Isabella and I sat awhile after the meal until a waiter gently informed us that people were waiting to use our table.

"You always seem to eat steak," she said when we got back to the car. "My father wouldn't touch it."

"Really?"

"He's a vegan you know."

"That sounds serious," I said. "I've heard of them. Were they anything to the Klingons?"

She pulled her hair back from her face and laughed. "You're a howl, Lllllexie. You don't need Groucho to write your stuff. You're a natural."

"It's just that you're on my wavelength Isabella," I said and my heart was light as air. "You're good for me, you really are."

"He's a health freak. He does these seven day detoxes to clear out his body, hardly eats anything except lemons and then he drinks gallons of water too. One time he fasted five full days in a row except for filtered water. Do you know something? He's got this big water filter in the house that's the size of ... oh." She opened her arms wide. I glanced across to see the size of it. She was lying slouched in her seat, arms reaching out and legs apart, completely relaxed.

"That big?" I said. "Well, you tell him this from me the next time you see him. Tell him there's no pleasure worth passing up for three extra years in the geriatric ward."

She screeched happily and her laughter rang through me. What she didn't know of course was that I had filched that little gem from somewhere. Where? Somewhere recently. It'll come to me.

Then, as we slowed behind a traffic jam, she began to yawn. "I could nearly sleep," she said. "Why am I so tired? I wasn't tired in The Rusting Nail."

"Rusty Nail. It's the big meal you had. Big meals always make people sleepy."

She suddenly sat upright. "You said the next time I see him. I don't want to see him again. It's over, it's all over."

I didn't respond to that. Better not to blacken her mood.

The road into Clonmany was lined with parked cars. "Must be something on," I said. "Clonmany Festival time I'd say." And so it was. There in front of us was a big banner stretched across the road. FIFTIETH ANNUAL CLONMANY FESTIVAL - 6th to 13th August 2017.

"Should we stop?" Isabella said. "Will this be good?"

"It's a big deal but I don't think it's my scene. Though maybe you ..."

"No, it's whatever you want. I wouldn't want us to stop here if it's not your scene."

The crowds were milling around in front of us and it took a while to get through. "I think we'll head onto Ballyliffin," I said. "There'll be no place to stay in Clonmany tonight."

"How far is Ballyliffin away?"

"A mile or so. It's got a few hotels so we should get in there."

But there was no room in Ballyliffin, not in the hotels or even the guest houses. We drove on and the landlady in the next guest house we tried, a place called Crabtree Lodge, told us she was full up but asked us into her hallway so she could ring around to see if there were any vacancies.

She was a woman of at least eighty, with a white mudpack on her face that gave her the look of an ancient Goth, especially with her long jet-black hair and staring eyes. And to top all that, she had a voice like the creepy little girl in the Halloween movie. I felt sort of glad she was full up. After a few minutes of trying she put the phone down and informed us that there were vacancies at a place called The Hunter's Rest about a mile down the road.

"It's after the fourth bend on your right," she said. "Or is it the fifth? And you'll have to go up a dirty oul lane to get to it. There's a sign telling you where the turn is. Serilda Doherty's the name of the woman but she gets Serilda the Mount here because there's so many Dohertys around."

"Thanks," I said. "I'm very much obliged."

"And don't be surprised if the guards arrive when you're there. She's got a drink licence and she runs an open bar and that doesn't mean the drink's free."

"Don't go there even if you're stuck." This from a wizened old guy that had just paused precariously in the act of tottering down a flight of stairs to the side of us. "She's an evil bitch" he rasped and promptly took a fierce fit of coughing. The old timer looked as if another clean shirt would do him.

"You'll have to excuse Rocky," the lady said. "Rocky's my husband. Rocky doesn't like her. Isn't that right Rocky? This is Rocky by the way."

"And neither does anybody else." Having said his piece the old gent turned on his heel and staggered gasping back up the stairs.

"I must go now if you don't mind," she said. "I'm in for the talent competition that's on in the Ballyliffin Hotel and my man has to hold the fort here. That's why he's so mad."

"What kind of songs do you sing?" I asked.

"Well, I don't really sing, except *Let's Get It On* to open my act. You know, the Marvin Gaye one. I do stand-up."

"Gosh," said Isabella. "That's terrific."

The Goth gave her a scary smile. "Thanks Darling. Anyway, must fly."

+++++

A mizzle started as we left Crabtree Lodge. "There's the rain now," I said. "Didn't I tell you? It probably won't stop for a week."

The Hunter's Rest was a patchwork sort of place the size of two houses and parts of it looked hundreds of years old. It had two crumbly chimneys on one side of the roof and a modern one on the other side and four newly fitted front dormer windows and there was dirty grey pebbledash all over its facade. When we were waiting for somebody to come to the door, Isabella said "Isn't it funny that old man being called Rocky?"

"Maybe he's called that because he's not too good on his feet," I said.

She laughed. "And so many people called Doherty too."

"That's right. And McLaughlin. From what I know, there's hardly anybody from down around here that's not called Doherty or McLaughlin. So they get nicknames. There used to be a pharmacist in Carndonagh on down the road that was known as Mary Teresa the Painter because her grandfather was an interior decorator, and somebody told me one time there was a doctor they called Paddy the Shoe because his great grandfather was a shoemaker. It seems odd when you're not from here."

Serilda Doherty greeted us in an offhand sort of way. She was a tall statuesque woman with short metallic blonde hair cropped like a boy's and she smelled like a bombed-out perfume factory. She wore a short tight revealing blue dress that I'd guess was made for someone thirty years younger and two stone lighter. I heard an intake of breath from Isabella and guessed that she liked what she saw, but my own impression was that our prospective hostess might just be anybody's for two large gins and a chicken curry; though it's possible, I suppose, that I was influenced by the alias the Crabtree woman had told us about.

"Now," she said, talking to me but looking at Isabella. "I only have the one room left though it does have its own en suite bathroom. Is this your daughter?"

Isabella and I replied at the same time.

"Yes," she said.

"Granddaughter," I said.

"So ... you'd better come in then."

"My granddaughter likes to make me younger than I am," I said hoarsely as we followed her into the wide hallway, walls alive with flocks of flying ducks.

"Whatever," said Serilda. "So the room has a double and a single bed. That's all I can offer. Bed and breakfast forty-five euro each. Choice of Irish or continental beginning eleven thirty am."

I looked at Isabella and she was smiling cheerfully at me and nodding hard. She had painted her lips with some kind of purple gloss. When had she put that on? In the middle of several missed heartbeats I said, in as controlled a voice as I could: "I think we're both in agreement. This should do us all right."

"OK." She flashed a business smile, disclosing yellow gums. "Now, if you'd just bring in your luggage? I'll show you to your room, and when you're settled you can go and make yourself a cup of tea in the kitchen and then you're more than welcome to use my bar. Don't be afraid to come in and enjoy the crack. And by the way, my bedroom is next to yours, so if there's anything you need during the night don't be afraid to shout."

+++++

"Did you hear her?" said Isabella. "She serves drugs. Imagine."

"The double bed looked more like king-size to me but the single bed was very narrow. ("I'll take that," she insisted. "You're bigger than me.") A dark brown candlewick spread lay rather untidily on the large bed and a small yellow-stained duvet covered the single bed. Beige lampshades with missing tassels sat on the bedside tables.

There were two grimy and quite shocking reproductions hanging above the bigger bed. I knew the one on the left well and the one on the right even better. The one on the left was a sketch by an inspired artist I'd studied called Gustave Witkowski of a naked man sodomising another naked man with his hand, a procedure that youthful research had told me goes by the name of fisting. The other one I remembered from my well-fingered copy of *Michelangelo: The Last Judgement - A Glorious Restoration* and it showed a naked man being dragged into hell by the testicles.

The bold Serilda was living up, or down - depending on what way you want to look at it - to my estimation of her. A homophobe too, obviously. But what a preposterous pair of pictures to have in the bedroom of a guesthouse. Isabella didn't seem to have noticed them.

"What do you mean, drugs?" I said. "Here, you use the built-in wardrobe. I can put any clothes I want over this armchair."

"We could share if you want," she said. "It's really big. Did you not hear her? They're using crack. It's no wonder those other two don't like her. Maybe they're jealous." She smiled. The gloss on her lips shone under the bare ceiling bulb.

"No, the kind of crack she's on about is something else completely," I said.

"What?"

"It mostly means good company. That's what it means in Ireland anyway."

"Oh." Was that a disappointed oh? Maybe just surprised. "I like that name. The Hunter's Rest. A place where men go after they've been out hunting all day."

"Could be. You know, there's something about the name that's been bugging me. It's as if I was here one time away back. Or maybe I read about it in some tourist guide."

"But what about her name?" she said. "Serilda? It's a funny one, isn't it? I've never heard it before."

"I have. I don't remember a lot of things too well anymore but I'm pretty sure it's a Teutonic name for a maiden in battle armour."

"That's her all right!" said Isabella. "Except she doesn't need battle armour. But she's very glamorous, isn't she? What's Teutonic?"

"It's funny you ask that," I said, "because the Teuton people originated in your country."

"In Denmark?"

"Yes, away before Christ. This story may be apocryphal, but I've read that when the Romans defeated the Teutons in battle, three hundred of the Teutonic women were to become sex slaves to the Roman top brass, but rather than do that they committed mass suicide."

Isabella giggled. "I can't imagine Serilda doing that. She'd probably be first in the queue." She had the grace to blush then and quickly got back to the subject. "You know so much Lllllexie, you really do. How do you store it all?"

"I've this little chip here in my head you see," I said, aware that she was looking at me admiringly. This excited me in ways I will not describe right now. "Actually, my memory has been slipping lately. It used to be nearly photographic, you know, when I was young."

"But you *are* young," she said. "You're younger than any of the dumb boys I've ever known." She opened her suitcase. "I'm going to put on another outfit. I only brought four with me and this is my last one."

"That's all right. I'll go down to the bar while you're changing. You can follow on. Is that OK?"

"No no. I'll change right now in the bathroom. I'm going to have a quick shower first. I'll only be ten minutes. Don't you dare go down there on your own." She grabbed some things from the suitcase and made to go past me. She was excited and happy. Her high heels suddenly seemed too high for her, making her step sound more coltish than ever.

I touched her elbow as she came close. She looked up at me expectantly, eyes dancing. "I've been thinking," I said, looking at a place on the wall behind her head. "It's not right that you and I sleep in the same bedroom. It's just ... what I mean is ... we should leave now and drive on to Carndonagh. It's only a few miles away and there are bound to be guest houses with separate rooms there. Let's just go. Serilda doesn't need to know a thing. We haven't even told her our names or signed anything."

"Why do you want separate rooms? Do you snore?" she said. "I'll bet you snore."

"I do. Terribly. But you know what I mean Isabella. It wouldn't be right."

She pressed her hand on the back of mine. "There's nobody I'd rather sleep in the same room with.

And in case you think I'm thinking something else, I know you won't take advantage of me. Anyway, I wouldn't miss the crack down there for anything."

"OK. No alcohol Isabella. You made the resolution, remember?"

She smiled, leaned forward and kissed my cheek. "No alcohol. I remember."

"I'm your guardian for as long as you're here, no matter how long that is."

"You're my guardian angel, Lllllexie. And I want to be here for a long, long time." She blinked and the blue in her eyes took on a different look. "The Hunter's Rest. It's a funny name, isn't it?"

She took her hand from mine and turned her back to me. My eyes strayed automatically to her little behind that seemed to give an extra wiggle just for me as she rounded the corner into the bathroom.

+++++

"How do I look?"

I'd seen near enough the same outfit on other nymphets online and knew what it had done to me, so I kept a tight rein, just smiled and nodded, not trusting myself to speak at first. She had on what to the best of my memory are called Saturday denim shorts and under them a pair of dark grey leggings. On top she wore a short, sleeveless, translucent, cream blouse with low neckline and soft white bra underneath, a bow below the breast and below that her bare midriff.

Leaving aside the blouse and pale brown cleavage and tummy and mind-blowing navel for now, but not for long, the inexplicable thing about the combination below her waist is that it wasn't just twice as titillating as denim shorts with bare legs or dark grey leggings without the shorts. It was a hundred times – no, make that beyond infinitely – more titillating.

So I sat on the big bed and looked and looked and finally (after five seconds? ten seconds? half a minute?) said in as natural a voice as I could muster: "You look enchanting Isabella. That's a lovely blouse. And I really like your leggings. What colour would you say those shorts are by the way?"

"Pacific indigo," she replied brightly, eyes alive with mischief. "Do you like them? You said you liked my blouse and leggings but you didn't say you liked my shorts. I adore them."

So did I. But I made a show of slow deliberation while sitting rigid on the edge of the bed eyeing them with carnal care. They caressed her little crotch as snugly as anybody could have wished and I had a sudden madman urge to rush forward and bury my face in her lap. This is beyond the beyond, I thought, and this is the girl that wants to be a boy. *Sacre Coeur!*

Say something. *Any*thing. "I think I would have preferred them lighter, but you know better than me Isabella."

"Oh," she said, pretending a scowl, "You're quite the connoisseur. I'll have to watch what I wear from now on when you're around." And then to make it clear she was only fooling she came over to me, put her arms tightly around my waist and rested the side of her head on my chest, just as any young girl might have done with her doting grandfather. Only this grandfather was but one more guileless move of hers away from exploding.

+++++

The bar was a big barn of a place and wasn't exactly buzzing. Seven silent heads turned to look at us and then turned away. Half a dozen men and one woman around three separate tables and not a sound out of them. And Serilda behind the bar washing away at glasses and whistling for all she was worth. Just to show that the crack was good.

"What'll you have?" she drawled.

"Ah, let me see. What would you like Isabella?"

"I'll have a ginger beer. Non-alcoholic please."

"Ginger beer. And I'll have a Cabernet Sauvignon thanks."

"On their way. Jeest you sit down there with your young lady and I'll bring them over," indicating a collection of empty tables.

We sat and waited and after five minutes the drinks weren't forthcoming. Serilda went on whistling and washing glasses and placing them carefully upside down to the side of her with a lit cigarette dangling out of the middle of her lips.

"Dinny, why don't you tell them about bringing your German shepherd to that vet in Clonmany, what do you call him, Manny McCausland?" said somebody.

"You talking to me?" said the man that must have been Dinny.

"Well now I'm not talking to the stool you're on. Who the fook do ye think I'm talking to?"

"Aye, right then. Quiet that crowd then and I'll tell them."

The man beside him addressed the silent drinkers. "Wheest there a minute would yeez till yeez hear about

Dinny taking the German shepherd to Manny McCausland."

"Well," said Dinny, then cleared his throat and spat on the floor, "as yeez know, I used to have a German shepherd name o' Shep that had a bad turn in his eye, and I was getting a bit worried about him, ye see, that he'd be seeing two sheep instead of one or a hundred sheep instead of fifty even. So this day anyways, I took him out to see Manny. Well, I toul Manny what the matter was – not that he couldn't see for hisself – and he come over and lifted Shep up in his arms so he did and looked him square in the bad eye. He held him that way for a right good while and then he turned round to me.

"'Dinny,' he sez, 'Dinny me boy, I think I'm going to have to put him down' and I sez 'Jesus Christ - God forgive me, and His Blessed Mother Mary for using His holy name in vain - but are you telling me you're going to put him down just because he's cross-eyed?' 'No,' sez Manny. 'He's too heavy.'"

The only reaction to this, not counting a loud giggle from Isabella, was from a heavy-shouldered, black-clad man in a cloth cap sitting near us that had the look of an off-duty undertaker.

"Aye, that would be the Manny that was all for Charlie Haughey."

"And what of it?" growled Dinny. "D'you see you Peadar? D'you wannae know what's wrong wae you?"

"What?" defiantly.

"You're bitter, that's what's wrong wae you. You're bitter. No man ever done more for the small shopkeeper in Donegal than Charlie Haughey."

"How come you're supporting the small shopkeeper all of a sudden?" shouted Peadar. "Wasn't it you that got barred from Joe Toye's shop in Carndonagh for calling him a right fooker? And Dick Marner nearly had a fight with you for squeezing his gooseberries? Going to send for the fooking guards and all so he was."

"Who's Charlie Haughey?" whispered Isabella. "And why are we not getting our drinks?"

"He was the Prime Minister of the Republic about thirty years ago, and I don't know why we're not getting our drinks."

"The poitín republic?"

"No, sure that was way back. The Republic of Ireland. The whole country."

"Here yeez are. That'll be nine euro sixty-five." Serilda left the drinks down heavily on our table and stood waiting, hands on hips. The top three-quarters or maybe more of her right nipple had come out and was showing dark purple above the neckline, not exactly the most erotic sight I've ever seen. I guessed the minor wardrobe malfunction must have happened during the vigorous washing up she'd been doing. Either that or she planned to lift her turnover by holding on to the males in the bar for as long as she could. I gave her ten euro and thanked her and told her to keep the change whereupon she returned wordlessly to her place behind the bar.

Peadar was looking as if he was fit to be held. "And what the fook would you know anyway about the small shopkeeper? Nothing! That's just a thing Haughey's tribe learned off like the two-times table."

"Ha!" shouted Dinny. "Sure, all your crowd was useless, charging big tax on children's shoes and letting them go to school in their bare feet. Charlie Haughey had the common touch so he had. Didn't he anchor his yacht off Leenan Bay and let a whole lock of fishermen come aboard for drinks didn't he?"

"Aye!" snorted Peadar. "Schemy bastard."

There came the sound of a rolling glass and Serilda marched out to the middle of the floor, nipple and all. "I'll thank you to keep a clean tongue in your head Peadar Tobin. We'll not have that kind of language here."

"Sorry Serilda, me tongue slipped." He turned back to Dinny. "As I was saying there, Haughey was nothing but a schemy basket. Didn't he know what would get into the papers and stupid fishermen going on about it on the TV? But tell us this now and tell us no more. Where did he get the money to buy a yacht like that? Half a million wouldn't look at it. How the fook could he afford a thing like that on his pay? And his island and his big mansion and his fooking racehorses and his bank accounts in the Gaymen Islands."

"What did you call that yacht anyway?" said Serilda. "*Irish Mist* wasn't it?"

"Aye, Irish mist," said Peadar. "The Irish missed a trick all right when they elected thon boy. Embezzled the whole fooking country so he did."

"Them were stories put out by your excuse for a party," countered Dinny. "The man worked for every cent."

"Stories put out? What about his Jarvey shirts from gay Paree and his island off Kerry and his big ranch in Kinsealy. What about them, eh?"

"Charvet," I said.

Suddenly everybody seemed to be staring at me and a woman's voice from somewhere said "What? Who in under fook's that?"

"Sorry," I said. "I was just saying. The shirts he got from Paris were Charvet shirts."

There was a silence that went on for a bit before the knockabout got under way again, and the company seemed to have forgotten about me except for one man with the jaw of a horse and a dour look about him that kept eyeing me suspiciously for a while. Isabella whispered "This all happened thirty years ago, didn't it? Why are they arguing about that now?"

"Wait till they get to the civil war," I said.

"What civil war?"

"The one we had here nearly a century ago."

It was clear from the look of him that Dinny was far from finished. He half stood and shouted: "Your bleddy crowd had nobody to come near him. The man could charm the knickers off of a nun, sorry Serilda, I meant tae say the birds off of the trees. Common touch you see."

"I heard," said a blue-chinned individual wearing a beat-out Crombie, "that Maggie Thatcher fancied him like mad."

"Swept her off her fooking feet so he did Philip," said Peadar. "She had him at Chequers and it wasn't chequers she was looking to play either, the ugly gurrier."

"I heard he slept with her once," said the Crombie man darkly.

"But no impropriety occurred," I whispered.

Isabella folded forward with silent laughter and her head hit the table.

"You OK?" I asked.

Her head was still down. I put my hand on her shoulder and felt the naked heat of it. *Oh mio Dio.* She sat upright again and looked up at me, eyes dancing. She loved being here with me.

"But wait till I tell yeez now what happened back in nineteen-eighty," Peadar said. "Onced back in nineteen-eighty I was out there in Clonmany starting me day selling ice cream. Yeez might member I got a secondy-hand ice-cream van for a snip and I called it The Dixie Pixie Ice Cream Heaven – d'yeez member? – and sold the stuff in the street in Clonmany.

"Well, this day anyways, the sun was splitting the rocks and I parked me van down near Comiskey's shop and was all set to do a roaring trade when these two big fancy limos rolled up and the bold Haughey and a crowd of other gangsters that looked like they'd just robbed Savile Row stepped out and stood waiting; and then these tribesmen left off beating their drums and come down from the hills wae this lorry and a fooking sound system, would you believe, and what did they do but park the whole fooking shebang right in front of me and me van.

"And you wanted to see the tan Haughey and the other crooks had on them. I'll tell yeez wan thing now. They nivir got a tan like that in Ireland nor they niver got it out of a bottle either. Anyways, nixt thing these fookers were sitting up on the back of the lorry taking turns tae spout shite out of microphones, sorry Serilda, spout crepe and them with their bellies hanging out over the tops of their trousers."

"I mind that day too," said the woman customer. She had a face like raw meat and yellow pustules growing out of her forehead and was all happed up with a big heavy black overcoat accessorised with a thick brown scarf round the top of her head. "I was there wae me three weans and I was going to buy them some of your pokes Peadar but we couldn't git near the van. The thing was all blocked off."

"Right first time Miriam," said Peadar. "But wait till yeez hear what happened. These boys started speechifying about us in Donegal having to tighten our belts if we wanted to get through these bad times – could yeez credit it? – cause we were living way above our means and if any of them on the lorry had tried to tighten their belts they'd have fooking exploded so they would, and that basket Haughey was sitting on a big green cushion chair at wan end of the lorry and he was the boy was creaming millions off of the whole country so's he could live in the lap of luxury."

"Tell us this Peadar," said Dinny. "Is there an election coming up, is there?"

"What?" said Peadar. "Not that I know of."

"Well I'm thinking there must be, with you coming out with your properganda. And here's something now I want to ask you, you being a Clonmany man and all."

"I am that," said Peadar, "and proud of it."

"Well then," said Dinny. "See if you can tell us the answer to this one. What would you call a Clonmany man with two sheep?"

"What?" shouted Peadar.

"A pimp," said Dinny.

"You shut your gob till I get finishing, you dirty wee scut," shouted Peadar and then turned to address the rest of the company. "I was telling yeez anyway. There was this man with a face like a rat and a fedora on his head that musta set him back a hundred euro up there on the lorry that seemed to be running the show, and I managed to get him by the turn-up of his Alexander

McQueens and toul him about Dixie Pixie Ice Cream Heaven being blocked off and could he get the lorry moved about ten feet please and the dirty munt turned round and toul me to go fook meself."

"He didn't say that did he?" said Miriam, coughing disbelievingly.

"Sure wasn't it me he said it to, Miriam, except fook wasn't the word he used."

"Shocking," said Serilda, hoisting up her bodice whereupon the nipple withdrew. "That's shocking. I'll never vote for Haughey's crowd again. Not that I ever did mind you."

"And right too," agreed Peadar. "But wait till yeez hear what happened after. I crawled under the lorry on me belly to get to the far end because I knew Charlie Haughey was over on that side with his fat arse on the big green cushion. And when I got there I sez to him 'Excuse me Mister Haughey' – basket and all as he was, I had to let on to show a bit of respect – 'excuse me Mister Haughey' and then I toul him me situation and I toul him as well that the other man had toul me to go fook myself, and Haughey looked me straight in the eye and he sez: "Well, I fooking second that."

There was a big throaty laugh from Dinny. "Serves you right, starfooker. You're nothing but a West Briton. Bleddy freestater."

Peadar half-rose and shoved his chair back. "D'you wannae go outside and repeat that, Master Dinny? Because if you do, you're a dead man and if you don't you're a coward."

Dinny shot back "You couldn't bate snow off of a rope, eejit. Sit down and catch yourself on Mister Softee."

Serilda flounced out from behind the bar. "That's enough out of yous two. I'm not going to have any political argyfying in The Hunter's Rest. It's not befitting so it's not. Yeez would be far better off ordering a drink instead of all that carry on." She pointed a nicotine-nailed finger at Dinny. "And d'you see you, Dinny Doherty? You've been sitting there this two hours with a half pint of Guinness in front of you that's as flat as a flipping pancake and you're not even halfway down it."

"I agree with you Serilda," said Philip. "We can argue till we're blue in the face and it won't change fook all. It's these fooking Europeans that's the problem. They're picking our pockets so they are. Them and their fooking bankers. Sure, look what they did to the price of wool. It's gone to pot."

"What's the price of wool got to do with anything?" shouted Peadar. "I cannae even sell me house now. There isn't a gypsy in Donegal would give me his caravan for it. The fooking thing's hardly worth a cent since Haughey's crowd did the deal with the fooking Europeans away back in ... when was it?"

"Och, I cannae mind. Sure our house is the same," said Philip. "I'm thinking of heading over to England nixt week agin. There's supposed to be plenty of building there now. And the Brits are getting shot of Myrtle and the fooking bankers and bondfookers too. We all got fooked by them crowd of basketing gamblers the time we got near drownded in the Irish fooking Sea, when was it, ten fooking years ago now, and we're still paying to bail the fookers out. D'you see –"

"Mind your language Philip," hissed Serilda.

"Sorry Serilda."

"Who's Myrtle anyway? said Peadar. "D'you mean Merkel? Is it Merkel you mean? The woman's name is Merkel."

"Merkel. Berkel. You know who I'm on about."

Isabella leaned her head towards me and shook with quiet laughter. I inclined mine to meet hers. "I'm glad they've stopped argyfying about politics," she whispered.

"Would yeez stop that now," shouted Serilda. "This gentleman and his young lady are laughing at yeez. Would you like another drink sir?"

I looked up at Serilda and straightened my face. "Just a ginger beer. Is that all right Isabella? Just a ginger beer thanks. I'll pass this time."

"Right," said our hostess. "Who else then?"

There was a scraping of chairs and Miriam said "Same again too for me and Willie. Wait. Make mine a double."

"Anybody else? I'll be closing the bar and turfing yeez out if yeez don't pay your ways."

Two more called for drinks. And suddenly there seemed to be a miraculous meeting of minds between the two main protagonists. "I'll tell yeez something now about that bucking Brexit," said Dinny, and Peadar nodding like mad behind him. "Brexit wrecks it. Them fooking Tories over there in England are going tae bring us all to wreck and ruination. Sure, there'll be no trade worth talking about. Them boys are going tae leave us wae food banks on every bleddy road in Ireland."

"Well now," said Peadar. "That's wan thing you're right about. The Tories is going down the tubes and they're going tae bring us down wae them. Brexit is Brexshit!"

“Fook Brexittania!” came a shout.

Isabella put her lips to my ear and whispered “I have to go to the ladies’. Where is it, do you know?”

“I think it must be that door down at the back on the right. Do you see it?”

She nodded and got up. As she walked her gamine walk I viewed with half-closed eyes the concave curve of her little spine. *Ma beauté maladroite.* That way she had sometimes of arching her body forward filled me with thoughts I shouldn’t have had. I quickly found myself imagining her standing for my inspection wearing nothing but a mini-nightie and just as quickly tried to put the picture out of my head.

It was a short distance to the toilet but my eyes still had just enough time to settle on the faded seat of her little denims and my head began to swim. Christ but she’s something. She’s streets ahead of even the teenagers that used to be, when so many of the girls seemed to be slender and feminine. We can live in a quiet little flat somewhere well outside of Derry where tongues won’t wag, and we’ll talk books into the night and I’ll give her intensive coaching if that’s what she really wants. One-to-one seminars. What’s the name some in the university have for them now? Hands-on seminars.

Yes. I’ll visit Henry often and pay for day and night carers. But what about me? How long before the final enchantment sets in and I don’t know who the hell I am anymore? Which reminds me, I must get Henry tested. I keep forgetting. And then the day will come when Isabella ups and leaves me and we’re just what are called good friends, and I’ll be able to take it because by that time she’ll be past the nymphet stage and she’ll have a new life in front of her with whoever and however many she decides. And that's as it should be.

When she was pushing the toilet door open, she suddenly turned right around and smiled straight at me. I tried to return it but all I could manage was the ghost of a nod. Because she had seen me looking where I was looking. And she still smiled. A radiant smile, innocent, open, but half-knowing at the same time I'd say.

And then would you believe it, as sure as I'd been watching her I got a feeling that somebody else was watching me. Serilda. Bitch. I looked sideways at her for long enough to tell me she had taken it all in. Yes, she had taken it all in and read me like a dirty book. I looked at her again, boldly this time, passing on the thought "what business is it of yours in your glass house?" but far from being disconcerted she thought back: "you're nothing but a filthy, filthy old man, don't think I don't know." It would take a lot to ruffle that one. And I wouldn't put it past her to have two sets of eyeholes in the Witkowski picture above my bed, one in the giver and one in the given.

Isabella came back as Serilda was serving the drinks and calling for a song. "Come on now Miriam. These men haven't a note between them. Give us *The Short Cut to the Rosses* wouldn't you."

Miriam barked out a cough. "Sure me voice is destroyed wae the bronchitis," she said. "I couldn't sing if you paid me."

"Not much danger of that one getting paid anyway," said Philip *sotto voce*.

Serilda looked at me. "What about you, sir, or your young lady? Can any of you two sing?"

I shook my head modestly. Serilda gave Isabella what was meant I think to be a warm look. "How's about you dear? Would you not set the ball rolling? Once these boys get somebody to start them, there'll be no shutting them up you know."

"He can sing," said Isabella, looking at me. "Can't you? Remember?"

Beautiful Dreamer. Yes, I remembered. And I remembered the time she sang too. I leaned to her ear and whispered "And so can you. Remember Lisfannon?"

I didn't think she was going to do it but she did. She kept her head down and suddenly began singing with the same amazing grace and in the same sweet voice that had set my senses racing as I sped down that hill to Lisfannon. How long ago was that? Sixty hours, give or take. How long ago that was!

Moon river, wider than a mile
I'm crossin' you in style some day.
Oh dream maker, you heart breaker,
Wherever you're goin', I'm goin' your way.

Two drifters, off to see the world,
There's such a lot of world to see.
We're after that same rainbow's end,
waiting 'round the bend,
My huckleberry friend,
Moon river and me.

Before she got to the end of her first line there was silence in the room, not a breath, not a whisper, not a bark. And when it was over, too soon, nobody applauded except for me. What sort of people are these? After a few seconds I stopped, embarrassed.

"Well now, that was very short," said Serilda. "You've got a good little voice Miss. But how about your gentleman friend? Can he not sing?"

"Maybe when someone else does," I said. "Maybe I'll have a go then." But I was already rehearsing melodies in my head. Then without introduction, Philip sang *God Save Ireland*, and as soon as he finished Dinny sang *Wrap The Green Flag Round Me* and then Peadar sang *The Boys of the Old Brigade*, and by that time the drink had started to flow and the rafters were rattling and I'd have been hard put to get a note in edgeways, even if I'd wanted to. Clearly a truce had been called.

And then when Serilda was coaxing Dinny to sing *The Fields of Athenry* and he was humming and hawing so as to get a bit more coaxing out of her, I thought I should explain the background of the song to Isabella. Because it's such a beautiful composition, and to appreciate it she should know something about Ireland's famines, about the potato blight and the million or more that died and the millions that emigrated.

So I told her quickly and then gave her a rundown of the song. And when Dinny did finally sing it, in tones as clear and heartfelt as you could find anywhere, her dark lashes went wet with tears. She held my hand under the table and didn't speak. Then without preamble I followed Dinny with *The West's Awake* and it went down well.

Before we left for bed I drank a pint of water to try and rehydrate, realising too late that between the water and the prostate I'd probably be in and out of the toilet for half the night.

+++++

I was reading in the dark.

This early novel by The Marquis de Sade tells the story of Justine, a beautiful and trusting twelve year-old girl who sets out to make her way in revolutionary France. On her journey she suffers a series of rapes by hypocritical men. Some of these occur after she goes to Confession in a monastery where she has sought refuge. Here she is forced to become a sex slave to the monks who subject her to countless sadistic orgies. After she escapes from the monastery she helps a gentleman who has been attacked and robbed in a field. To show his gratitude he takes her back to his chateau and promises her paid work caring for his ailing wife, but then imprisons her in a cave where he ravishes and beats her repeatedly. As the novella nears its climax Justine finds herself facing the death penalty when she stands in court begging the judge for mercy after being found guilty of theft and arson.

"Denise."

Damn. I switched off the torch and lay still.

"I know you're awake Denise. Why won't you speak to me?"

She's dreaming. The beautiful dreamer is dreaming and I could do without it. She was crying in her sleep when I came back from the bathroom and now she's dreaming. I can't even get bloody reading and anyway I should have been asleep an hour ago. But that crowd are still singing their rebel hearts out and I've a two-hundred mile round drive ahead of me and I have to talk to the father and then face her afterwards. Why in God's name didn't I drive on to Carndonagh?

"I love you, Denise."

I'd do a quiet diddle that might put me over only it would be just my luck she'd waken up in the middle of it and know what I'm at and she'd be filled with revulsion and I don't think I could survive the looks she'd give me till the moment they leave and she'd never want to see me again. But I suppose that might be the best for everybody.

To hell with it anyway. I put *Justine* and the torch on the bedside locker and slipped off my Babydolls and thong and did a U-turn and put one of the pillows under me and hoped the bed wouldn't waken her. Then to give myself a good kick start I thought of Gustave Witkowski's masterwork looking down on me. And that's when her lamp came on and suddenly she was standing right there at my bed.

"Please don't do that Denise. You don't have to do that."

I turned over and looked up. Her long hair, silver in the sudden light, half covered her face and hung all rumpled down one side of her. She was partly in silhouette and leaning over me and I could see the dark purple on her underlip.

"You're asleep Isabella. Just go back and lie down now."

"I'm not asleep."

"Then why are you calling me Denise?"

"Because that's who you are. You are Denise."

"You're shivering Isabella. Go back to bed. You've a long journey ahead of you tomorrow."

"I can't sleep. My bed's cold. I think it might be damp too. Can I lie in this bed? I'll never be able to sleep if I don't."

"Of course. You can if you want. I'll sleep in your bed. Here, wait till I get –"

"No. That bed will make you sick. You'll get pneumonia. Is your bed dry?"

"Yes."

"I'll soon warm up then. Can I lie on the part of it you're lying on?"

"If that's what you really want."

"That's what I really want. Let me in quick. Please. I'm frozen."

I scrabbled for my Babydolls and thong and had them nearly on by the time she'd got in. I shifted to the far end of the bed pulling the pillow up from under me. The undersheet was like ice. The crowd below were starting another song. I hoped this one would be their parting number.

When boyhood's fire was in my blood (they roared)
I read of ancient freemen
When Greece and Rome who bravely stood
Three hundred men and three men
And then I prayed I might yet see
Our fetters rent in twain
And Ireland, long a province, be
A nation once again.

A nation once again, a nation once again
And Ireland, long a province, be a nation once again.

"Oh this is lovely. This is like heaven. I think I'll sleep now. What are they singing?"

"It's an Irish rebel song. The rivals seem to have set aside their differences in the face of the common enemy across the Irish Sea."

"You're funny, Lllllexie. Oh it's so cosy in here."

"That's great." I could smell her. She was at least two feet away from me and I could smell her. I knew that aroma. It was a particularly pungent one that I recalled from being on a school bus that I flagged down in desperation one flashflooding day shortly after the heavens opened and the driver took pity on me and stopped.

And the heavens truly did open that day for this middle-aged celibate pervert breathlessly ensconced for twenty steaming minutes with what seemed like fifty or more second and third year girls from Saint Philomena's, at least a quarter of whom were crammed together with me in the blessed aisle. Two girls offered me their seats, I remember, but I waved them away with a weak smile. Anyway, that was the smell. To be honest it was a blend that wasn't without its drawbacks, but the overriding effect was like some kind of a hormone thing that got me both in the area of the groin and at the back of the throat, from their pores I think, or maidenhair was it? To do with their cycles or the full moon maybe. Christ knows. My memory isn't the best these days but I seem to remember from the time I used to read religiously about these things that pubescent girls' hormones go absolutely haywire sometimes and their testosterone can leave a man's for dead, *O Dio Onnipotente.*

"Do you know how I knew you were Denise?"

I didn't speak. I drew my knees up to my chest. God but it's cold.

"Do you know how I knew?

I didn't answer.

"One of the things happened up at Grianan fort and the other one happened on Dunree beach."

"What do you mean?"

"At Dunree you knew the joke Denise and me had about King Cnutcase."

"Oh. I must have sneaked a look at her computer then."

"And the other thing was at Grianan when you said you found the bit of paper with the handwritten love poem on it between two stones of the fort. Remember? *My heart would hear you and beat.* Remember?"

"What about it?"

"It was your handwriting."

"My handwriting? What makes you say that?"

"I was beside you in the hotel when you wrote your name and address at reception."

"Are you a handwriting expert then?" (cried the rumbled old rat).

"No, but nobody else could write like you. You've got a really cool style of writing. And do you want to know what that poem told me?"

"No, tell me."

"It told me that you loved me. I think you fell in love with me at first sight. That poem was from you to me, wasn't it?"

I was so busy working on how to wriggle my way out that I didn't respond at first.

"Wasn't it? Answer me. Please."

"Did it not occur to you," I said, and I could hear my voice thudding inside of me, "that maybe I was seeing you as an object? You're very beautiful after all. What a girl thinks of as love from someone else might not be love at all. And apart from all that, you're out of my league Isabella. Look at your age and look at my age. It's preposterous. It doesn't make sense. And don't be thinking it does."

"It does. It does make sense. It makes sense to me. And I would love being your object. You're a man, aren't you? You like looking at girls. I'm so flattered you think I'm beautiful. If you told me to my face that I was the object of your love as well as ... as well as ... as well as ... that, then I'd be the happiest person in the world. Did you not know that girls my age fancy older men like crazy?"

"Yes, but there's older and then there's really old." How do I stop this heart going off the scale? She wants to make love, a blind man could see that. She wants to make love and I'm not up to it. I'd need some kind of a splint for God's sake. "Listen Isabella. I know what I'm talking about. This is infatuation. It used to happen to me all the time when I was your age. You can't possibly love me. You've known me for less than three days for heaven's sake. It'll pass. Please believe me."

"Don't you be talking down to me! How do you know what I can and can't feel? You're not me! And what does time matter anyway?" I could hear the tears now. And she seemed to have got closer, so close I could have reached out and pulled her under me. She'd let me take off that pink pyjama top, of course she would, and then, then there'd be no stopping.

"But you have to see it Isabella. I'm an old man and you're a young girl. You should be having crushes on boys your own age."

"I had crushes and the boys were all so immature. And mean. All they wanted was to use you and boast about it and get pictures of you with no clothes on and show them around. Boys are useless. And you're not an old man. You're middle-aged and I love that. You're experienced and clever, but you never once talked down to me except for that time there now and you explain things so brilliantly and you're the funniest man I ever met. And I never told you before but you have the most gorgeous brown eyes. Like Orlando Bloom's. And Jeremy Corbyn's."

"His are green," I said. "Jeremy Corbyn's are green."

"Are they? I thought they were brown. Who else? Yes, Colin Farrell's. Colin Farrell's. And ... and do you want to know where I fell in love with you?"

She's taking for granted I'll be able to do it. But I won't. I know what's going to happen.

"Are you listening? Denise, are you listening? Do you want to know where I fell in love with you? I fell in love with you in that pub on the way from the airport."

"*The Ponderosa*."

"Yes, *The Ponderosa*. I knew then. I read one time that it can happen just like that with some people. I knew right away I wanted to talk to you and listen to you forever."

"But how could you know? You're only fifteen for heaven's sake. How could you know?"

"Sixteen. I'm sixteen. I told you before."

"You told Denise you were fifteen."

She didn't respond at first. Then she giggled and reached over and shook me by the shoulder and I smelt something oniony. Christ, don't tell me that's what it was all the time. Did she have fried onions in The Rusty Nail?

"You caught me out, Denise. It's my turn to be caught out."

"Don't call me Denise, Isabella. Please."

"All right. Lllllexie then. Is your name really Lllllexie?" Her hand was still on my shoulder.

"Yes. Lexie."

"Why did you pretend about your son and his wife and the suicides?" She didn't sound mad, just curious. Could she be so much in thrall?

"I can't answer that."

"You mean you won't?"

"Partly. Partly both."

"Oh, Lllllexie. Why did you invite me anyway?"

"I didn't. You invited yourself, remember?"

"Oh. You're right. So I did. But Denise was so real and so sexy. And Huncan! Oh my God. How did you make them up?"

"It was a fantasy that got out of hand. I probably needed something to keep me going. I needed ... I don't know ... I needed ... company? Maybe that was it. I needed company."

"But what about your wife? And have you no sons or daughters?"

I didn't reply.

"Your shoulder feels so cold Lllllexie. Can I come over to you?"

"Yes." *O mia santa zia.*

She was beside me in a blink. "Turn round and face me. Please."

I turned and right away her arms were around my shoulders and she was all against me. Point of no return Lexie. She kissed my chin, my cheeks and my lips and I kissed her lips back. And then softly she tickled the inside of my mouth with her tongue.

"I love you Lllllexie. Oh. Your teeth. Where–? ... You have ... no top teeth. Oh my God, you have no top teeth."

What could I say?

"Lllllexie, you have no top teeth."

"That's right."

"So ... so what was it that Bastar did? I thought you said he knocked out two of your top teeth."

She was embarrassed. What I'm telling you here is, *she* was embarrassed. I said "He knocked two of the false teeth out of the plate. I have a full row of bottom teeth though" (a little white lie, *entre nous soit dit.* It's actually a bridge held in place by my last two remaining teeth, one at each end of the lower gum).

"Oh." Her legs were tighter to me now and I felt her little crotch nuzzling mine so the teeth thing clearly wasn't putting her off. I think it was at this point it came into my blazing head that she would have been just starting nursery school the summer I retired and that there were fifty-six years between us and that I was losing control and that she didn't really smell like onions anymore because what I was getting now was much closer to mackerel.

And then, maybe sensing that we might be on the verge of an accident that would put a serious damper on things, she drew back a little. That's when I began to see her better, partly lit by the bedside lamp behind her. Lying there with her warm breath on me she was more beautiful than I'd seen her at any time in the last three days. Flushed face, long chestnut hair curling dark against the lamplight, purple-stained lips, eyes dancing, elfish eyes dancing. *Dolce Gesù!*

"Wait till I do something. Do you mind if I do something?"

"I don't know," I said. "It depends what it is." What I actually meant was: you can do absolutely anything you want, my Love.

"This is something Teresa and me used to do after the Joggers had done their night patrol in the convent. We'd take it turn about to go to each other's bed when the coast was clear and we'd massage each other. It's the loveliest feeling. Do you mind if I do it on you?"

I managed to get out "No, I don't mind. Who were the Joggers?" (as if I cared).

"That's what we called the *John of God* nuns. You know, *Jay-O-Gee. John-of-God*. We called them the *Saint John of Godders* at the start but then it got changed to Joggers. They'd sort of run round the dormitories at night like they were on roller skates to make sure there was nothing funny going on, so we called them the Joggers. They were like penguins on wheels with their big long habits and you couldn't see their shoes."

She laughed, quickly disengaged herself a little more and reached down to the hem of my Babydolls. When she got there she momentarily touched the instep of my right foot which sent some kind of charge through me. She then moved her fingers slowly and gently up my right leg.

"You're so tense Lllllexie. Try and relax. This is what we did to each other. First the shins, then the knees.

Remember, you'll have to do it to me after – oh dear, what's that on your leg? What are those? Oh dear."

"What?" She was running her fingers through the hairs of my shin and I felt as though I was on fire and every ounce of blood was heading for the one place. *Grands serpents en vie!* Maybe I can do it after all. If I can only just time it right.

"It's like lumps under your skin. What are they?"

"Ah, those are varicose veins. Some people get them."

"But that's terrible. Poor Lllllexie."

She fingered the lumps tenderly for a few seconds and then seemed to dismiss them as she headed further north. But almost immediately she stopped. After a short hesitation she said matter-of-factly "Can you take off your jammy bottoms please Lllllexie? I can't get to your knee properly. These bottoms are too tight."

Hold on, I'll have to think about that, my Dear. Like fun I will. I moved so fast I nearly slipped a disc getting them off. Slight delay pulling them over the bit of an erection I had going but I don't think she noticed.

Some of what came next is a blur, but most of it is as clear as a bright blue day. So I'm going to set down as much as I can remember, starting here. By the time she'd finished with my knees I was so far gone I hardly knew where I was. And when she wrestled my thong to my feet and pulled it roughly off and flung it on the floor, my brain felt as if it was leaving my head and she began whispering all hoarse with her tongue in my ear and I couldn't make out a fucking word she was saying.

And then as God is my witness, she got half up and knelt between my knees looking down at me and she took every last stitch off of the two of us and then lay down and drew me against her, oh Christopher, and pushed herself into me as if she was the man and kissed me hard and groped me like mad and guided my hands to particular parts of her she wanted seen to and suddenly shouted: "Do it, Lllllexie! Now! Do it now!" and I croaked back: "I don't think I'll be able to, Isabella. I haven't ..."

"You haven't what?"

"I haven't done it in years" and she rubbed her young breasts up and down aggressively on my chest and asked "How many years?" and I said "Many many" or something like that, and she cried and told me it was me and not her she was crying for, and next thing she was everywhere on me and it was nearly like being in bed with some kind of a snake if you can imagine it, and out of the blue she bit me on the John Thomas.

And then I had this amazing sensation that she had swallowed my scrotum and its contents, but she let it all out again after I don't know how long and next thing was I got her on her back till I had her spreadeagled like a starfish using my hands and elbows and knees, and then after a minute she flipped me over and did the exact same to me – think of the size of her and she did that! – and then she slid right down the front of me till her feet must have been sticking out at the bottom of the bed and that's when she made it all come with her mouth and she took in every last millilitre of it, I swear; and then she moved my fingers till she had them deep inside of her, *Geronimo!* and I heard her call my name and shout something out of her and I wish to God I could remember now what it was because whatever it was it meant she loved me but I can't and never in my whole life had I anything to compare with it all, not ever, not ever, not even those times with Henry and the love poems before the embargo.

I slept then. It must have happened very suddenly because I don't remember kissing her goodnight. And I awoke just as suddenly with my bladder about to burst and rushed naked to the bathroom. And when I finished a long and luxurious pee and went over to the mirror to admire myself (because I'd done very well considering everything) a leery old man looked out at me and I saw her breath on him again right there in the mirror and he was dipping and delving again like billy-o and of course he was getting roused as hell thinking about it.

And funny, it was then looking in at the toothless old reprobate and thinking of the sleeping girl not knowing what was in store for her this very morning that I began to get the feeling something wasn't right. Or shame was it? Was it shame I was feeling? Maybe that was it. Shame. Yes, that was it. Shame. Oh, she shared it, she shared it all right but the big share was mine.

Forget about her skin-deep innocence – for let's face it, she was never the innocent – because the real shame belonged with me. I'd had carnal knowledge of a minor and that was bad enough; but worse, much worse, I was going to have it again right now, right now again when I left the bathroom and then again and again and in every possible way with her, my schoolgirl supplicant who would look up at me always with those worshipful eyes and let me do anything I wanted.

But wait, said the man in the mirror. What are you beating yourself up for? Every minute of the day and night in some part of the developed world, there are voyeurs of all sexes posing as fashion connoisseurs sitting ogling gamine-looking girls parading their bored little bodies along the catwalk.

And another thing. While Isabella may well be a minor in British and Irish law, she has far more intellectual and emotional maturity than most twenty-year-old female undergraduates you ever dealt with. And maybe the old rake was right. So reader, fair-minded though understandably sceptical reader, bear with me while I follow this train of thought. Just give me a minute, would you?

Let's imagine Serilda the Mount had indeed defaced Witkowski's masterwork by cutting eyeholes in the faces of both the debaucher and the debauched above my bed and as a result got an eyeful of Isabella and me going at it like rabbits and decided to report me to the guards. Well, I would simply say as they slipped the handcuffs on me (**THE HUNTER'S ARREST**, the tabloids might well put it): "I'm sure you think this is a fair cop, lads. But how fair, I ask you, how fair? OK, you've got me dead to rights on the letters of the law – but these very letters, as you well know if you dally of an evening with your bit on the side, often spell out the word ASS."

And then at my trial, when the judge asks if there is anything the prisoner wishes to say before sentence is passed …

(twenty years in the slammer I reckon; I could be ninety-one when I get out. Good God. Imagine, twenty years with the ever-present possibility of being buggered day and night by my fellow inmates because of the nature of my offence. But enough of this daydreaming) …

I'd first of all remark: "Your Honour, please look at the relativity of all this. I beg you to consider the case of the much-loved David Bowie and his thrilling threesome with fourteen-year-olds Lori Lightning and Sable Starr; and remember also the brilliant bassist Bill Wyman (born William George Perks. Didn't know that till I looked him up, always thought Wyman was his real name), ex-Rolling Stone, having a sensitive and loving thing going with convent-educated Mandy Smith, fourteen, away back when he was a kid of forty-eight; and also that amazing rocker Jerry Lee Lewis – widely admired for his *Great Balls of Fire* if you recall – wedding and bedding his thirteen-year-old third cousin Myra Gale Brown who still believed in Santa Claus at the time.

"And consider also Jerry's intrepid old trailblazer Edgar Allan Poe whisking *his* cousin Virginia Clemm off on honeymoon when she also was sweet thirteen. And I have to ask you, Your Honour, did any of these gentlemen ever serve time as a result of their amorous activities? I think not.

"But I suppose we shouldn't forget that Lewis and Poe were US citizens and were in no way breaking the law there. In fact, Your Honour, there is no definitive minimum age for marriage in any of the fifty united states. You doubt me? Look it up and doubt no longer.

"This strange situation is managed by means of a trick called 'exemptions', otherwise known as parental consent, sometimes called parental coercion. For even in the case of a little girl crying her heart out while her parents sign the application form that forces her into marriage with a foul-smelling lascivious old lout who has a bit of money about him, the town hall clerk doesn't have the power to intervene. Thank you, Your Honour."

I'd gone to the bathroom in such a hurry that I hadn't noticed Isabella was back in the single bed. When? When had she switched? It didn't matter. I went over and looked down at her. She was snoring softly and her mouth lay half open. Her chestnut hair was gathered around her like a halo and her lips and upper teeth and part of one cheek were smudged a dirty purple.

I had an unsettling picture for a moment of a sleeping young harlot after a night's work and a ripple of lust ran through me. I knew I could do it right, right here, right now. And why not? I was ready. Just pull back the eiderdown. My very nakedness had made me ready. When she woke to find herself in my arms she would smile and kiss me like she did last night and hold me even tighter than I had held her, and I'd smooth her hair and we'd do it all again, only this time it would be perfect.

I went over to the dressing table and looked at my watch. Ten past ten. That gave us a full hour and twenty minutes before breakfast. But then I got this unstoppable urge to wear something sexy. Silently I put on my bedtime clothes from last night and the black silk dressing gown over them, then took the dental plate and deodorant from my suitcase and returned to the bathroom to do the needful. In less than a minute my mouth was right as rain and smiling gap-toothed at the mirror. No problem there. I knew from the morning after my experiences in room 344 that she thought I was cute without those two front teeth. Probably my body wasn't that important to her anyway, she'd only pampered it to get to my heart.

And it was then that something occurred to me. Her bed was damp. Why had she gone back to it? Had I been bothering her in my sleep? Or had she only pretended it was damp to get lying with me? Yes, that would be it. I heard a loud drawn-out half-awake yawn. No time to waste. I gave myself a quick dose of the Herban Cowboy, praying it would be enough to neutralise the stale spunk that I could still smell coming off me.

"Lllllexie."

"Yes?"

"Are you in the bathroom?" Another long yawn.

"No, I'm right here my dear," I said as I rounded the corner and went to the side of her bed. She was half sitting and rubbing the sleep from her eyes. And when she opened them wide they were avoiding mine. Her face was flushed and I could see that she was flustered. Her lips were lined and dry and she was wetting them in a hurry with the tongue that I remembered with a delicious shudder. I saw the movement of her legs under the eiderdown, now together, now apart, and I felt her thighs live in my hands again.

"Did you have a good night?" she said, rubbing her little knees together.

"Ah... wonderful my dear. What do *you* think?"

"I don't know. I think ... I think you were restless. You kept turning over and over."

I smiled, bent forward and kissed her on the forehead.

"Oh, Lllllexie." She stretched like a kitten, sat upright and tried to smile, still not looking at me. "Am I staying Lllllexie? Please tell me I'm staying."

"Of course you're staying," I said. "I would never let you go." She smiled properly this time but still didn't look at me.

"What time is it?" She humped her knees to her chest the way I'd seen her do before. Oh my God. Every movement. Henry never did this to me. "We're not late for breakfast, are we?"

"No. We've got over an hour."

"Oh I must shower then. I have no more changes of clothes Lllllexie. Which of my old outfits should I wear do you think?"

"Ah, let me see. How about –"

"Are you sure you're all right to drive? You were dreaming over there. I heard you talking in your sleep too. Do you remember anything?"

I stared down at her. "Talking? What was I saying?"

"Oh, lots of things. Things you never say when you're awake." She giggled nervously and quickly stopped herself.

All at once I had the feeling that my legs were about to go from under me. I felt my weight fall heavily on the edge of her bed.

"I'm sorry," I said. "I'm sorry. Is it all right if I sit here for a minute?"

"Of course it's all right."

"Things I never say when I'm awake? What sorts of things?"

"I have to go to the bathroom. Would you be thinking when I'm in there? I'll bring my outfits with me and you can shout in. You'll be thinking, won't you?"

"Thinking?"

"Lllllexie, you're not listening to me. About what I should wear. And will it definitely be all right for me to stay with you till Denise comes back? Oh Lllllexie, it's so exciting. She'll be helping me to find an apartment in

Buncrana and showing me the best places to go at night and where to shop for clothes. I'm going to need more clothes. I've lots of money saved, you know."

+++++

"Just wait till you hear this," she said, leaning away back, heels on the seat, knees together in the air as she flipped over the pages of a tabloid. "I took it out of The Hunter's Rest. Do you think Serilda will mind?"

"I don't know."

The same skintight jeans as before, the same black crop top, the same bare midriff, the same ripped thighs. The little vixen has been running rings round me for three days now. No, what am I thinking? Not three days. Longer than that, far longer than that. She started back on *Steam 4 Teens* and she hasn't let up.

What was it she wrote? I think I love you a little bit? What do you wear in bed? Bloody tease. And look at her now. When she isn't walking in that coltish way she has that drives me out of my mind, she can move with a grace beyond her years, all that dignity. Yes. Except she wouldn't look so dignified if I ripped those jeans right off her and gave her, what is it they call it, a good seeing-to? And it may come sooner than she could ever imagine. Little prick teaser. She's going to push me to the limit one time too many.

"Here it is." She gave a little cough. "Police in the city of Rostock in northern Germany yesterday freed two men who became entangled with a hat stand and a large toy fire truck. The officers were alerted after cries were heard coming from an apartment on Saturday morning.

"They found the sixty-two-year-old tenant and a seventy-year-old visitor hopelessly locked together with the toy fire truck and a hat stand which was draped in net curtains." She put her feet on the floor again, spread her legs out wide and laughed. "Isn't that something?" she said.

"Yes."

"You're very quiet, Lllllexie. Are you in bad mood?"

"Bad mood? What makes you say that?"

"You've hardly said a word since we left Serilda's. Oh look! Isn't that so dramatic?"

"What?"

"The scenery. The wildness. And look, see the way that water rushes round and round? Look! Oh my God. I think the Glenshane Pass is just as nice as ... what do you call it, Mamore Gap?"

"That's right. Mamore Gap."

"Will there be time for us to stop in Derry?"

"We've already bypassed Derry. Why did you want to stop there?"

"You told me you were going to take me to see the place where Shane Mullan and his sons were hanged. In The Diamond you said. Remember you told me all about Shane Mullan the highwayman?"

"We wouldn't have had time. Anyway, there's far too much of this morbid tourism in Derry. I'm sick of it. Mindless Americans and Japanese pointing their cameras at places where two of my friends were butchered by British paratroopers. And just because it's three hundred years since the Mullans were hanged doesn't make that kind of ghoulish fascination any less morbid."

"Oh. I didn't know that. Oh Lllllexie. Oh Lllllexie I'm sorry. Wasn't it thirteen they killed?"

"Fourteen. And murdered is the word. These tourists are vultures."

She fell silent then. This gave me time to think. What was it that was in my head before she spoke? Yes. There's no fool like an old fool, that's what it was. Carried away by a street-smart congirl, all those 'Oh Lllllexies' and flatterings, all those provocative outfits, all those little hugs that promised so much and gave so little. The oldest tricks in the book and I fell for them.

I'll tell her father to take her with him. Because if I don't, I'm finished. She'll have me running around like a doddering idiot up and down to Buncrana just for her nearness and the smell of her and the sound of her and the little embrace at the end of each coaching session, enough of it to bring me back the next time. And why did she take that tabloid from The Hunter's Rest? To read a weird news item to me? What was all that about?

How will I be when she goes? What's in front of me? I'm done with *Steam 4 Teens* anyway, none of that again. I remember back before I started it I used to get a kick out of reading the problem pages, but I don't think I could do that anymore. There have to be better turn-ons. As far as I remember, most of the pubescent girls writing agony letters were as horny as cow buffalos. And some of them nearly as gross too I'm guessing, thighs on them as broad as my back. I'd rather feast my eyes any day on a frail little fourteen-year-old than waste my time even giving a passing thought to any of those ones.

And to think that more and more of them are paying out good money for whatsitsname, butt-augmentation services? As if their arses weren't big enough already. Butt augmentation. What a name. Is my bum big in this? Please tell me it is. I read a letter one time from some poor desperate guy. He said he kept falling asleep at work and was in danger of losing his job because his girlfriend had him up for hours seven nights a week. He told about her bum and all. "Her lovely big bottom is what always starts me." Jesus help us.

What else was it he wrote? Something like "But she insists on a really long session every single time before we go to sleep. It's very satisfying but exhausting too. Then when she comes back from the bathroom at about four in the morning she has to get doing it all again. And on top of that she sets her mobile alarm for three quarters of an hour early so we can have a quickie as she calls it before we get up. This is every single time. It's like clockwork. Please help me. Yours sincerely, Suicidal."

"I think you've missed the turn."

"What?"

"I saw a signpost for the airport back a bit. Maybe there's another turn further on."

"You're right. I missed it. And this is a bloody busy road. And I don't think there's another turn. Oh God, I'll have to find some side road I can reverse into. What time do you have to check in at?"

I heard a sharp inhalation and then a loud gasp. "Check in? What do you mean Lllllexie? I'm not getting the flight."

"Christ, I don't know if we're ever going to get turned on this road. Sorry, I meant what time were you supposed to meet your father?"

"Half past three at the information desk."

"It's nearly that now. He'll be gone."

"Well that's great – brilliant. Look. There's a side road – before that bend. See?"

"Right." I indicated, pulled in and slowly reversed. The place was thick with traffic. "OK. Now how the hell are we going to get onto the road again?"

We sat there for what seemed like ages and then I began to nose out. This was very risky of because a car coming round that bend wouldn't have had time to stop before hitting us broadside and Isabella would have got it full on. But I managed – just. Isabella had her hands over her eyes and didn't take them off till I told her it was all right.

+++++

"You wait in the car and I'll go see him."

She was bolt upright now and very jittery. I tried not to look at her. I'd been aware the whole journey of her body smells and the unmistakable Jasmin Rouge filling the car even when I opened my window. To say that these things hadn't affected me would be a lie. All those miles coping with that. So I'd filled as many of them as I could trying to think of what I would say to him.

I was hoping he'd look just like his pretty boy picture. The last thing I needed was to find out that the photo was taken twenty years ago and that he'd morphed into a hairy beast. Things were tricky enough without those kinds of complications. But as it turned out I needn't have worried. He was still pretty – small, pale and pretty like one of those troubled matinee idols from the fifties, you know, when men were boys. Hair dyed a sleek black, perfect posture, elegantly dressed in a three-piece pinstripe. The bastard could have stepped right onto the catwalk.

"Mister Batty?"

"Yes?" Silky soft voice. Like Liberace. Exactly like Liberace. Gay? Wouldn't it be funny now if he was? But what's that fragrance? *Soleil Blanc*? Yes, it is. *Soleil Blanc*. This guy has money. Or maybe it's a free sample. Didn't Isabella say he was in the perfume business?

"Isabella gave me your photo so I'd know you. I'm Lexie Cheddy, Denise's grandfather. I'm sure she told you all about Denise." I smiled and extended my hand. He shook it limply, frowning.

"Oh. Yes." He looked around. "Where is she?"

"She had to travel with my wife to care for a relative who's very ill."

"Who are you talking about? Where is my daughter?" He blinked rapidly, then glared at me with her bright blue eyes. His jet-black eyebrows met in the middle. Odd for someone so well-groomed.

"Sorry, I should have explained. She was quite hysterical and didn't want to see you just yet, so I let her wait in the car to calm her. Don't worry, I'll be fetching her shortly. I just wanted to talk to you a minute if that's all right. How soon do you have to go through security?"

He glanced at his wristwatch, pulling his jacket sleeve well up so I could have a good gander at his Patek Philippe. Strap alone would get you a long weekend in the Bahamas. "Twenty minutes. Bring my daughter in now, please. She was supposed to have been here a quarter of an hour ago. You and I have nothing to talk about, sir."

"Would you have a coffee with me? Please. We'd have time for a quick coffee before I get her. I take it you've checked her in online?"

"Yes. And what's this about her not wanting to see me? Bring her in here now."

"If you'd just have a quick coffee with me. All I wanted to do was ask you something, if that's OK."

"Ask me right here. Whatever it is you wish to say, say it now. I haven't time for chitchat."

I drew a deep breath. "It's just that I've got to know Isabella while she's been here and she's confided in me and told me what she wants to do which is to study in Ireland and live here permanently. Now of course I know that's out of the question at present and I fully realise she has to go back with you …"

"Got to know her? What does that mean? Was she with you all the time?"

"Well, yes. She wanted to see Donegal so I tried to entertain her as best I could. It was the least –"

"Entertain her? Is that what you say?" His beetle brows rose like a circumflex. "Well, I say you're an opportunist. What's an old man like you doing for three days with a naïve fifteen-year-old girl? Sleeping around Donegal? Bring her in now before I report you to the airport police. You're an abductor, sir. I'll soon find out from her exactly what you've been up to."

To say you could have knocked me down with a feather would have been to greatly understate the situation. But I was more than shocked. I was incensed, as incensed as any law-abiding citizen could be. So I responded in kind. And the words were out before I'd even thought of them.

"Yes, and while we're talking to the police, perhaps you'll tell them about the hard porn films you forced her to watch and what came after. You're looking at twenty years under the Sexual Offences Act, *sir*. Now if you'll excuse me."

I moved a little away from him and in a loud voice said to the information lady "Could you help please? I'm wondering if you'd contact the airport police for me. This gentleman here is a Mister Batty. He has committed incest with his underage daughter. She ran away from him but he's now planning on taking her back to England by force. She's waiting outside in my car and is prepared to testify against him. Would you ask the police to come as quickly as possible? The gentleman has a plane to catch. I would make a citizen's arrest myself except that I'm elderly and infirm."

"Sorry? Say again?" The lady was clearly taken aback. So I said it again, slowly and rather more graphically, turning the screw as tightly as convention allowed and adding for good measure that the girl should be made a ward of court for her own protection.

Miss Information was staring hard at me, no doubt trying to decide whether or not I was a crank.

"W-w-well," she began. "Where is this gentleman you're referring to?"

"Right here," I said. "Goodness, he's gone. Looking for security, I imagine."

The lady's eyes narrowed. And she blinked several times, no doubt still wondering what to make of me. But then, as it happened, a man and woman came and stood behind me, waiting their turn.

"Go right ahead," I said to them. "I'm done here."

I went back to the car in a state of high excitement. Reader, I don't mean to be brusque here, but I want you to stop thinking what you may well be thinking right now and simply read what I have to tell you. Twenty seconds will do it, I promise, and then you'll understand.

In a few years' time – sooner in the event of a stroke perhaps – a carer will in all probability be wiping my bottom. Yes. And grateful and all as I would be for that service, I'd obviously be hoping for somebody and something infinitely more satisfying and rather more personal than that. I'm referring of course to Isabella. The great French writer George Sand once said: "Try, my friend, to keep your soul young and quivering right up to old age." And George is the girl who did that very thing. By God she did. Because as well as producing magnificent novels, plays and essays, she cross-dressed in private and public with a soul that quivered like nobody's business. And mark you, this was the nineteenth century.

My friend George had multiple lovers who included composer Frederic Chopin and actress Marie Dorval (to whom she wrote by the way: "I want you in either your dressing room or in your bed.") I do so wish I'd known her in that masculine part of her persona.

Isabella had her knuckles in her mouth when I got to the car. First time I'd seen her doing that. She nearly jumped off her seat when I opened the driver's door. So not wanting to keep her in suspense I said "I don't think he'll be bothering you anymore."

Her eyes widened. "What? Say that again. Please. Say it again."

"I don't think he'll be bothering you anymore." I smiled, sat down and closed the door. "Well, I suppose we'd better get moving. This car park costs a small fortune."

I put the key in the ignition, but before I could start the engine she was sitting on my lap with her arms around my neck. She had navigated the handbrake and gearstick as if they weren't there and now here she was, jiggling blissfully on my John Thomas and pressing hard on my stomach with one of her nipples. "Oh Lllllexie," she cried. "How did you do it? What did you say to him? You're the most wonderful man, you really are."

"You can't do that Isabella!" I gasped. "People will see you."

She kissed my cheeks and my eyelids and my ear lobes. "Pardon?"

"People will see you. You can't –"

"Pardon?" She kissed my forehead, my nose and my chin. The windscreen was beginning to mist up now, further impairing my vision which had been so-so anyway from the moment she landed on my fevered lap, though I was still able to make out the suitcase-wheeling middle-aged couple who had paused in their tracks right in front of us. The woman was staring and pointing at our windscreen and her partner was staring too.

"That man and woman Isabella. They're looking at us. See them? You're going to get me arrested." Another three inquisitive people suddenly stopped to join them. This had the makings of a mob.

"Move. Please. You have to."

"Oh I'm sorry. Oh dear. You're sweating Lllllexie. Do you want to go now?"

"We'd better, I think."

She was back in her seat in the blink of an eye and smiling angelically across at me. I took the cloth from my dashboard and wiped the windscreen and driver's window. The condensation was still there so I opened all the windows full and sat back, breathing hard.

"Those people are all away now," she said. "Weren't they nosey?"

"Yes. They were, weren't they?" She hadn't kissed me on the lips. Keeping that for later?

For the first few miles of our journey to Derry I gave an imaginative account of the conversation between her father and me, an account which left her in no doubt about the power of my personality. And for most of the rest of the time she talked excitedly about her life ahead with Denise and Huncan. This monologue depressed me more than I can say and when we neared Derry I knew the time had come so I pulled into the forecourt of a shop in Drumahoe village.

As soon as I applied the handbrake I let my shoulders slump and right away felt her eyes on me. She started to speak, something about fashion shops in Buncrana I think, but I interrupted in a rush. "I've got something to tell you Isabella, and I don't think you're going to like it."

I'd been avoiding looking at her but now I turned to face her and she was gazing at me open-mouthed. And she was so beautiful at that moment, maybe more beautiful than she really was, and so beholden to me, so powerless and so fragile. When I look back now, which I do often, when I think of how I want to remember her, this is the moment, not the crazy dream, not *Moon River*, not the holding hands under the table, not the hero worship, not the closeness of her embraces, but this. And if this makes me a control freak and a chauvinist creep, then those are what I am.

"It's about Denise," I said.

+++++

I'd had plans. Pie-in-the-sky plans, but plans nevertheless. She would live alone in her Buncrana apartment and I would travel there three evenings a week to help her with her A-level studies, and I'd stay awhile after each tutorial. Wouldn't you? But at the same time I was realistic. In six months to a year, she'd be shedding her nymphethood and would become a regular young lady and a free agent to boot. However, it was those precious months that had preoccupied me since she first mentioned Buncrana as a place to live.

She took it badly. She cried her little heart out and I had to give her first my hankie and then what was left of my box of tissues. She told me through bitter tears and runny nose that she never wanted to see me again and why hadn't I just raped her when I was taking advantage of her anyway?

She used language that I wouldn't have believed she was capable of and called me a dirty old man and a fantasist, prefixing the latter word with a particularly obscene epithet. And then when she had blown her nose for the umpteenth time she put her hand down into the front of her crop top and plucked a folded sheet of pink paper from her cleavage.

"There! There's your poem, you brute. Take it" – she threw it on my lap – "and keep it for the next one. I wonder what your wife would say if she knew. And where is she anyway if she's not in Cork, or Kerry, or wherever it was you lied about? You left her to look for something young. And I trusted you! The things I told you! You're slime! No, you're worse than slime!"

She wrenched the door open and I heard her going round to the back of the car. I got to her just as she was pulling her suitcase from the boot.

"Isabella. Please. Let me drive you."

"I'm hitching a lift," she shouted. "I'm hitching a lift to Buncrana."

"But you'll never get there this way. You'll get picked up and ... and ... you'll never be heard of again."

"Oh, you're so worried about me, aren't you! Spare me that stuff."

"Please. I'm so sorry Isabella. Please, please forgive me. I was lonely. I needed company. That's why I started the online thing. I would never have done anything to you. You can't risk hitching a lift. You wouldn't know what might ..."

She was rolling her case towards the shop with me following. "I'd never know what might happen?" she shouted back. "Like, some old pervert might pick me up! Wouldn't that be terrible!"

I stood at the newspaper stand and listened as she spoke to a lady behind the counter. "Can I get a bus from Derry to Buncrana?" I heard her ask. "Oh, that's great. But how do I get to Derry from here? Are there buses? Or will I have to hitch it?"

"It'll be ... let me see," said the shop assistant who then called out: "Angie, what time is the next bus for Londonderry? That long? You'd have to wait about an hour and a half dear. But don't be trying to thumb a lift whatever you do. There's trouble between here and Londonderry. Policemen getting attacked and God knows what else. And sure you wouldn't know who'd be driving the car anyway. You'd be wise to wait for the bus, Love."

I went quickly back to my car and waited. After a couple of minutes she came out of the shop, looked around and came to my open window. "I'm taking your offer this one last time," she shouted and her face was red and puffed, "and I'll pay you for whatever petrol you use."

+++++

There wasn't a word between us till we got to near Buncrana. As the Inishowen Gateway came into view I said "You could have a meal here by yourself while I make inquiries about some place for you to live. Is that all right?"

"I'm not going in there," she said.

"What do you mean? Why?"

"Are you stupid or what? He could still be there. No way am I going to set foot in that place."

"OK," I said. "Do you mind waiting in the car then? I'll ask at the desk to see if the receptionist would have a look on the computer to find somewhere for you. Then I'll bring you to any apartments that are available and let you decide."

She didn't respond but she didn't refuse either. When I left her, she was violently flipping over the pages of her tabloid.

The he she had talked about was preoccupying me as I stood waiting at the empty desk. Was it possible he hadn't yet left? It's amazing the things that can dart in and out of you at times of stress. I didn't have to collect

Henry from the nursing home till tomorrow, so if I was able to deposit Isabella safely in an apartment, there was no reason why I couldn't …

"Can I help, sir?"

I recognised him, the young man who had given me the replacement key card. "Oh. Yes please. I don't know if you remember me. I stayed here with my granddaughter for a couple of nights and we were really delighted with the service."

"Of course I remember. And thank you sir. It's very nice of you to say that."

"We'll certainly be recommending your hotel to all our friends."

"Thank you sir."

"A – A – there was a Bulgarian gentleman that we got to know quite well during our stay. Very interesting character. Is he still here by any chance? I wanted to …"

"Ah yes. I think I know who you mean." He ran his finger down a list of names in an open book. "Mister, let me see ... here we are. Mister Draganov. Mister Angel Draganov. Yes. He and his daughter actually checked out this morning."

"Oh. Oh I see. I ... I ...."

"Yes?"

"Ah, sorry. Nothing. But there was one other thing I wanted to ask you about if you don't mind."

+++++

Things could be worse. They'll never be the same as they were, of course, but they could be worse. In some ways they may even be better, I suppose. It took some time but two things happened. Isabella stopped being a nymphet and I was able to open out to her about how I got to be the way I am. Even though it's been humiliating at times, she understands my situation almost as well as I do myself.

But strangely, she has no suspicions about how I see Gerald. Gerald is her live-in boyfriend and he's irresistible except that I'm resisting him. He has an upper body far superior to George Clooney's for example, a face like, who shall I say, the young Robert Redford's maybe? An ass like Matt Damon's, legs like David Beckham's, a member (I tell myself) at least the equal of friend Draganov's and the sweet nature of a Leonardo DiCaprio. We swam alone together at Dunree beach one day last week – Gerald and I that is – and I nearly had a seizure looking at him.

But what makes it really difficult at times is that he admires me so much. He's studying for his Masters in Philosophy but has this fascination with the Romantics that he feeds by getting me alone and picking my brain. Seems he can't open out about Byron and company for some reason unless we're alone. Can you imagine it? Naturally I wouldn't dream of making a pass or letting him or Isabella discover how I feel about him.

But here's the killer. I know that every time I leave the apartment to go back to Derry after coaching her that they will very shortly be making beautiful love. I was near to crashing the car thinking about it on my way back to Derry one night. Yet I'm not jealous of either of them anymore, only envious of what they have. Because from what I can see, their love for each other is as close to heaven as makes no difference. That's if there is a heaven. There'd bloody well need to be because it's hell out here.

And as for *Steam 4 Teens*, there'll be no going back to that. I plan to live on my memories now, my memories and my daydreams. I don't care what Buddhists say. Daydreams are the nearest thing in this world to proper meditation. And the nearest thing out of this world to heaven.

All of which reminds me. *Google Daydream*. *Google Daydream* is my new-fangled life-raft and from what I can pick up, it has the best navigation system that there is. Because I've been thinking ahead, looking into Virtual Reality you know. I've got it nearly all worked out but there's still some thinking to do. This is where my teeming brain will really come into its own before dementia sidles up and blows it to nothing.

And at the risk of this little journal turning into a commercial, I have to tell you now that I'll be doing in-depth investigations of all the possible porn avenues that *Google Daydream* has to offer. They don't do adolescent girls under sixteen. That's one good reason for being here: because that age-group would kill me. But their social apps and 360-degree videos will be the gateway to the action and Lexie will be right there in the middle of it.

So while Henry is jabbering away to herself up there in her lonely, lumpy bed, I'll be down here living it up on my studio couch. I've read cowards and killjoys who say that this kind of venture could turn out to be the thin end of the wedge to some personal dystopia or other, and even if that's so, I'm still prepared to take the chance. I've been cautious for far too long. It's time to live. But only for as long as it's worth living.

Printed in Great Britain
by Amazon